The SORCERER KING

Also by Frewin Jones

The Faerie Path
The Lost Queen

The
SORCERER
KING

Book Three *of The* FAERIE PATH

FREWIN JONES

An Imprint of HarperCollins*Publishers*

For John, Jack, Eric,
Alan, and Michael

Thanks to Rob Rudderham

for allowing me to use a verse of his song

"The Man in the Moon"

Eos is an imprint of HarperCollins Publishers.

The Sorcerer King
Copyright © 2008 by Working Partners Limited
Series created by Working Partners Limited
All rights reserved. Printed in the United States of America.
No part of this book may be used or reproduced in any manner whatsoever without
written permission except in the case of brief quotations embodied in critical articles
and reviews. For information address HarperCollins Children's Books, a division
of HarperCollins Publishers, 1350 Avenue of the Americas, New York, NY 10019.
www.harperteen.com

Library of Congress Cataloging-in-Publication Data
Jones, Frewin.
    The Sorcerer King / Frewin Jones. — 1st ed.
    p.   cm. — (The faerie path ; bk. 3)
    Summary: Sixteen-year-old Tania returns to the realm of Faerie with her mother, Queen
Titania, only to find that it has been overtaken by the Sorcerer King of Lyonesse, an
ancient enemy of the Faerie Court.
    ISBN 978-0-06-087108-6 (trade bdg.)
    ISBN 978-0-06-087109-3 (lib. bdg.)
    [1. Princesses—Fiction. 2. Kings, queens, rulers, etc.—Fiction. 3. Wizards—Fiction.
4. Fairies—Fiction. 5. Fantasy.] I. Title.
PZ7.J71Sor 2008   2007021236
[Fic]—dc22   CIP
                                                                                 AC

Typography by Al Cetta
1 2 3 4 5 6 7 8 9 10
❖
First Edition

Faeries tread the faerie path
Immortal souls in timeless amber sealed
Mortals dwell in flux of Mortal World
Through life and death, their destiny revealed

One soul is torn between the worlds
A road to take, a doom to dare
A flashing blade, a warrior-maiden's choice
Shall lead to heart's desire or heart's despair

YNIS BOREAL ⟹

Highmost
Voltar

Rhoth

Ynis
Maw

Tongue   Hob's
Tongue

Fidach Ren

Gallowshead

Beroald Sound

PRYDEIN

Caer Liel   Reganfal
R. Lych

WEIR

Caer
Circinn

MINNITH
BANNWG

LLYR

Caer Rivor

The
IMMORTAL
Realm of
FAERIE

The Cloud
Scudder

the hospital; later that same morning, believing herself to be experiencing a vivid dream inspired by the story in the book, she followed a young man in Elizabethan clothes, who took her into Faerie.

The young man introduced himself as Gabriel Drake and explained that Evan was in fact his servant Edric Chanticleer, sent into the Mortal World to find and retrieve Anita. Gabriel believed she was his lost bride, Princess Tania: the *seventh daughter* of Oberon and Titania, with the power to walk between Faerie and the Mortal World. For five hundred years, ever since the disappearance of Princess Tania and the subsequent loss of her mother, Queen Titania, the Eternal Realm of Faerie had been plunged into a sad and gloomy twilight.

When Gabriel took Anita to meet Oberon, the king was so overjoyed that his lost daughter had returned, light and life came back into Faerie once more. Soon after, Anita met Princess Tania's six sisters. As she learned more about this strange world—and *remembered* things she could not possibly have known—her certainty that this was all a dream began to waver. At last she was forced to confront the fact that she was truly Oberon's lost daughter.

Full of pain and anger at Edric's betrayal, Tania grew closer to Lord Gabriel. It was only when Edric told her the true purpose behind Gabriel's dramatic rescue of Tania from the Mortal World that she was saved from falling under Gabriel's spell. Gabriel Drake had planned to marry Tania and use her power

What Happened Before . . .

On the eve of Anita Palmer's sixteenth birthday, her boyfriend, Evan Thomas, took her for a speedboat ride on the River Thames. Her birthday surprise turned to terror when they saw a ghostly shape on the river and Evan, swerving to avoid it, sent the boat crashing into a bridge.

Anita woke up in hospital. Her injuries were superficial, but Evan, although otherwise physically unhurt, remained unconscious.

At the hospital Anita's parents brought her a curious parcel: a birthday present sent with no card and no name. It was an old leather-bound book with blank pages that mysteriously became filled with words when Anita started looking.

The book told how Princess Tania, seventh daughter of King Oberon and Queen Titania of the Realm of Faerie, disappeared from the Royal Palace on the eve of her wedding to Lord Gabriel Drake. While reading this story, Anita learned that Evan had vanished from to enter the Mortal World and bring back a terrible poison called Isenmort, known to mortals as metal, a substance so deadly in Faerie that a single touch meant instant death. The Faerie Palace was torn apart with treachery—even Tania's own sister Princess Rathina tried to force her to marry Gabriel.

In the end Gabriel's plans were thwarted and the evil lord was banished by Oberon. Peace returned to the Realm of Faerie but Tania was convinced that her mother, Queen Titania, was still alive, trapped in the Mortal World. She and Edric returned to mortal London to seek her out.

Returning to her old life was not easy—Tania had been missing for several days and it hurt that she could not tell the truth to her mortal parents. She was also haunted by the dread that Gabriel Drake would be able to harm her from afar.

Clues led Tania and Edric to the Pleiades Legal Center, where they discovered that Queen Titania worked under the name Lilith Mariner. Their hopes of a swift reunion with the Lost Queen were dashed when they learned that she was away on business.

Things took a sinister turn when Tania found that she could no longer "walk between the worlds." Soon after, three of Tania's faerie sisters—Zara, Sancha, and Cordelia—appeared in the Mortal World with terrible news: Princess Rathina had released the Sorcerer King of Lyonesse from the palace dungeons, Oberon had been imprisoned, and Lyonesse's evil Gray Knights had been set free. The princesses hoped that, with Tania and Queen Titania's help, they would be able to return to Faerie and defeat the Sorcerer King.

A band of Gray Knights broke into the Mortal World—with Gabriel Drake as their captain. Despite several perilous encounters with the Gray Knights, Tania, Edric, and the princesses managed to find the Lost Queen and together outran their murderous pursuers and found their way back into Faerie.

Part One:

The Palace

I

Tania stared through the arched stone window at the vast blue skies of Faerie. She could hardly believe that her sisters; her mother, Titania; and her beloved Edric were alive, and that they had all managed to get back into the Immortal Realm. They were safe for the moment in the upper room of Bonwn Tyr—the brown tower that stood in the parklands between the deep, dense vastness of Esgarth Forest and the expanse of the Royal Palace.

Her joy at their miraculous escape did not last long—she saw immediately that something was badly wrong in Faerie.

Zara stood at her side. "Some great evil has befallen the land," she said. "High summer should lie over Faerie. It is not yet the Solstice Day, and yet the trees are withering as if in the grip of a premature autumn."

Tania had been in Faerie only a few days ago, and then the slender aspen trees surrounding the tower had been in full leaf and the grass had grown thick and lush on the hill that sloped down to the palace. But now the aspens were dying and the ground was brown and yellow, the grasses shriveled as if from a whole season of drought. Farther away, the leaves of the forest were shrouded in dark, autumnal colors.

"What did this?" Tania asked in dismay.

"It is the influence of the Sorcerer King," said Queen Titania, coming up behind her. "Sickness and death follow wherever he treads. Let us hope that the whole Realm is not so badly affected." The Queen's eyes glinted. "But while the Royal House of Faerie survives, Faerie will never be completely ruined."

Tania leaned from the window, peering through the bleak branches. Her heart quickened. "There are some Gray Knights down there!" she hissed in alarm. "Two of them. In the trees."

Edric caught hold of her arm and drew her back. "Don't let them see you," he said.

"Why should we not?" declared Cordelia. "It is time to take the battle to the Sorcerer King. Let us destroy the evil creatures and be done with it."

"I'm not sure it's such a good idea to pick a fight right now," Tania said. "They don't know we're in Faerie. We should try and keep it that way for as long as possible."

"Tania is right," said the Queen. "We'll make our way to the palace without being seen. If the Sorcerer King's forces are alerted to our presence, it will make our search for Oberon all the more difficult." She looked at her daughters. "But we should take a few moments to assess our injuries." She frowned. "Cordelia, your arm is bleeding."

"We have no time for licking our wounds!" Cordelia exclaimed.

"Yet it would avail us nothing were you to faint from blood loss," said Sancha. She stooped and tore a strip off the hem of her skirt. Reluctantly, Cordelia allowed her sister to bind the cut on her left arm.

"And now let us be gone from here," said Zara. "But there is only one way out of the tower. How are we to pass the guards unseen?"

"By giving them some other quarry to chase," said Cordelia. "Come, I will show you how we may escape." She walked to the winding stone stairway that led down to the ground floor and up to the flat roof. She stared upward for a moment, then looked uneasily back at them. "We must prepare ourselves for the worst," she said. "It may be that we will find Eden's body on the roof."

A terrible, horror-struck silence filled the tower at that dreadful thought. Titania put her hand over her mouth, her eyes hollow with anguish.

Eden had led Zara and Sancha and Cordelia here and had opened a hole between the worlds—but she had not followed them into the Mortal World. It seemed all too possible to Tania that the Gray Knights that had been pursuing them had killed her.

"If she is dead, then we must bear the pain of it," Sancha said, her voice trembling. "But let us pray it is not so."

Cordelia began to mount the stone steps. Titania followed, and Tania could see the dread in the Queen's eyes as she climbed toward the hatchway in the roof. Tania and Edric came next, and finally Sancha and Zara. The trapdoor had been forced open and smashed—damage that Tania guessed had been done when Eden and her sisters had fled here with the Gray Knights on their heels.

Tania's heart thumped sickeningly and a horrible pain grew in her stomach as she approached the broken trapdoor. But when her head came out into the open, she saw that the flat stone flags of the roof were bare, save for a ring of blackened markings like fire scorches on the stones.

"Eden did not die here," Cordelia said.

They all came up onto the roof. "Was she captured, mayhap?" Sancha asked. "Could it be she is their prisoner?"

"She may have escaped them altogether," Zara said. "She is very powerful."

Edric touched Tania's arm. She turned to him and saw that he was staring southward with an appalled look on his face. Titania had moved to the southern side of the waist-high stone balustrade, her body stiff and tense, her hands tightened into white fists at her sides as she gazed at the Royal Palace.

Tania let out a gasp of shock. A scene of utter devastation met her eyes. The Privy Gardens that lay between the parklands and the palace had been laid waste. It was as if some hideous disease had passed over the flower beds and lovingly tended groves of trees, leaving only bare bones and blasted earth. The fountains were dry and many of the statues that decorated the pathways had been broken or knocked down.

Beyond the blistered gardens, a haze of dirty gray smoke hung over the palace. Here and there from blackened windows and collapsed roofs, spirals of darker smoke curled into the sky. The palace was vast, and Tania could see that much of it was still undamaged—the high red-brick walls of countless towers and turrets and buildings and halls still standing proud along the river's winding course—but the Royal Apartments, the parts of the palace that Tania knew best, had been seared and scarred by fire.

"How has the Sorcerer King wrought such destruction is so short a time?" murmured Zara, coming up beside Tania. "In but a few brief days . . ."

"I knew that he was mighty in evil sorcery and that he would wish harm upon us," said Sancha. "But not like this . . . not like *this* . . ."

"The menagerie is deserted," Cordelia said, shading her eyes as she peered to that part of the gardens. "If he has harmed the animals, I swear I will cut the very heart out of him."

"Perhaps they got away," Tania said. "I can't see any bodies or anything."

"I pray it is so." Cordelia turned away. "There is work to be done." She moved to the far side of the roof and let out a series of lilting high-pitched whistles.

A few moments later a pair of crows came flapping up from the trees and landed on Cordelia's out-stretched arm. She spoke briefly to them in a low voice. They each gave a single caw in response and flew away.

"It is done," said Cordelia. "The birds will create a diversion so that we may escape this place. Let us go down to the doorway and wait."

Tania was glad to get away from the sight of the palace. As she descended the spiral stairs she saw in her mind the glorious halls and chambers of the Royal Apartments; it was hard to believe that all the beauty and splendor of the place that she had only just accepted as her second home had been destroyed in just a few days.

They gathered in the lower level of the tower. Cordelia opened the door a fraction. Tania stood at her shoulder, peering out through the trees to where two Gray Knights sat astride their skeletal steeds. Edric was close beside her. Their eyes met and she knew he was thinking of their recent encounters with the undead Knights of Lyonesse.

The sudden screeching of birds and the sound of beating wings took her attention and she looked back at the Gray Knights. Scores of different birds were attacking the silent watchers; Tania recognized ravens and starlings and crows and magpies rising and falling and whirling about the heads of the knights and their horses. A frantic neighing came from the animals as they were attacked by beak and claw. The knights drew their swords, shouting and howling in their half-human voices as they fought. The gray horses reared and bucked. White swords slashed this way and that. Black feathers flew and birds fell.

"Now is the time," Cordelia said, throwing the door wide. "Follow close!" She ran through the doorway, Tania and the others on her heels, following her through the leafless trees toward the palace.

Cordelia's eyes blazed with anger. "I curse the Sorcerer King that he has made me ask such a sacrifice from living creatures!"

She halted where the trees ended. Tania and the others gathered behind her, staring out from behind the slender trunks. The great northern gatehouse of the palace stood about a mile away from them, a crudely painted version of the banner of Lyonesse billowing from its high turret: a black serpent on a bloodred background. Two mounted knights guarded the gate.

"We can't cross all this open space," Edric said. "We'll be seen."

"We should keep to the edge of the forest," Titania said. "Head east to the orchards and vineyards. We can use the trees and vines as cover to get to the palace from there." Her voice hardened. "And once Oberon is free, I swear we will have such revenge that the damnable island of Lyonesse will tremble to its deepest foundations!"

Tania looked in surprise at her Faerie mother—at that breathtakingly familiar face, the face that was a mirror to her own, with the green eyes and the high slanted cheekbones, and the frame of tumbling red hair. A change had come over Titania; already Tania could hear the formal elegance of Faerie speech in her mother's voice, as though the five hundred years of her exile were melting away. In the Mortal World, Titania had established herself as a powerful business woman specializing in human rights law, but now it was brought starkly home to Tania that this woman was the Immortal Queen of Faerie, prepared to do whatever it took to save her husband and her kingdom.

"And once in the Palace, what then?" asked Sancha. "Where do we begin the search?"

"We must go by stealth to the Royal Apartments," said Cordelia. "And down to the dungeons below, for it is there that our father will have been imprisoned, be most sure of that."

"And Eden also, pray it be so," added Sancha.

"Then let's go," said Titania. "Follow me, and keep to cover."

"Hang on," Tania said. "Wouldn't it make more sense for just a few of us to go down there, at least till we know what we're up against?" She looked at her mother. "It's crazy for us *all* to go—and it's especially crazy for *you* to risk it. If something bad happens to you, how do we get Oberon free once we find him?"

"You're wrong, Tania, if you think I have any special powers to help liberate the King from the Sorcerer King's enchantments," Titania said grimly. "The strength that we have between us *may* be enough to defeat Lyonesse, but it cannot be used until after Oberon has been set free. So long as he is imprisoned in amber the bond between us is severed and the power of the Sun King and the Moon Queen is broken."

"Then it makes even more sense for you to stay clear of the Palace," Tania urged. "We *think* he'll be in the dungeons, but what if he isn't? What if it takes us a while to find him? We could run into all kinds of trouble."

"A smaller group would be less likely to be seen, Your Grace," Edric said. "If the King is too heavily guarded, we may need to make our way up into Anvis, to Caer Ravensare, to fetch reinforcements."

"Let us hope that is not the case," said Titania. "Every hour we lose only helps the Sorcerer King to tighten his grip on the land." She looked thoughtfully at Tania. "You have a good head on your shoulders." She sighed heavily. "It burns my heart to send my children into danger, but I will do as you say and remain in the forest."

"Not alone," said Cordelia. "I will remain with our mother lest the enemy come upon her by stealth." She drew her crystal sword. "They shall not harm her while I stand at her side."

Sancha swung the backpack she had been carrying off her shoulder and held it out to Cordelia. "Guard our mother's crown till we return."

Cordelia took the bag. "I will."

"Then it is agreed," said Titania. "Edric, Sancha, Tania, and Zara will go to the Palace, and Cordelia and I will wait here and pray that you find the King and return safely."

"A party of four, with but two swords," said Zara. "Who of us will go unarmed into such peril?"

"I'll do without a weapon for the time being," said Edric, holding out his sword for Tania. "I'd rather know that you'd be able to defend yourself."

"I also will forbear a weapon," said Sancha. "Let Tania and Zara be our warrior maidens."

Tania took the sword from Edric's hand and stared out toward the smoke-hazed palace. What harm had the Sorcerer King done in that sad, defiled place? She tightened her grip on the sword hilt, pushing away her fear as she prepared to confront the horrors that she knew must be lurking in the palace.

"Ready?" Edric asked her.

She nodded, her lips pressed tightly together. She had to be ready.

The Realm of Faerie needed her—what other choice was there?

II

Tania and Edric and the two princesses made their way stealthily down through the orchards and vineyards. The evil power of the Sorcerer King had wrought havoc here, too: Tania saw fruit hanging wrinkled and rotten from the trees, and the grapes were shriveled on the vine, gray and furred with mold. The foul stench of decay hung in the air, a miasma of bitter and sickening odors that came from the putrid juices and the maggoty pulp.

They reached the vast palace half a mile or more from the Royal Apartments.

"I'll go first," Tania said as they passed under a tall, arched entranceway. "Keep in single file behind me. Zara, you guard the back. Edric? I don't know my way around this part of the palace—how do we get to the dungeons?"

"I'll explain as we go along," he replied.

She looked into his eyes for a moment, gathering her courage for what was to come.

"I love you," he murmured softly, holding her gaze.

"I love you, too," she whispered with a smile. "Let's go."

They moved forward, Tania in the lead with her sword ready, Edric close behind, and Sancha and Zara at the rear. Tania brought them to a halt at every corner and intersection and doorway, judging the safety of the next open space before moving on.

It filled Tania with sadness and dismay to see her home so empty of life as they made their way through the great staterooms and banqueting halls and chambers. A few days ago these rooms would have been filled with people, but now they were deserted and ominously still. A creeping dread grew in her as they moved cautiously along the desolate halls and across forsaken courtyards silent under a smoke-hazed sky.

They passed the open door of a small private chamber where the signs of violence were all too obvious: A table was overturned; a window was shattered. An arrow jutted from the doorpost and a fine tapestry had been slashed by a sword.

"Do you think everyone got out safely?" she whispered to Edric.

He looked at her with hollow eyes. "No," he said softly. "I don't."

She shivered. "Me neither."

"I know our quest is to find and rescue our father," Zara hissed. "But I would gladly meet with our enemy and pay them back for what they have done here!"

"So would I," Tania said between gritted teeth. "But we can't."

"Nay," said Sancha. "We four against ten score Gray Knights? Cordelia may think those fair odds, but I do not." She stared down the long curving corridor. "We are nearing the Royal Apartments. My heart tells me that we shall encounter the filth of Lyonesse soon enough."

It wasn't long before they came upon more signs of the brutal revenge of the Gray Knights of Lyonesse: spatters of dry dark blood, broken Faerie swords lying on the rich carpets, a torn and bloodied cloak strewn on a stairway, a woman's shoe fallen on the parquet floor of a ballroom. Tania's chest grew tight and a bitter taste filled her mouth as she gazed at the forlorn slipper. People had been killed here, she felt certain of that. Part of her wanted to turn and run from this dreadful place—but a stubborn determination made her stay despite her fear.

It was clear that fighting had taken place in this room. There were no bodies, but among the upturned furniture and trampled ornaments, Edric and Sancha found undamaged crystal swords. Tania looked apprehensively at the discarded weapons, wondering how they had come to be lying there. Had trapped Faerie knights thrown them down in surrender—or had they been pried from dead hands? She shuddered and turned away. She would have a chance to avenge their deaths, she promised herself.

Several doors led out of the ballroom. "Which way now?" she asked.

Edric pointed to open double doors at the far end of the room. "A corridor leads from there," he said. "If we follow it to the left, it'll take us to a stairway and then out to a courtyard you'll recognize."

He was right. When they came out into the open, Tania remembered the wide grassy courtyard very well. The last time she had been here, children had been playing—Faerie children with their childhood wings.

Now a blackened pile of burned furniture was heaped in the middle of the courtyard. Wisps of smoke still snaked up into the dull brown air. The grass was burned and parched. Every window that overlooked the courtyard had been smashed and as they skirted the reeking pyre, broken glass crunched under their feet.

"This is our *home*," Zara said, sobbing, under her breath. "See what terrible things they have done to our home."

Sancha put an arm around her shoulders. "The Sorcerer King takes pretty revenge for a thousand years imprisoned," she said. "But he will not prevail. This evil will be defeated, never doubt that."

Tania looked at her sisters for a moment, pierced by Zara's sorrow and disturbed that Sancha's hopeful words sounded so unconvincing. "He's free now," she said. "Why doesn't he just *go*? What's the point of all this destruction?"

"The Sorcerer of Lyonesse is a creature of lust and anger and greed and fear," Sancha replied. "He dreads light and laughter and beauty. He is tormented by joy and grace and compassion. While the Realm of Faerie survives his heart is burned by it. He has to destroy us utterly." Her eyes were huge and dark. "He is other than we are, Tania—he is a monster."

"I want to kill him," Tania said, a white-hot rage filling her mind. "I want to find him and kill him for what he's done here."

Edric took her hand, lacing his fingers with hers. "We can't fight them all," he said. "We have to find King Oberon, that's the most important thing."

"I know," she said. She took a long, deep breath. "But I hate all this; I hate it so much!" She broke away from Edric, clenching her fist around her sword hilt as she made for the doorway that would take them back inside.

But there was no relief in here from the devastation of the Gray Knights. They were in the Royal Apartments now and the smell of burning drifted through the air. In room after room, ugly scorch marks blackened the walls and stained the ornate plasterwork of the high ceilings. Everywhere, furniture had been smashed; broken ornaments were strewn across the floors, tapestries and paintings and wall hangings torn down and ripped to fragments.

They came out into a lofty atrium where a grand oak staircase led to an upper gallery. They were halfway across the tiled floor when Tania heard from above the echoing sound of heavy footsteps.

"Gray Knights!" Zara hissed.

Nothing more needed to be said. They ran soft-footed back to the doorway through which they had come. Tania leaned against the open door, out of sight of anyone coming along the gallery. The sound of footsteps grew louder. She closed her eyes as memories of the Gray Knights of Lyonesse came flooding back into her mind. They were thin as ghosts, clad in mail that glistened with a sickly light. Their long wispy hair hung like cobwebs around their sunken, ash white faces. Their eyes were red as fire and their cruel mouths spread in perpetual lunatic smiles.

Tania's heart pounded. It sounded as if several of the Gray Knights were marching along the high wooden gallery. What should they do if the creatures came down the stairs? Turn and run? Fight them?

But the clatter of booted feet receded and the ominous silence returned. Tania opened her eyes, shocked by how scared she had been. Edric was looking anxiously at her.

"Are you okay?" he asked.

She nodded, smiling to reassure him. "I'm fine." What was the point of admitting her terror? "Where do we go from here?" she asked.

"Follow me," he said. "It's not far now."

He led them across the atrium to a side passage. At the far end there was a stone doorway. The door itself was scattered in fragments across the floor of the passage. Tania saw that a narrow stone stairway wound darkly down. A reddish glow flickered at the bottom.

"This door was broken from the other side," Edric said. "The Sorcerer King must have come this way when he was first released."

"I think you are right," said Sancha. "My skin crawls and the very air is tainted by the memory of his passing."

Tania shivered as she stared into the gloomy well of the stairs.

"Wait here for me," said Edric. "I'll check it out." He slipped through the doorway and down the stairs, his receding shape black against the red light. A few moments later his voice called up softly. "Come down; it seems safe."

Tania led the way. Edric was standing at the foot of the stairs with a flaming torch in his grip. A long, low stone corridor stretched to right and left, lit by torches in blackened holders along the walls.

"We must be vigilant," Sancha said. "If our father is here, then he may be guarded."

Walking in a line, Edric first with the torch, then Tania, then Sancha, and finally Zara, they crept along the corridor, listening for any sound in the gloomy darkness. A black door stood open, bent and twisted on its torn hinges. Tania knew where they were: This was the Adamantine Gate, the entrance to the dungeons. Clearly some enchantment had blasted the stone door open, a deadly enchantment that had been buried for long ages in the shadowy place that lay beyond. Tania shivered, remembering only too clearly the endless maze of corridors and the low, barrel-roofed chambers with their terrible contents.

"There are no guards on the gate, at least," Edric whispered. "That's good."

"I know the design of the dungeon," Sancha said. "It was built as a maze, but there is a logic to it. Follow, and I shall lead us true." Her eyes gleamed in the torchlight. "Fear not: if our father lies within, we shall find him."

Tania felt the chill air of the dungeons crawl over her skin as she followed Sancha through the Adamantine Gate. There was a smell also: a burning, sulfurous stink. She had smelled it once before, when she had come to this dreadful place to rescue Edric from the Amber Prison into which Gabriel Drake had cast him. It was the stench that came when an Amber Sphere was broken open, and the dank air of the dungeon was heavy with it.

They came to the first of the prison chambers: long, low rooms with deep niches cut into the walls. When last Tania had been here, many of the dark niches had contained Amber Spheres—some so ancient that they were black, others less old and showing a faint orange light through the crust of years, and some where the prisoners crouched within were visible through the glassy surface, their limbs locked, their faces frozen, their eyes staring blankly.

But there were no spheres here now, just a scattering of yellow fragments that crunched under their feet, and everywhere the stifling odor of sulfur.

"What is that smell?" Sancha asked.

"The stink has been all around us since first we entered this forsaken place," Zara said. "'Tis brimstone."

"No, there is another smell," Sancha insisted. "Worse than that."

Tania sniffed. Sancha was right: There was a new smell in the air, quite different from the sharp stinging odor of sulfur. A smell that was like rotting flesh and putrescence—a smell that filled her head and made her feel sick.

They walked onward, more slowly now, and it was as if they were wading into a stench as thick as stagnant water.

"I cannot stand this," Zara protested. "Let us go back."

"No, we must keep going," said Sancha, one hand covering her nose and mouth. "We are approaching the last few chambers."

"Shhh!" Edric held up his hand, warning them to halt at a junction between several passages. *"Listen!"*

Tania held her breath. At first she could hear nothing apart from the sputter and hiss of the torch, but then other sounds came to her ears: a soft, rasping, slithering sound from an adjacent passageway, as if something was being dragged over the stones, and a sharp clicking like the rattling of impatient fingernails. No, it was too hard for fingernails. . . . It was like claws—claws on the stone.

It faded and she was able to breathe again. "What was *that*?" she whispered.

"I do not know," Sancha said. "Some foul beast of Lyonesse, mayhap. Be thankful it did not come upon us."

"How many chambers are there yet to search?" asked Zara.

"Few," Sancha said. "Four, maybe five."

They rounded a curve and found a body lying in the middle of the floor. It was a man, clad in the black uniform of a prison guard.

"His face!" Zara gasped. "Look at his face!"

Reluctantly Tania looked. Bathed in the ruddy torchlight, the dead face looked less than human, stretched and distorted like melted wax. The man's eyes were wide open as though caught in a moment of absolute terror and his mouth was locked in a grimace of agony.

Sancha let out a breath. "I know this death-mask," she said. "I have read of it in the ancient bestiaries in the library. It is called the *rictus basiliskus*. It is the look that is found upon the faces of the victims of a basilisk."

"A basilisk?" said Edric. "How can a basilisk have got here? They only live in the far north."

"Cordelia had a basilisk locked up in the menagerie," Tania said. She thought back to her encounter with the strange beast in the wooden hutch. All she had seen of it was the glittering red eye that had peered out at her, draining the strength from her limbs, clouding her mind with darkness, until Gabriel Drake had pulled her away.

"It must have escaped and made its way down here to be out of the sunlight," Edric said.

"Indeed it would do that," said Sancha. "Those creatures thrive on cold shadows and bitter darkness. This dismal place would suit it well."

"I shall be ready if it should come upon us!" Zara said, swinging her sword.

"There is no sword that could harm it," Sancha said. "Its feathers are as hard as stone, and where its flesh is bare of feathers, it has scales that would thwart the keenest of blades."

They moved even more cautiously now, waiting at every corner, ears straining for any sound, eyes constantly staring into the dark tunnels, seeking out any movement in the flickering torch-flame.It wasn't long before they encountered another dead guard—facedown, thankfully. But they heard nothing of the creature and saw nothing but leaping shadows on the walls.

Sancha came to a halt in a long, low chamber. She turned, her face drawn and pale, her shoulders slumped. "We are done with our search," she said, her voice full of despair. She pointed to a tunnel mouth. "That way leads us back to the Adamantine Gate." Her voice cracked. "Alas, but our father is not here!"

Tania remembered what she had said to the Queen before they had entered the palace. *We* think *he'll be in the dungeons, but what if he isn't?* It seemed that she had been right to doubt their hopes. Oberon was *not* here.

She looked determinedly at the others. "Then we've got to search the whole of the palace for him," she said. "We can't quit now."

"The entire Palace?" Zara exclaimed. "Such a task would take us many days."

"No!" Sancha said sharply. "I am such a fool! There is another way of learning where our father is. Had I but given it thought earlier, I could have saved us this fruitless sojourn." She strode quickly toward the tunnel that led to the Adamantine Gate.

"What is it?" Zara called, following her.

"We must go to the—" But Sancha was given no time to finish. A dark, screaming shape came leaping from the tunnel entrance.

"Cover your eyes!" Zara screamed. "The basilisk is upon us!"

As she threw her arms up over her eyes Tania had only a split second to take in the shape of the monster. The basilisk stood over four feet tall, like a hideous blending-together of a bird and a snake: a huge bird whose bullet head wove back and forth on a long, scaly, sinuous neck; the red eye gleaming with an ancient evil; the long curved beak open; a forked black tongue flickering. It was plumed with hard dark feathers, more like the spines of a porcupine than the feathers of a bird, and its long, thick legs were covered in black scales. Great, curved black claws clicked on the stones as it moved forward, its head tilted upward and to one side, one eye fixed on Sancha. The wings ruffled with a sound like clashing iron. A long whipping, naked tail dragged on the stones, hooked at the end with a fearsome barb. A sound like scraping fingernails vibrated in its throat.

"Sancha!" Tania heard Zara scream. "Look away!"

Squinting between her fingers, Tania saw Sancha standing alone and helpless in the face of the terrible monster, stiff and unmoving as though she had been turned to stone. Without even thinking, Tania lifted her sword and ran forward, shouting. She remembered what Sancha had said about the impossibility of harming the beast but she didn't care; she had to do something to try and help her sister.

She was vaguely aware of Zara standing to one side with her arms over her face. She heard Edric shout. "Tania! No!"

"Leave her alone!" Tania howled as she ran across the stones.

The monster let out a hideous screech. Sancha swayed for a moment and fell sideways to the floor.

There was nothing now between Tania and the basilisk's malevolent gaze. Time seemed to slow. She could hear Edric calling frantically, but his voice was almost drowned by the throbbing of blood in her ears. As the basilisk's red eye caught her gaze and held it she felt the strength draining from her body. She crashed onto her knees.

And then a woman's voice sang out in the darkness: "Come summer sun, come heaven's bright orb, come morning's golden light!"

A blaze of sunlight burst out from the tunnel entrance behind the basilisk. The monster's long, lithe neck writhed and its wings spread, beating frantically as it stumbled away from the source of the light.

The woman stepped into view with one arm lifted, a golden ball of light held in her fingers, its burnished rays flooding the long hall with golden arrows. And strutting at the woman's feet was a gold and scarlet feathered cockerel.

"Come, fearless harbinger of dawn, come crested lord to welcome the new day! Sing aloud in your ancient voice!"

The basilisk let out a screech, but the grating noise was drowned out as the cockerel lifted its head and crowed loudly. The basilisk shrank back, its wings jerking, its legs stumbling, and as Tania watched, the beast began to shrink and shrivel like burning cellophane. The sound of its voice turned to a high-pitched whine as it fell.

It writhed for a moment on the stones, small and withered and horrible to look at, and then, blackened and dried-up as though blasted with fire, it lay still.

The golden light faded and now only the red flames of the torch that Edric was holding lit the hall.

"Well met in evil times," said the woman.

Now that the blazing light was gone, Tania could see long white hair and piercingly blue eyes set in a pale, narrow face.

It was her eldest sister, Princess Eden.

III

Zara was the first to run toward Eden. "You are alive!" she cried.

Eden smiled grimly. "I have walked the line between life and death many times these past few days, but the filth of Lyonesse has not done for me yet." She knelt at Sancha's side, resting her hand on her tumbled hair. "She will recover," Eden said. "She looked into the monster's eye for but a few moments." She gazed hopefully from one to the other. "Did you succeed in your mission? Is the Queen in Faerie?"

"Yes, she's in the forest with Cordelia," said Tania.

Eden gave a gasp of relief and for a moment the stern lines of her face softened. "'Tis well," she said. "I feared all might be in vain. But we must quit this place. The Sorcerer King's men swarm the halls above us like vermin."

"We came to find King Oberon," said Edric.

"He is not here," said Eden.

"That we know, dear sister," said Zara, kneeling at

Sancha's side and pulling strands of chestnut brown hair off her sister's pale face. "With Sancha's guidance, we have searched the Dungeons most thoroughly."

"The King is not anywhere in the palace," Eden explained. "His whereabouts are hidden from me by the Sorcerer King's enchantments, but I know he is not close." Anguish burned in her face. "He has been taken to some dark place, but I cannot guess where. The sorceries of Lyonesse fog my senses."

"When you did not come through the mystic opening into the Mortal World, we feared the Gray Knights must have killed you," Zara said. "How did you escape them?"

"I had power enough after opening the portal between the worlds to throw a glamour of sleep over them. I fled the tower and found refuge in the western fastnesses of the palace. I stayed hidden from them, waiting for your return." She looked curiously at Tania. "How did you defeat the Sorcerer King's enchantment against passing between the worlds?"

"We melted some black amber onto a sword and I managed to cut my way through," Tania told her. "We only just made it."

"That was bravely done," Eden said, and then she frowned. "We cannot linger here." She looked at Edric. "Master Chanticleer, will you bear the princess until she awakes?"

"Of course I will." Edric crouched and, with Zara's help, he gathered the limp form of Sancha in his arms. He got cautiously to his feet, holding Sancha against his chest with her head lolling on his shoulder.

Eden stood and walked over to the cockerel. She held out her hand, palm down over its head. "Well done, good and honest creature," she murmured. "Go now with my blessing and find light and grain."

The bird dipped its head, then went strutting off into the corridor with a clatter of claws on the stones.

"I don't get it," Tania said, glancing at the blackened shape on the ground. "What killed it, exactly? I thought those things were meant to be . . . well, kind of *invulnerable*."

"Indeed they are," Eden said. "To all but the first light of dawn and the crowing of a cock. These things they cannot endure. I knew the basilisk had fled into the dungeons, so I called the cock to me and fed it grain to keep it close lest I encountered the monster. The Orb of the Dawn is a brief enchantment, but it sufficed for our needs." She reached out to touch Sancha's trailing arm. "Would that I had come upon you a few moments sooner. Come, let us find somewhere less noisome until Sancha awakes."

Eden led the way as they headed along the low corridor to the blasted Adamantine Gate.

"We will not take the route that leads to my apartments," Eden said. "Gray Knights guard my sanctum and the Oriole Glass is secured against us. But we cannot attempt to leave the palace until Sancha recovers."

"Mayhap to one of our bedchambers?" suggested Zara.

Eden's face twisted. "I have seen what they have done to those rooms," she said. "Your chamber rages with an endless storm, Zara. They have burned the forest in Hopie's chamber, and slaughtered the animals in Cordelia's."

Tania's heart ached at the thought of those wonderful, living chambers being defiled. Each princess had a chamber that was like an exquisite reflection of her innermost self: Zara's room was a serene seascape beyond a shingle beach, Hopie's was a dark forest, and Cordelia's, a garden world where magical animals prowled. The walls of Sancha's room had teemed with flowing script and whispering voices, tales and lore from every age of Faerie. Dancers circled endlessly in Rathina's room. Tania's own room was hung with living tapestries, faraway scenes that were like windows onto the wide world.

"What about the others?" Tania asked.

"Evil spells swarm the walls of Sancha's chamber," Eden said, "and the whispering voices speak of terrors beyond understanding. I have not entered Rathina's chamber—I would not wish to see what dread things writhe and ferment beyond her door." She looked at Tania. "The foul curse of Lyonesse has fallen on your chamber, too, Tania, but I believe that there we could endure it for a short time. Yes, let us go; I shall take us by a route that will keep us safe from the hoards of Lyonesse."

They made their way through abandoned halls and up deserted stairways. Now and then Eden brought them to a halt in corridors where distant voices could be heard speaking or shouting or laughing harshly. Tania shivered. She had encountered those half-animal voices before, most recently as they had clamored to break their way into her bedroom in London while she wielded the black amber sword.

Eden made sure they were not seen, and it wasn't long before they came to the door of Tania's chamber.

"Do not look into the tapestries," Eden warned, her fingers gripping the door latch. "You will not like what you see."

Steeling herself for the worst, Tania followed Eden into the room. A grayish light filtered through the shards of the broken windows. Tania looked around and felt her heart ache. Her bedding had been slashed and torn and the overturned furniture showed signs of ax blows. Her personal items—jars and bottles and jewelry—had been smashed; even the washstand had been thrown to the floor and the water jug crushed.

Despite Eden's warning, Tania couldn't help but glance at the tapestries that adorned the walls. They had been so beautiful before, with landscapes and seascapes, mountain ranges and wide plains, arctic regions with cliffs of blue ice reflected in indigo water. It was not just the beauty of the scenery that Tania loved—it was the sense of yearning that pervaded the tapestries; it spoke to something deep in her heart. And they had been alive, every thread and stitch a vibrant, changing thing so that woven clouds slid over the woven sky while leaves moved on woven trees and birds of delicate gold and russet thread soared against far mountains.

But the landscapes were dark and dreadful now. A volcano belched ugly red flames into a dour, smoke-wracked sky. Evil things crawled across a benighted countryside, riven with pits and fissures that belched yellow fumes. Forests were aflame. Disgusting feather-less birds lurched across yellow skies clutching naked writhing creatures in their beaks. Monsters swam in polluted seas filled with dead things.

Tania looked away, wishing she had heeded her sister's advice.

Edric carried Sancha to the bed and laid her gen-tly on the ruined covers. Her eyes flickered and she murmured.

Eden sat at her side, one hand on her brow. "She awakes," she said. "She should be able to walk soon, but it may be several hours before her mind clears. The evils that lurk within a basilisk's eye are not easily sloughed—and had I come but a few moments later, our sister may have never returned to us."

"How did you find us?" Tania asked.

"The enchantments of the Sorcerer King lie like storm clouds in my mind," Eden said. "But they do not entirely blind me. Some hours ago I felt the air dancing to the north—thus I knew you had returned. Even the most powerful sorceries cannot keep me from my sisters. I was hiding in deserted passageways to the west when I sensed your presence within the palace. I hurried to be with you, but I had to take care lest the Gray Knights captured me."

"And yet our father is hidden from you," said Zara. "That is ill fortune. How shall we find him?"

"I think Sancha had an idea," Edric said. "But the basilisk got her before she was able to tell us what it was."

"Then we must await her recovery," said Eden.

"Has this all been a total waste of time, then?" asked Tania. "Are we just going to go running back to the forest?"

"Our labors here have not been entirely without profit," Zara reminded her, nodding toward Eden.

"Oh, right! Sorry," Tania said. "It's really great that you're in one piece, Eden, and that we're back together again, but where are we with the Sorcerer King now? How are we supposed to fight him if we can't find Oberon?"

"You speak true," Eden said. "Knowledge of the Sorcerer's full intentions would serve us well, but I am diminished by his powers: My sight is dimmed and my Arts desert me. Would that I could get close enough to the King to pierce his thoughts and know his mind. That would be a thing worth doing." She frowned. "It *is* possible," she said under her breath, as though speaking to herself. "An Altier Glamour might suffice. But I do not know. The risk would be great."

"What's an Altier Glamour?" Tania asked.

"It is a way of transforming a person's true shape so that she may pass unnoticed among her enemies."

"And you can do it?"

"Yes, given time and peace, I can do it," Eden replied.

Sancha gave a small moan and her eyes fluttered open. Zara had her sister's head in her lap. She stroked her cheek. "Wake up, sweetheart," she whispered. "The darkness is all gone and Eden is with us."

"The bodies are torn. . . ." Sancha murmured in a faraway voice. "They lie cold in the dawn . . . all frozen and lost . . . and winter-storm tossed. . . . No grave for the brave . . . no tear for the fearful . . ."

"What's she saying?" Tania asked.

"I know not," said Zara.

"No! No! No!" Sancha shouted suddenly, her eyes wide open and her arms flailing. "I see them riding away over the blackened hills. . . . They beckon to me . . . I must follow . . . I must . . ."

"Sancha, be still!" Eden commanded.

Sancha fell back on the bed, her head in Zara's lap again. Her eyes were open but there was no intelligence in them.

"Help her up," Eden said. "See if she can stand. If she is able to walk, you must get her away from here. I will stay and attempt the Altier Glamour and come to you in the forest when I may."

"No way," Tania said. "I'm not going to leave you here on your own. The others should get Sancha out, but I'm staying. Can you do that glamour thing on both of us?"

"Indeed," Eden said. "But the risk of capture is not small."

"That's exactly why I'm staying," Tania said. "Someone has to watch your back."

She looked at Edric. An uneasy frown had gathered on his face. "You know I'm right," she said. "We can't just run away and leave her."

"Then I'll stay as well," he said.

"No," Tania said firmly. "You've got to help Zara get Sancha back to the forest."

Edric took her hand. "Promise me you'll be careful."

Tania nodded. "You bet I will." She touched her fingers against his cheek. "You be careful, too, okay?"

"Let good fortune attend us all," Eden said briskly. "Get you gone from here, Master Chanticleer. Take Sancha to safety."

They managed to get Sancha to her feet and to get her walking, propped by Edric and Zara.

"Be swift!" Zara urged Tania and Eden as they stood at the door. "If you are not with us by the time the sun is at its zenith, Cordelia and I will bring such a bane of swords to this place that it will make the Sorcerer King wish he had never been set loose!"

They shuffled along the corridor, Sancha drooping between them. At the corner Edric gave Tania one last, lingering look, then the three of them moved to the left and disappeared from view.

Tania looked expectantly at Eden. "Well?" she said. "What happens now?"

Eden lowered her head, pressing two fingers to her forehead between her closed eyes. She stayed like that for a long time.

At last, Tania had to break the silence. "Eden? What's going on?"

The fierce blue eyes flashed open. "I sense him," she said. "He is in the Great Hall, and there are many knights with him. Come, I will take you to a place where I can work the glamour without fear of discovery."

"What exactly does an Altier Glamour do?" Tania asked as she followed Eden along the corridor.

Eden glanced around at her, and there was a strange light in her eyes. "You will see," she said. "It will be . . . *interesting*."

IV

Tania crouched in half darkness, her back bent under the low slope of the roof beams, her eyes gradually becoming accustomed to the trickle of light that seeped in between the roofing tiles above her. Dust hung in the air and filled her nostrils. Her feet were balanced on wide joists between which stretched the upper surface of the lath and plaster ceiling of the Great Hall of Faerie. In better times Tania had danced with King Oberon in that grand hall to the music of lute and drum.

She looked at Eden. Her sister was crouching close by, her eyes closed, her lips moving in a soundless incantation.

Tania's ears were full of discordant noise, shouting and laughter and occasional screams welling up from below them. It sounded as though most of the Gray Knights of Lyonesse were gathered in the Great Hall for some sort of feast or celebration.

Eden's eyes opened, their intense blue like sapphires

between the snow-white curtains of her hair. "It is almost done," she said.

"Do you want to let me in on exactly what's going to happen?" Tania said. All she knew was that the Altier Glamour would make it possible for them to move among the Gray Knights without suspicion.

"We will be transformed into small animals," Eden said, her eyes fixed on Tania. "It will feel . . . *strange . . .*"

Tania's eyes widened. "Animals?" she echoed. "What kind of animals?"

"Rats."

"Oh."

"I can do this thing alone if needs be," Eden said.

"No, no. I said I'd help and I will," Tania said. "Will we be able to talk to each other . . . afterward?"

"Indeed we will."

"Okay, then." Tania swallowed hard. "Go for it."

Eden lowered her head and the white hair swept across her face. Tania heard her speaking in a lilting fashion, as though reciting a lullaby to a child. She didn't understand any of the words. Then Eden spoke one word three times:

"Vasistabel! Vasistabel! Vasistabel!"

Tania let out a gasp. Something was happening. A hollow cavern yawned in the middle of her body, a sensation that was like cresting the highest peak of a roller coaster and tipping downward into a stomach-churning plunge. She doubled over, a screaming wind rushing through her brain. She had the impression of falling and of her clothes exploding outward from her in all directions. It was as if her skin was becoming the wrong shape and size for her body. She could feel hair spinning out from her flesh, her eyes bulging from their sockets, the whole of the bottom half of her face pushing hard against her lips, stretching them, tearing the upper lip in two as her teeth grew long and sharp. Her fingers grew, her nails extending and curling into claws. Her legs bent up under her, the knees pressing to her flanks, her feet becoming narrow and spindle-boned. Her heart raced.

And then everything stopped. She was crouched in darkness with a heavy weight lying over her. She lifted her head and sniffed. Her whiskers twitched. She could smell human being all around her, powerful and instantly recognizable: the scent of herself.

She suddenly realized what was covering her. Her own clothes. She began to burrow through the creases and folds of her jeans, scuttling down tunnels and conduits of cloth, seeking a way out. It wasn't just her own scent that filled her head as she ran through the maze of her clothing; there were many, many other smells, and somehow she knew and recognized each of them: detergent, car exhaust fumes, a scent of Edric, the dankness of the corridors far below the palace. . . .

At last, a white glow appeared ahead of her and she came out into bright light. She ran along an uneven surface and sprang onto a joist.

A brown rat stood on its haunches on the next joist

along, whiskers quivering, black eyes bright as berries.

"Eden?"

"Indeed," said the rat. "How do you fare?"

Tania blinked. "I feel very peculiar. It's so bright in here."

"You have a rat's eyes now, Tania."

"I didn't expect to lose all my clothes."

The Eden rat gave a gentle laugh. "You thought we would roam the palace clad in tiny garments?" she asked. "That were the way to go unnoticed, indeed!"

Tania looked down at herself. Her light brown fur was sleek and smooth, and long claws grew out of her paws. When she flexed muscles she had not possessed before, her naked tail whipped from side to side.

"Are you recovered from the transformation?" Eden asked.

Tania nodded. "Kind of."

"Follow me, then, little sister, and be wary—we are going into great peril."

Eden led her in a scuttling run along a joist. They squeezed through a crack that Tania would not have believed would take them; she was finding her rat body amazingly flexible. They climbed headfirst down the inside of a wall, claws gripping on every ledge and ridge to stop them from falling. On the other side of the wall, Tania could clearly hear the noise of the Gray Knights at their revels.

Other sounds came to her sensitive ears: she could hear the scampering of spiders and roaches in the wall cavity, the creak and groan of the timbers. She could hear every sound that Eden made. And yet the quality of the sounds was quite different—there were no deep noises, and the air seemed to be filled with high-pitched squeakings and shrillings.

They reached the level of the floor of the Great Hall and pushed their way along a narrow channel that led between cold stone and rough woodwork. They were in utter darkness, and yet Tania was vividly aware of her surroundings, her whiskers and ears and nose and paws feeding her more information than her human eyes ever could have done. Ahead of them, she saw that a ragged hole had been gnawed at the foot of the woodwork. Bluish light flickered beyond.

Eden turned her long head and the blue light burned in her round black eyes. "Stay close to me," she warned. "We enter now into the very heart of evil."

With a flick of her long tail, she slipped through the hole. Tania sat on her haunches for a moment, her forepaws rubbing fretfully together, her heart running fast in her narrow chest. Sudden images of her mortal home filled her mind, pictures of her old life in London; thoughts of her Mum and Dad, whom she loved so much. What if something went wrong? What if she and Eden were discovered and killed? Her parents would never know the truth of what had happened to her. They would come home from their holiday to a wrecked house and a daughter who wouldn't ever return to them. It would totally destroy them.

She wished fleetingly that she had told them everything about herself and that their last few weeks together hadn't been clouded by secrets and lies. At least then if they never saw her again, they might be able to believe she was safe and happy in another world.

If they could ever have believed such a crazy story. *Don't think things like that! Just don't!*

Tania got a grip on herself, pushing her bad thoughts away. Taking a deep breath, she followed Eden through the hole.

An endless expanse of wooden flooring stretched out in front of her. She sat back on her haunches, overwhelmed. The legs of chairs and tables soared higher than the tallest tree. The people in the hall were colossal, their voices like thunder, their movements huge as an arm swept the air far above her head or a massive leg went surging by, the booted foot as huge as a moving hill, shaking the boards.

She realized that she couldn't see red at all. The flames of the torches that lined the walls had a fierce, hard white heart, sheathed in a flare of luminous violet. The shapes that filled the world in front of her eyes were in shades of blue and gray and dull yellows and greens.

And the smells! A thousand different scents assaulted her nose. Wood. Brick. Plaster. Stone. Cooked meat. Bones. Sweat. Blood. Rotting fruit and vegetables. A horrible, pervasive stench of something worse than dead. And a powerful stink that threatened terrible danger, a stink Tania instinctively knew to be that of dogs.

She stared nervously around the Hall. Yes! It was dogs! Fortunately, there were none close by, but she could see them roaming on the far side of the dizzying stretch of floor: great black dogs with lean flanks bunched with muscle, short-haired with blunt muzzles and small evil eyes. Some of them sprawled at ease beneath the long benches, waiting for scraps to be thrown from the tables. Others roamed the floor, snuffling through the filth, fighting over discarded food or gnawing bones.

"Morrigan hounds!" Eden hissed. "Be vigilant, Tania. I know of these beasts. They are fearsome creatures."

"Will they be able to smell us?"

"The glamour should mask our scent," Eden said. "But I know why these half-demon hounds are here. They were bred with but a single purpose: to scent out black amber. The Sorcerer King means to use them to hunt down the mine of Tasha Dhul."

Tania knew about Tasha Dhul; it was the hidden black amber mine, the only source of that precious mineral in the whole of Faerie. Black amber was the only protection against Isenmort—against metal— and it was the Sorcerer King's intention to equip an army with black amber jewels and send them into the Mortal World to conquer and destroy.

"Come," Eden said. "We must keep to cover or we will be seen and crushed underfoot."

"I'm right behind you," Tania said.

Eden scuttled off, keeping tight to the wall until they came under a table. There they paused, hidden in shadowy shelter. Gradually, Tania found herself growing accustomed to her surroundings. The noise and the smells and the sheer size of everything was no less alarming, but as she peered out from under the table, she began to be able to make sense of it all. And the things she saw were worse than her darkest nightmares.

The glorious Faerie tapestries had been torn from the walls, and ugly emblems had been daubed on the white plaster: swaths of red and crude representations of coiled or striking serpents. A smell of blood hung in the air like a foul gas. The Gray Knights of Lyonesse sat at tables laden with food and drink; debris from the meal was scattered on the floor—bones and hunks of gnawed meat, spatters of food lying in the accumulated filth, trodden underfoot, snatched up by the roving dogs—all foul and stinking.

Tania's stomach twisted in disgust when she saw the food that filled the tables. Impaled on a wooden spike on one long platter of roast meat was the head of a unicorn. She pictured the delicate little unicorn that she had met in Cordelia's menagerie. The beautiful violet eyes were dead now, the soft pale blue mane clogged and tangled with blood. And there were other things on the tables—the butchered remains of more of Cordelia's animals.

But worse was to come. On the far wall, briefly

revealed when the crowds shifted, Tania saw rows of Faerie folk chained in bonds of Isenmort. Their moans were drowned in the noise, their strength all but gone so that they could do little more than hang from their fetters while the poisonous bite of Isenmort burned into their flesh. Some were ominously still, their legs bent under them, heads drooping.

And there were more Faerie folk in the hall, unchained but prisoners nonetheless. Dull-eyed and bruised and dressed in the ragged remains of their once-fine clothes, they moved among the tables, waiting on the reveling knights of Lyonesse—spat at and reviled and struck for no reason as, with dragging feet, they carried jugs and trays and bowls of food to their tormenters.

At the far end of the hall, on the raised dais where the thrones of Oberon and Titania still stood, a figure watched over the feast with hooded eyes.

Tania didn't need to be told that this was the Sorcerer King. He sat leaning to one side, his long, narrow chin propped on one hand, his elbow on the arm of the throne. A dark red cloak with a dull leathery sheen swathed his lean body. His limbs were long and spidery, his face skull-gaunt with cavernous eyes and hollow cheekbones framed by thin gray hair that hung past his shoulders.

Another figure sat at his side, wearing a gown of what looked to Tania's rat eyes like dark blue velvet—although Tania recognized the gown and knew that it was actually a vivid scarlet. An agony of grief filled her mind and her small body trembled with shock as she found herself staring into the pale, expressionless face of her sister Rathina. The princess sat stiffly in the Queen's throne, her hands gripping the arms and her back straight, her long black hair disheveled around her blankly staring face.

"Such treachery!" Eden hissed, crouched at Tania's side. "Such wickedness. How could she do us such harm, how *could* she?"

Tania's throat was too tight for speech. What had happened to Rathina to bring her to this point? She had known that Rathina hated her, that she blamed her for Gabriel Drake's banishment. But to think that Rathina's hatred had grown until it had led her to help in the destruction of her entire family and of the whole Realm of Faerie—that was beyond Tania's understanding.

"I have to get out of here," she said, feeling sick. She turned to Eden. "Are you close enough to read his thoughts or whatever you were going to do?"

Eden sat huddled in a shivering ball, her long nose toward the Sorcerer King, her eyes intense, her whiskers swiveling. A long time seemed to pass, then the rat's head dropped and the eyes turned to Tania.

"Alas!" said Eden. "I cannot penetrate his mind."

"What about one of the others?" Tania asked. "Can you try it on them?"

"They have no thoughts. Their minds are dead. They have only the need to obey their master."

"So what do we do now?"

Eden's black rat eyes gleamed at her. "I do not know."

Tania stared across to where Rathina and the evil King sat. Eden had failed. This had all been a waste of time.

As she watched a Faerie woman in a ragged gown stepped onto the dais, carrying a tray of food bowls and goblets. She offered the tray to Rathina, but the princess waved a dismissive white hand. The woman held up the tray to the King. His eyes turned to her and the woman became stiff, the tray clattering to the floor. The King lifted his hand and the woman rose into the air. Despite the clamor of the hall, Tania was able to hear the King's voice with perfect clarity.

"Would you dance for us?" he asked, his voice as cold as ice under a waning moon. "Would you show us some pretty steps, my lady?"

The woman turned slowly in the air and, with a shock of horror, Tania realized who she was. It was the beautiful and gentle Lady Gaidheal.

The lady's face was ashen and drawn with despair, her eyes lifeless as she hung there at the Sorcerer King's will. The faces of many of the Gray Knights were turning toward the dais, their eyes burning with sinister joy.

"Mayhap wings will aid you with your dance," the Sorcerer King said. He made a curling gesture with his left hand. Lady Gaidheal screamed in pain, her back arching, her limbs flailing. Tania could hardly bear to watch as something dark red and sharp-edged came bursting from the woman's back, stabbing out like spindly fingers of bone, webbed with veined leather the color of dried blood.

They were wings: hideous, dark red bat wings, torn out of her body in some monstrous parody of the iridescent gossamer wings that grew from the shoulders of Faerie children.

The lady writhed in agony for a few moments as the horrible wings expanded and flapped, then she fell heavily to the floor with a single stifled groan. There was a howl of dark joy from the Gray Knights. The red wings shrouded the unmoving form. Blood spread slowly over the floorboards.

"She likes not her wings," the Sorcerer King said impassively. "This is poor sport indeed. If the birds cannot fly, then we shall build pretty cages for them and they will sing their hearts out for us."

He stood up, the cloak spreading open to reveal dully gleaming crimson mail. It was only now that Tania realized how very tall he was, far taller than any of the other knights. He stepped to the edge of the dais and opened his arms. He began to chant words in a language that fell like splinters of ice into Tania's ears. She shivered, feeling a strange stirring in the air.

Flecks of darkness floated from the corners of the hall, coming together and spinning slowly in a heavy column of dancing black light. Tania heard a sound that was like claws scraping at the inside of her skull. She brought her rat paws to her ears, trying to block out the noise. A disturbing new smell filled her head—dangerous and sharp and as toxic as poison. As she watched the jerking dance of the black light began to change, to shift into patterns like a dark grid work that was forming from the shivering air. A kind of moan came from the watching knights, a low guttural sound of pleasure and approval.

The black lines wove together and became firmer and harder until Tania realized that she was staring up at a large iron cage that hung unsupported in the air. Blue-gray threads spun upward from the cage, forming a linked metal chain that wound over the roof beams. The Sorcerer King lowered his arms. The cage dropped slightly, the chains rattling and vibrating as they took the weight.

A howl of appreciation came from the throats of the Gray Knights—some clashed sword hilts on the tables and stamped their feet, others pounded the tables with their fists until the platters and cups jumped while the baying of the Morrigan hounds added to the cacophony.

"It's metal." Tania gasped, staring at the cage. "How did he do that?"

"Only *he* has the power to draw Isenmort from the Mortal World and bend it to his will," Eden said, and her voice was shaking. "What devilry does he intend?"

"Fetch the pretty birds!" the Sorcerer King called. "I would hear their sweet music."

A small group of Gray Knights left the Hall. The others began to shout and chant, their fists beating rhythmically on the tables.

They did not have to wait long for their entertainment. A group of Faerie folk were herded in through the door. Tania could see the pain and despair etched in their faces. More knights rose from the tables and the Faeries were hurled bodily into the cage. As the Isenmort burned them their screams rose above the raucous laughter of the knights.

"Oh! Horrible! Horrible!" Eden whispered, turning away. But Tania forced herself to watch; hard as it was for her not to cover her eyes, someone had to bear witness to this cruelty.

After all the prisoners had been crammed into the cage, the iron door swung closed with a brutal clang. The Sorcerer King raised an arm and the cage went winding into the air on its long chains. The agonized cries of the trapped Faeries filled Tania's head. Adults tried to lift their children, to protect them from the burn of the Isenmort bars, but it was impossible for them to stay upright as the cage swayed. Numb with horror, Tania recognized the oarsman who had rowed her and Zara to the Royal Galleon on the night of the Traveler's Moon festival. She saw a gardener she had spoken with once, a woman who had been attending red flowers while white butterflies danced around her head.

Tania turned to look at Rathina. The princess had lowered her head, averting her eyes from the horrors. But the Sorcerer King came to her throne in two long strides. He caught her chin in his hand, forcing her head up so that her dark eyes were fixed on the swaying cage. There was no change of expression on Rathina's pale face as she was forced to look at the torture of her people. How could she bear to see such suffering? It was as if their agony meant nothing to her.

Finally, Tania had to look away, as a stony hatred for her sister hardened inside her. She was suddenly aware that the dog smell had become stronger. One of the Morrigan hounds was moving toward them, its great blunt snout to the floor as it snuffled its way across the wooden boards.

Eden had seen the creature, too. The two of them crawled back into deeper cover under the table. The hound was only a man's length away now. It lifted its head and sniffed, turning its muzzle from side to side as if trying to capture an elusive scent. Tania kept her eyes on the hound as it took a few ponderous steps closer to their hiding place, its huge paws pounding down in front of them like black pillars. Had Eden been mistaken about their scent being masked by the glamour?

Every nerve in Tania's body quivered. To fight was not an option: The hound could easily snap them both up with one bite of its massive jaws. But if they broke cover, did they have any hope of getting back to the hole in the wall before they were run down?

"Eden?" Tania whispered. "I'm sure it can smell us. What are we going to do?"

Eden's long head turned to her and the eyes stared bleakly, hollow with despair. "What do we do? We die,

Tania. That is all. We die."

The dog was only a few steps away now, its gigantic head almost coming under the table. As its slavering jaws were lowered and its wide nostrils flared the stench of its breath nearly made Tania faint.

A harsh blare of trumpets rang through the Hall. The dog looked up, distracted by the noise. There was the sound of doors being thrown open. The dog trotted away, its tail wagging. The doors opened wide and a small group of figures strode into the Hall.

The Sorcerer King turned, opening his arms in welcome. "Gabriel Drake!" he called. "You are most welcome, honored servant. What news of your quest in the Mortal World? What news of the lost Queen and her errant daughters?"

Tania huddled against the wall, paralyzed with terror. The man she feared more than anyone else, the man to whom she had been betrothed for five hundred years and who had been freed from exile by the King of Lyonesse to pursue her into the Mortal World, had returned to Faerie.

Gabriel Drake strode up the long Hall with his Gray Knights at his back. Tania saw that the knights still wore dark jewels on bands at their foreheads—the black amber stones that had protected them in the Mortal World. Drake walked proudly with his head held up, but Tania noticed that his right arm was pinned against his body by a crude sling of gray material and that there was blood on his sleeve where Queen Titania had thrust a sword into his flesh.

The Sorcerer King watched him intently as he approached the dais. Drake knelt—a little stiffly—and bowed his head as he spoke. "My lord."

"How fare our fortunes in the Mortal World, Drake of Weir?" asked the Sorcerer King. "Are our enemies dead as I instructed you?"

"No, my lord." Drake's voice trembled as he spoke, and as he looked up at the towering figure of the Sorcerer King, Tania could see the fear in his eyes.

"Are they captured, then, good my Lord?" There

was an ominous edge to the King's voice now. "Have you brought them to us as helpless chattels to be the subject of our will and judgment?"

"I fear it is not so, my lord."

"Then you have failed us!" The voice hissed like a snake. The King thrust out his arm and although Drake wasn't touched, he sprawled forward onto the floor as though a huge weight had come crashing onto his back. "Did we not tell you when we sent you hence into the Mortal World that you should not return until your duties to our sovereign person were fulfilled!" raged the King. "And yet you come crawling back to us with tidings of a task unfulfilled and a quarry not found? Damn you to a sleepless death!"

The Sorcerer King opened his hand and Tania saw a ball of blue flame spinning in his upturned palm. His face contorted with anger, he flung his arm down—but as he did so Rathina threw herself forward, snatching at the King's arm with both hands, pulling it to one side so that the hurled ball of fire missed Drake and burst like a thunderbolt on the boards beside him.

The King swung his arm back, striking Rathina a savage blow to the side of her face. She fell backward with a stifled cry. "Do not impose upon our favor, *Trechla*—traitor-woman," thundered the Sorcerer King. "You live only by our will."

But Rathina's actions had given Drake time to get to his knees. He glanced at the circle of fire that flickered on the burned boards, then turned to face the King. "Kill me indeed, if it is your will," he exclaimed. "But in your wisdom, allow me to speak first." He got heavily to his feet, his good hand cradling his injured arm.

The Sorcerer King glared down at him for a moment, and Tania saw the anger fade a little from his face. He stepped back and sat in Oberon's throne. "Speak, then, and mayhap save your life," he said.

Drake stepped up to the dais. "Your enemies are powerful and cunning, my lord," he said, and his voice was as smooth and even as velvet. "I did not engage them in full battle, for I wished for them to lead me to the Queen, so that all could be ensnared and slaughtered. My lord, you told me that the way between the worlds was shut, but they summoned some enchantment to their will. I know not what it was, save that it took the form of a black sword. The Seventh Daughter wielded the sword and cut a path into Faerie. They passed through and the way closed behind them. I tried to open the door again by my Mystic Arts, but it was in vain."

He paused, licking his lips, and Tania knew he was watching for a reaction from the silent King. "I gathered the Knights and we rode swift as arrows through the Oriole Glass to bring you these tidings." His head lifted a little and he looked clear-eyed into the Sorcerer King's face. Clearly he was encouraged by the silence with which his words were being received. "They entered Faerie in Bonwyn Tyr, my lord. They have been in your Realm for but a brief time. Send out your Knights, and upon my word, the women will be dead within the hour. I wish only one favor: that you do not kill the traitor Edric Chanticleer, who came through with them." His silver eyes glinted. "I would beg that pleasure for my own, and I promise much sport ere his soul be teased forth!" He spread his arms and bowed his head. "And now, my lord, kill me if that is your will."

An expectant hush came over the Hall, pierced only by the groans of the Faerie captives. All eyes were on the King as he sat looking at Drake with his deep, hooded eyes. Tania saw fire flash under the dark brows. A cold, thin smile curled the King's lips.

"'Tis well," he murmured. "The woman and her brats are within our reach at last." He surged to his feet, his cloak billowing. He pointed to one of the Gray Knights. "Gristane, take three of your most trusted knights and go with all speed to the Royal Library. Mayhap the Queen will go there to retrieve the Soul Books of her family. Burn the library—wood, leather, and paper! If she comes, let her find only ruin!" His hand curled into a fist as he stared around the Hall. "Knights of Lyonesse, go now. Hunt down the Royal Family and put all to the sword. Our favors upon he who brings us the Queen's severed head!"

He lifted his arms and shouted words that Tania didn't understand—harsh words like axes ringing on stone. A black mist formed in front of him, swirling and condensing as the bars of the iron cage had done. Moments later, a half circle of gray swords hung in the air around him, their blades shining dully in the blue torchlight. The King made a sweeping gesture with his arms and the swords glided through the air until they hovered above the Gray Knights that stood at Drake's back. The other knights shrank back—without the power of black amber to protect them, they were as vulnerable to Isenmort as the Faerie folk.

"Weapons of Isenmort we give to you!" howled the King. "Use them well to destroy our enemies. And know this: once the woman and her brats are dead, nothing shall stand between us and the mine of Tasha Dhul! And upon that day, all our knights shall bear black amber upon their brows, and nothing in Faërie nor in the Mortal World shall be able to stand before us!"

Pandemonium erupted in the Hall as the Gray Knights streamed out, the baying hounds running along with them like a black tide. Now that the King's attention was turned away from him, Tania noticed that Drake's expression changed, his face betraying the relief he must be feeling at having survived his master's anger. Shivering in fear, she turned her eyes away from him and looked to where Rathina had fallen from the Sorcerer King's blow. She had lifted herself on one elbow, her hungry eyes on Gabriel Drake.

But Drake seemed completely unaware of her as he bowed to the King and then turned and swept from the Hall. His knights followed close behind, each of them wielding a sword of darkly shining steel.

"We must go," Eden hissed at Tania's side. "We must warn the others before this hell-spawn falls upon them."

Tania looked up at the captives in the iron cage. "Can't we do anything to help them?"

"No, alas," Eden said. "We can do nothing."

Tania felt sick at heart that they had to leave those poor prisoners to their fate but she knew Eden was right: How could they possibly rescue them from the Sorcerer King? If they attempted it, they would be discovered and killed—and then what of Faerie? She turned away and, trying to block out the sounds of their cries and moans, she went scudding along the floor in her sister's wake.

VI

The transformation back into her human shape was no less shocking to Tania than the change into rat form had been. If anything, it was worse. For some moments after Eden had cast the reversing spell, Tania lay panting on the roof beams, trying hard not to be sick. Her stomach was churning, hot and cold flushes wracked her body, her limbs shook. She watched with bleary eyes as Eden dressed herself.

"Come, Tania, make haste. Time is against us."

Trembling from head to foot, Tania struggled into her clothes in the confined roof space. Gradually the fever left her and she managed to gasp out a single question: "Why did the King tell them to burn the Library? I don't get it."

"He fears the power of the Soul Books," Eden replied. "He has no understanding of what the books truly are, but he fears them and would have them destroyed rather than risk their falling into the Queen's hands."

"Are they powerful, then? I didn't know that."

"They have power, but not in the way that he thinks. For him power is but a means to an end—a way to conquest and destruction. The books are not weapons; they cannot be used against him." Eden frowned. "But to destroy them would be an evil deed that would strike at the very heart of Faerie. It would be as if we had never existed."

Tania looked at her sister in alarm.

"Let us be gone," Eden said. "Death stalks this place."

They made their way down from the roof space, always on the alert for Gray Knights as they ran along the upper corridors, heading eastward to the part of the palace where the orchards would afford cover for them to get back to the forest. From a window in a corridor, Tania glanced down into the ravaged gardens. Gray Knights were riding hard through the withered flower beds, heading no doubt for the brown tower with Morrigan hounds following in a black flood. From other windows she saw more knights on horseback, swords in hands as they rode, and they all had the familiar, joyless grins fixed on their faces: the battle-smiles of Lyonesse, a grim mockery of mirth.

The hunt was up—and the Royal Family was the prey.

They were halfway down a wide staircase when Eden stopped, her arm coming across Tania's chest. From the stairwell below them came the sound of booted feet. Without a word they turned and ran back the way they had come. Tania leaned over the banister and saw two Gray Knights on the stairs. Beckoning, Eden led her through a series of interconnected rooms and along a gallery above a broad, high-ceilinged atrium. An ornate oak stairway led down. The floor below them was of red and green tiles, lined with tall candelabra. Light poured in through broken doors under a stone archway.

Tania recognized the room; those doors led to the gardens. She looked at her sister. "We can get out this way," she said. "Can you do that glamour thing again? Maybe turn us into birds or something this time?"

Eden shook her head. "I have not the strength yet for another such enchantment," she said. "I will need time and rest to summon my powers." She stiffened suddenly, her hand coming onto Tania's shoulder, her fingers biting into her flesh.

"What?" Tania stared around, afraid that Gray Knights were approaching.

"Zara is close by," Eden said. "I feel her. She is running. She is full of fear."

Tania gasped. "She's still here? How come?" Edric and Zara were meant to take Sancha back to the forest—they should all be long gone by now.

"I do not know. She is close. Very close. Come, we must go to her aid." Eden turned and ran back along the gallery.

Tania followed her. "What about Edric and Sancha?" she panted as she ran alongside her sister. "Are they still here as well?"

"Indeed they are," Eden told her. "Sancha is desperate. Edric fights for his life."

Twice they had to backtrack to avoid Gray Knights. Then they came to a long spiral stairway. As they descended Tania heard the patter of feet approaching. Not booted feet this time, but the soft sound of shoes on the stone treads.

Moments later, Zara appeared on the stairs below them. She stared up with desperate eyes. "Angels of mercy, I have found you!" she said. "Come. There is little time." She turned and ran back the way she had come. Eden and Tania followed hard on her heels.

"Sancha and Edric are in the Library," Zara explained breathlessly. "Gray Knights are upon them."

"Why aren't you in the forest like we agreed?" Tania demanded.

"Sancha recovered swiftly after we left you," Zara said. "She said we must go to the Library and take our father's Soul Book away with us. She said it would hold the secret of his imprisonment."

"Indeed it will," panted Eden. "I had not given thought to the Soul Book. Sancha will be able to read it. The story of our father's life will lead us to him."

"If she has the chance to cast her eyes upon it," Zara said. "We had only just entered the Library when four knights of Lyonesse fell upon us. I was outside, keeping watch when they came. They had torches with them. I fear they mean to burn all the books. While I fought with one the others entered the

Library. I slew the one that remained outside, but the others had barred the door against me and I could not get in. I heard Edric shout that I should seek you out."

"How long ago was this?" Tania asked.

"Not long, though we may yet be too late."

"Have no fear," Eden said. "They live still. I would know if it were otherwise."

They reached the corridor that led to the Library without encountering any Gray Knights. The tall doors were shut but there was the smell of burning from beyond them. A sword lay on the floor alongside a guttering torch and crumpled gray garments: boots, a suit of mail, and a broad cloak. Of the knight Zara had slain only a scattering of white ash remained. The Gray Knights of Lyonesse were not alive in any real sense; they were animated only by the will of their Dark Master. When their hearts were pierced, they turned to dust.

The sisters could hear the sounds of combat from beyond the doors. Tania hurled herself at the wooden panels. She was thrown back, her shoulder throbbing with pain.

Eden stepped in front of the doors. She raised her arms and pressed her spread-fingered hands over the wood. Her head dropped and Tania heard her speaking soft words. Eden stepped back and shouted a single word of command. The doors burst open, the wooden bar that held them closed splintering into flying fragments. Smoke was billowing through the

Library, spiraling up to the glazed dome of the roof. The circular galleries with their carved wood balustrades and shelves laden with thousands upon thousands of books could just be glimpsed through the thick gray fog. One whole side of the Library was already ablaze, the greedy yellow flames swarming up the ornate stairways and leaping over the galleries. Curled and blackened pages were falling through the smoke, ash white scraps leaping in the heat.

Smoke caught in Tania's throat and stung her eyes as she ran into the burning room. She saw Edric fighting with two knights who had backed him against a wall. One hacked at him with a slashing sword while the other sought a way through his defenses with a long spear. The swordsman's head turned at the sound of the door being blasted open, and Edric lunged with his sword. There was a gust of exploding ash and the knight's empty clothing collapsed to the floor, his sword ringing on the tiles.

Tania ran forward, shouting and brandishing her sword. The spearman turned quick as a snake toward her and she almost ran onto his spear-point. Edric's blade sang through the air and the spear was broken. A following thrust took the knight in the middle of his narrow chest. A burst of white ash foamed where his face had been. The gray mail slumped and the broken spear rattled on the ground.

"Where is Sancha?" Zara shouted above the roar of the flames.

"She went up to get the King's Soul Book," Edric

called. "She may be trapped by the fire."

Tania stared up into the smoke. The upper galleries couldn't be seen now; the fog of the burning surged and rolled against the roof. She threw down her sword and leaped for the winding wooden staircase. "Don't follow me!" she shouted. "I'll get her."

The heart of the fire was still some way off, but the flames were spreading fast, feeding greedily on the ancient books. Tania tried not to think of all the wisdom and knowledge that was being devoured by those leaping yellow tongues. She began to cough as she pounded up the stairs. She had been to the gallery where the Soul Books were kept and knew it was four flights of stairs up. The smoke wrapped around her like ghostly hands and the stench of burning filled her head, clogging her throat. She coughed, doubling over, clinging to the banister rail. She was almost there.

She ran along the fourth gallery, the fire licking at her heels. The aisle in which the Soul Books were kept was full of smoke.

"Sancha?" Tania shouted, trying to sweep the smoke aside with her arms as she ran.

She heard weak coughing from somewhere near the floor. The wreaths of smoke parted for a moment and she saw Sancha huddled in the corner. Her head was hanging and she was coughing and retching.

Tania reached down and dragged Sancha to her feet. Her sister's eyes swam in her pale face. The air crackled around them. Putting her arm around

Sancha's back, Tania half towed her toward the stairs.

"No!" Sancha struggled against her. "The King's book. We must get the King's book."

"It's too late!" Tania coughed.

"No!" Sancha pushed away from her and ran back into the burning niche.

"Sancha!" Half blinded and with her lungs shredded by heat and smoke, Tania stumbled after her sister. The flames surrounded them now and all the shelves seemed to be ablaze. She found her sister snatching down the heavy Soul Books from the upper shelves. Sancha already had three or four in her arms, and she was reaching for more. Dark smoke rolled into the gap where the books had been.

"Get away from there! You'll be killed," Tania shouted.

"Help me," Sancha said choking. "The Soul Books must be saved." A flickering tongue of fire leaped from the shelves, curling around the book that Sancha was pulling down. Tania heard a high-pitched scream as the flames took hold. At first she thought Sancha had cried out in pain, but the wailing voice did not belong to her sister. The Soul Books themselves were screaming.

The other books fell from Sancha's grasp, but one remained in her hands, burning her flesh. Tania flung herself forward, smashing the book out of Sancha's fingers and slapping at the flames that smoldered on her sleeves. She could see that her sister's hands were burned—but it was the look of horror in Sancha's face that terrified her the most.

"Tania!" Edric's voice sounded through the smoke.

"Here!" she shouted back.

Edric came plunging out of the smoke. Sancha was sagging in Tania's arms, her face a mask of unbearable misery.

"Help me," Tania said, gasping. "She's hurt."

Edric caught Sancha up in his arms.

"No—the King's book," Sancha groaned. "You must bring the King's book." Her arm swept down, her hand pointing to the smoldering floor where the books had fallen. The books were all aflame now, their cracked pages withering to black shreds.

Tania could just make out the spine of one of the books, the green and red letters standing out in the gloom: *Oberon Aurealis Rex*. She snatched at the book, but as her fingers grasped the spine the flames surged. Tania dropped the book again, her fingers seared. It fell open, the pages fluttering in the deadly fire wind.

Edric shouted to her. A wall of fire leaped forward. The heat beat her back, but not before she made one final effort to snatch hold of the book. She felt paper crumpling in her fist and she felt the weight of the book. Then the weight was gone as the pages tore loose and all she had in her fingers were a few crushed scraps.

It was too late to do any more. She fell back, her arms up to protect her face from the fierce heat. "Go!" she shouted to Edric.

He stumbled ahead of her through the smoke, Sancha in his arms. They came to the stairway and Tania took the lead, helping Edric to keep his footing in the darkness, helping him to support her sister.

Zara met them on the second stair. Eden was at her back. A well of clear air surrounded them, a bubble of oxygen in the dark clouds of smoke.

"Quickly!" Eden said, gasping. "I cannot hold the fire back for long."

As they ran across the Library floor Tania could see the flames hurling themselves at the outer skin of Eden's ball of pure air. The whole place was alight now. Sancha's beloved books were all burning. There was the crash of a collapsing gallery and the flames roared with triumphant laughter.

They reached the corridor. The smoke was less dense here.

"Follow me," Edric ordered. "We can go through the servants' quarters and the kitchens. I know the way. It'll take us right away from here."

They ran. Behind them the Great Library of Faerie burned like a furnace.

VII

Tania stared down through the trees that formed the southern edge of Esgarth Forest. Dark smoke was rising from the broken dome of the Library. Here and there on the long slope of heathland that rolled away into the west, she could make out the shapes of Gray Knights on horseback hunting for them with swords and spears at the ready. And running among the gray horses, she saw the black shapes of the Morrigan hounds.

They had escaped, at least for the time being. Edric had led them through underparts of the palace that she had never seen before—through kitchens and sculleries, washhouses and laundries, larders and storerooms that must once have rung with the cheerful bustle of the palace servants but were now bleak and deserted and disturbingly silent. The food left to rot, the overturned milk churns, the rancid butter, and moldering bread all told their own sad tales, as did a cook's apron Tania spotted on the floor, stained with blood.

Sancha had been able to walk after a while,

although she had clearly been in pain from her burns and weakened by the amount of smoke she had inhaled. She had stumbled along with Zara on one side and Edric on the other, her pale face soot-blackened, her hair tangled and filthy, her eyes hollow with agony at the loss of her beloved Library. Several times they had heard the sound of knights nearby but none found their trail, and they had made their way up through the orchards without encountering any of the murderous brood of Lyonesse.

Tania turned from the appalling sight of the palace and followed the others into the forest. They headed silently through trees withered by an unnatural winter, the dead leaves hanging from the branches like shrouds. There was no birdsong, no sign of life at all. Tania had folded the torn pages she had snatched from Oberon's Soul Book and slid them into a pocket. As they walked she took them out and opened them.

"Oh, no," she whispered, staring down at the blank pages.

Zara turned at the sound of her voice. "What is the matter?"

"Look." She showed the pages to her sister. "There's nothing on them. It was a total waste of time."

Zara gave a faint smile. "Nothing that reveals itself to your eyes, perhaps," she said. "Did you not know? A Soul Book can be read only by the one whose story it tells. These pages could teem with words, and you and I would see nothing. It is part of the mystery of the books."

"Then what was the point of trying to get Oberon's book if no one can read it?"

"One of us can," Zara said. "Sancha has the gift. There is not time for her to peruse these pages now; that can wait until we are deeper into Esgarth. But do not despair; put them away safely now, Tania. You may yet have in your hands all that we would wish."

Tania had just slipped the pages back into her pocket when Eden's voice rang out. "Cordelia and the Queen are close at hand." She pointed to the right. "This way, not three furlongs hence, and they have found water!"

A little while later they came to a place where the ground folded in on itself and they had to walk single file along a narrow valley, almost a trench, filled with the rattling and scratching fronds of dead ferns. But as they moved slowly onward Tania saw that the forest was beginning to change, as if bleak midwinter was giving way to glorious summer in the space of just a few footsteps. One step and all was brown and dead; a second step and the leaves and plants were yellowing and failing; a third step and all was green and growing.

"We have come to the edge of the Sorcerer King's pestilence," Eden said, looking back at Tania. "You see? His power is not yet absolute. He cannot kill all."

The vale met another fold in the land and now they could hear the trickle of water over stones. Below them, in a bowl-shaped dingle of lush grass and spread-fingered ferns within a sheltering ring of oak trees, they saw Cordelia and Titania seated on a rock beside a rippling stream. The two women jumped up at the sound of their approach, their eyes filled with relief and delight.

"Mother!" Eden's voice choked with emotion as she scrambled into the dell and embraced the Queen, bringing to an end five hundred years of separation and heartbreak.

"My beloved child!" Tania could see tears running freely down Titania's face. This meeting, after such a long and wounding parting, meant as much to the Queen as it did to the daughter who for five centuries had believed she had been the cause of her mother's death.

Cordelia helped them get Sancha down the slope. "Her poor hands," she said, staring at the red raw burns that disfigured Sancha's skin. "What happened?"

"The Gray Knights burned the Library," Tania said, helping the others ease Sancha down so that she sat with her back to a large stone. "And Drake is here. It's really bad in the palace. People are still alive in there." Her voice shook. "They're torturing them."

Cordelia's eyes blazed and her hand reached automatically for her sword hilt.

"They know we're in Faerie," Edric said. "The Sorcerer has sent all his knights out to find us."

"Then let them find us," Cordelia spat. "They will rue the discovery!"

It was Sancha who spoke next, her voice faint and rasping. "They are hundreds, Cordelia. We are but seven. It would be folly to face them in battle." She looked up at them. "We must flee."

"To what place?" Cordelia demanded. "Where

shall we be free of them? To the crags of Leiderdale in the uttermost west? Or maybe north to the wastes of Fidach Ren? Would that be far enough, think you?"

"Calm yourself, Cordelia," Eden said with gentle authority. "We must be prudent, though our hearts would have it otherwise. You know this forest better than any of us; is there a place where we might find shelter for the night?"

"The House of Gaidheal lies only a few leagues hence on the forest's northern edge," Zara said. "We will find a warm welcome there, if the lord and lady have not fled."

Tania bit her lip. "I don't think they'll be there," she said quietly. "I think they were in the palace when . . . when Rathina freed the Sorcerer King."

"Gaidheal House would not be a safe place," Titania said. "We need to find somewhere the knights may not think to look."

"Listen!" Edric's voice was like a whip crack. He was standing stiffly on the edge of the dell, his hand raised in warning.

"What is it?" Zara asked.

"Hounds," came the short reply.

Tania held her breath, straining her ears. The distant sound of baying drifted through the trees, sending a cold shudder up her spine.

"The Morrigan hounds are on our trail," said Eden. "Our options diminish."

"I know where we may find shelter," Cordelia said. "There is an old hunting lodge not far from here. A forester has made it his home now for many a long year. Rafe Hawthorne is his name and he is a good man and true. But it will not shield us from the tracking skills of the Morrigan hounds."

"Have no fear," Eden said. "I will protect us once we are there. Sancha, can you walk?"

Sancha pulled herself to her feet. "Yes," she said through clenched teeth.

"Master Hawthorne will tend your wounds, sister," Cordelia said. She looked at the others. "Let us pray that he is not fled."

The eerie baying of the hounds came floating through the trees again, a little louder now, and with a slightly different tone to it.

Cordelia's eyes widened and she let out a soft hiss. "Can you not hear it? They are merry—they have found our scent."

"Then let's get out of here," Tania said.

"No," said Cordelia. "Wait a moment." She turned and went leaping up the side of the dell. She vanished into the trees. For a few moments there was the rustle of movement, then silence.

"Where's she gone?" Tania asked.

"I know not," Zara said. "We must trust her."

They waited in silence, all of them staring up to where Cordelia had disappeared. Tania felt Edric's hand slip into hers. She looked at him and he gave her a reassuring smile.

"Eden wasn't able to read the Sorcerer King's mind," she told him.

"I guessed not," he said. "Was it bad?"

Tania swallowed; it was too soon to speak easily of

the things she had seen in the Great Hall. "Rathina was there," she said. "Sitting next to the King."

All eyes turned to her. "As his consort, do you mean?" Zara whispered. "Pray that it is not so!"

"I'm not sure," Tania said. "Maybe she's under a spell or something. Her face was . . . I don't know . . . it was totally blank."

"Aye," said Eden. "Until the traitor Drake entered the hall. Then the love-light brightened her eyes swiftly enough."

"The poor child," Titania murmured. "Imagine how she must feel, knowing she caused all this."

Sancha's eyes flashed. "It is by her actions that they burned my Library," she said in a low, flint-hard voice. "It were best Rathina came not ever within my reach. I would rejoice to see her writhing in flame!"

Titania reached out a hand and rested it on Sancha's arm, her face full of sadness. Sancha frowned at her and shook the hand off. Tania also hated everything that Rathina's wickedness had caused—but deep within her a small voice reminded her that they had once been the very best of friends. She sighed, comforted a little by the feel of Edric's hand in hers. Had all the wonder and glamour of Faerie come down to this: to be hunted through the forest and murdered by the Sorcerer King's undead minions?

The terrible music of the approaching hounds sounded out clearly from the south. Death was approaching fast.

There was a rustle in the trees and Cordelia burst out. Tania noticed movement at her feet: a blur of red fur in the long grass. Foxes. Five, six, seven foxes came tumbling down into the dell, their pink tongues lolling, their eyes bright with cunning.

"Come!" Cordelia called, beckoning. "The scent of fox is stronger than the scent of Faerie folk; they will mask our trail and leave the hounds bereft!"

They made their way up quickly to where Cordelia was standing. Tania looked over her shoulder as they went into the trees. The foxes were rolling and cavorting in the grass, erasing all sign that they had been there.

She smiled gratefully down at them. "Brilliant!" she whispered. "Thank you."

Cordelia led them at a great pace through the trees, pushing on and on as the afternoon waned, not allowing them to stop even for a moment. At first they could still hear the faint baying of the hounds, but after a while the forest became quieter, although Tania still felt the threat of pursuit close behind them.

The forest seemed to go on forever; the ground rising and falling as they made their way northward, the trees thick around them, the branches always stretching over their heads, the afternoon light dappled green through the leaves. As evening approached and the shadows lengthened, birds began to sing, and soon the whole forest seemed to ring with their voices. It was such a joyous, untroubled sound that it lightened Tania's heart. Even though horrors stalked the land at their backs, at least something of light and beauty remained to hold back the oncoming dark.

But she was tired. So very tired. When had she last

slept? Fitfully, two nights ago. But a true, deep, untroubled sleep? She couldn't remember. Days and days ago, it seemed. She stumbled, her aching legs betraying her for a moment. Edric's arm circled her waist, saving her from falling.

"Can you manage?" he asked softly.

She stepped gratefully into his arms and they held each other for a moment, her face against his neck. "I'll be fine," she said. They kissed and she broke away from him, giving him a rueful smile. "It's not like I have much of a choice, is it?"

"I could carry you."

She touched his face with her fingertips. "You look as tired as I feel," she murmured. "Perhaps I should carry *you*?"

Cordelia's voice came ringing out from up ahead. "Rejoice! We are at journey's end!" she called. "Behold the Royal Hunting Lodge."

They emerged into a wide clearing hemmed with chestnut trees. Above them, the dome of the sky was cloudless: a deep, sultry blue to the east, glowing with purple and violet light in the west. The crescent moon sailed high and a few stars were already glittering as the sun went down.

A thatched building was set back toward the rear of the clearing, a large half-timbered house with two floors and many windows. Warm yellow light glowed behind the glass, and even as they stood on the fringe of trees the door of the house opened and the light of a lantern poured out. A heavyset man came striding out, the lantern held in his upraised hand.

"Travelers, ho!" he called in a rich, deep voice. "No weary friend was ever turned from my door, and although I play host to many lost souls, I shall find room for you in my . . ." As he came closer his voice faded away and a look of astonishment transfixed his face. He stumbled forward and dropped to his knees in front of Titania.

"Your Grace!" he said. "From beyond the veil of death you return to us in our darkest need." He looked up at the Queen and Tania saw tears welling in his eyes. "Save us, Your Grace. For pity's sake, save us."

Titania stooped and drew the man to his feet. "I hope that I shall find the strength for that," she said. "But meanwhile we are tired and hungry, and one of my daughters is hurt. Show us into your house, Master Hawthorne. Quickly now, Lyonesse hunts us close by."

Fear showed starkly in the man's round face and Tania saw him glance into the forest. "Only over my dead body will any of that evil brethren cross my threshold," he said, but his voice was trembling.

"That were bravely said!" Eden responded. "But they will not find us. Go you all now into the house; I will follow shortly."

Tania saw faces appear at the windows as they approached the house. A plump woman stood at the door; her face breaking out into a smile as they came closer. Tania recognized her immediately—it was Mistress Mirrlees, the seamstress who had made the gown Tania had worn at her welcoming ball. But she was sadly transformed: her blue dress tattered and grimed, her hair unkempt and her eyes shadowed with lack of sleep.

"I did not look for such joy to come at the end of such evil days!" Mistress Mirrlees cried, running out to meet them. "Your Grace—and my beloved princesses!"

Zara threw her arms around the small woman's neck. "I prayed that you had not fallen to evil," she said.

"Nay, not I, my lady, but many have," Mistress Mirrlees said, patting Zara's shoulders. "So many."

More people came out of the house now: waifs and strays from the palace who had fled here in hope of refuge. Tania was glad and relieved to see that at least some of the palace folk had escaped alive. She recognized many of the faces. They were mostly servants and retainers: women from Mistress Mirrlees's workrooms, some stable lads, people from the kitchens. And a maid that Tania remembered very well: a timid, sweet-faced girl who had once taken Tania to the King's privy Dining Room. They all crowded around the Queen, a new light in their eyes as they curtsied and bowed to her. Titania stood among them, taking their hands, speaking to them, bringing them hope.

Eden was still standing at the edge of the clearing. Her back was to the house and she held her arms spread wide, fingers splayed. Her thick white hair hung heavy as snowfall down her back. She was chanting in a slow lilt, and Tania could just about make out the words:

I call upon you who dwelt in Faerie when Faerie was yet young

I call upon you who drank the seas when the
seas were sweet
Who ate the fruit of ancient trees and breathed
first the wholesome air
You spirits of root and branch and blossom and
leaf
Aid me now and preserve me from my enemies.

As Tania watched, a soft, pale green light began to glow all around her sister, as if she was a hollow figure carved from jade and lit by an inner flame. Moments later, light poured out from Eden's fingers, sparkling with emerald points, like a filigree-fine spiderweb spinning out into the night, jeweled with green stars. The net rose and spread and curled upward and over and down in a smooth arc, forming a shimmering dome over the clearing. Tania felt the air ripple. A spicy smell tickled her nose. The forest beyond the dome went dark.

Eden turned and walked toward the house. Her face was pale and drawn, but she was smiling as she came up to Tania. "I am weary beyond measure," she said, resting her hand on Tania's shoulder. "But it is done. The Emerald Shield is only a temporary enchantment, but neither hound nor horse nor undead thing shall find us here for the time being." She sagged and Edric was quick to catch her arm and help her as they followed the others into the welcoming light of Rafe Hawthorne's forest home.

VIII

Beyond Eden's twinkling emerald dome, night had fallen over the land of Faerie. A couple of times through the evening Tania and Edric had gone to the perimeter of the enchanted force field, listening for any sounds of pursuit. The first time, they had heard only birdsong; the second, a single howl, definitely a Morrigan hound, but too far off to be of concern.

Inside, the hunting lodge was large yet cozy, with long, low-beamed rooms and winding stairs to the upper level. Warm yellow candlelight banished shadows, and the scores of people who had come to Rafe Hawthorne's home for refuge from the Sorcerer King tended to Queen Titania and the princesses and Edric with all the care they had shown in more peaceful times. The refugees had harrowing tales to tell of their own—of fleeing the palace in the night, of plunging in blind terror into the forest. Of losing friends and family in the chaos that followed the release of the Gray Knights. Of seeing companions being cut down, of flaming torches flung into rooms where people were trapped, of the doors being locked on them. Of the mad rampage of Lyonesse through the palace.

Sancha was taken to an upstairs bedchamber, where several women tended her wounds, salving the burns on her hands and wrapping cooling bandages around them. Tania went to see her once she had been made comfortable but by then Sancha had fallen into an uneasy sleep. Tania didn't like to think of the dreams that were disquieting her rest.

There was only a limited amount of food to go around with so many people, but enough was found to give the seven newcomers something fresh to eat: apples and pears, grapes and damsons and strawberries and blackberries from the forest. Mushrooms, eggs, and venison, too, were cooked and set before the Queen and her daughters, along with springwater and a glass or two of the rich red cordial of Faerie.

The people were eager to hear Titania speak of what had happened to her after she had gone through the Oriole Glass five hundred years ago. Until only a few days ago, they had all thought her dead—and now, to find her alive and well and back in Faerie, was like a miracle. They listened in rapt silence, sitting on the floor and on every table and chair, others on the stairs, more standing at the walls, as she stood with the green-lit window at her back and spoke to them at length of the Mortal World.

As the evening progressed people began to drift off to sleep—some in the beds, others on makeshift palliasses, and a few hardy young lads and lasses content to curl up in warm corners with blankets thrown over them. Tania learned from Rafe Hawthorne that the Royal Hunting Lodge had many fine bedchambers under the eaves of its long, stooping thatched roof, though not enough for all its guests now. He told her that the house had not been used by the Royal Family since the Great Twilight began—those bleak centuries when Oberon had brooded upon the loss of his wife and youngest daughter and time had stopped throughout the Realm.

At last, when the night was fully come, only Edric and the Queen and the princesses still remained awake with Rafe Hawthorne.

"Many of your folk escaped the palace, Your Grace," he explained as they sat around a long oakwood table in flickering candlelight. "From what I have been able to find out, some fled south across the river into Udwold Forest. One ship at least managed to set sail from Fortrenn Quay before the Knights descended, but I do not know where she fared nor what became of those aboard."

"And the *Cloud Scudder*?" Zara asked. "Is she safe?"

"Nay, my lady. She was burned by those devils, rig and rigging."

Tania felt a terrible pang of loss; the Royal Galleon, *Cloud Scudder*, had been a beautiful, wonderful ship. Tania had sailed on her just once on an enchanted voyage to the island of Ynis Logris to celebrate the festival of the Traveler's Moon. It made her heart ache to think she had been destroyed.

"A few followed the line of the Tamesis west, meaning to make for the fortress of Caer Marisoc, but most came north over the heaths and through Esgarth," Rafe Hawthorne went on. "I scoured the forest for lost souls; those you have met were all that I found. I was told that a good many folk were heading north to Ravensare and some others to the east coast to find refuge in Caer Gaidheal. Lord Gaidheal was leading them, so I was told, but his lady was not among them. It is hoped she found another way out of the palace."

"She didn't," Tania said softly. "I saw her in the Great Hall. The Sorcerer King wanted her to dance for him . . . he did something horrible to her . . . he made red wings grow out of her back." She put her hands to her face as the memories came flooding into her mind. Edric's hand rested on her shoulder and she leaned against him.

"Lady Gaidheal was killed for the sport of the Sorcerer King," Eden said. "I fear for anyone left alive in that place."

"Can we not mount a rescue?" Cordelia asked. "I do not say we go there to do battle, but is there no way we can save our people from this scourge?"

"The hunt is up now that the Sorcerer King knows we are here," Edric said. "I don't think we'd even get out of the forest now. And what if one of us was captured?" He looked around the table. "We might wish ourselves dead rather than meet such a fate."

"Master Chanticleer speaks truth," Eden said.

"Bravely endured pain will not save us if one is taken alive. The Sorcerer King will shred our very minds to learn where the Queen may be found."

"Our only hope is that word is spreading quickly enough through the Realm," said Titania. "There are people who will be able to rally armies. Earl Marshal Cornelius for one, and Hopie and Lord Brython will gather more troops in the west."

"My husband will not be slow to heed the call to arms if asked," Eden put in quietly. "The men of Mynwy Clun are fierce and loyal—they will follow Earl Valentyne and come to our aid if anyone can be spared from here to make the journey west to Caer Mynwy."

Tania had forgotten that Eden was married; all she could recall being told was that Earl Valentyne had quit the palace when the Great Twilight had come down. Eden had not spoken of him before, and seemed reluctant to mention him now, judging by the tone of her voice and the pensive expression on her face.

"And what of Weir?" Titania asked. "Will Lord Aldritch send help?"

Tania looked up sharply at the mention of Gabriel Drake's father.

"The northern borderlands have ever been debatable territory," Eden said.

"But surely they are loyal?" said Zara.

"Lord Aldrich is an honorable man," Edric said thoughtfully. "He won't ally himself with Lyonesse, but Weir is a long way from here. He may decide to use his army to defend his own borders rather than risk sending a force south to help us."

"And will he not take it ill that our father banished his only son?" Cordelia pointed out. "That news will have reached him by now, surely."

"Gabriel Drake's crimes were great beyond measure," Eden said. "Even a father could not excuse them."

Titania shook her head. "He may not be able to excuse them, but he will still love his son, no matter what terrible things he has done. Edric is right: We should not rely on Weir's aid."

Tania looked around at her mother and her sisters. "Exactly how powerful is the Sorcerer King?" she asked. "He's only a got a few hundred knights with him right now. If everyone you're talking about gets together and helps us attack him, won't we be able to beat him?"

"Only Oberon and Titania together have the power to defeat the Sorcerer King," Eden replied. "Lyonesse has rule over the Four Elements—over earth, water, fire, and air. Only the strength of the Sun King and the Moon Queen in unison can stand against such fearsome might. And as for his army—it is true that they number only in the low hundreds now, but the Sorcerer will have sent word to Lyonesse. An armada will come and an army thousands strong will sweep across Faerie like a dark plague."

"The people of Faerie are far flung," Rafe Hawthorne added. "It will take time for our forces to gather."

"And even then the Sorcerer may prove too deadly to assail," Zara said. "We have seen how the land withers around him."

"Yet his power has its limits," said a new voice from

the far end of the room. They all turned. Sancha was standing at the foot of the stairs. She looked tired and haggard, but there was a fierce light in her eyes.

Zara ran to help her, but Sancha gently pushed her sister's hands away. "I can walk," she said. She seemed stiff and Tania could see the pain in her face as she came over to the table. Rafe found her a chair and she sat with a sigh.

"How are you?" Titania asked, looking anxiously at her daughter's bandaged hands. "Are you in a lot of pain still?"

"It is somewhat better," Sancha said.

"Would that Hopie were here." Cordelia sighed. "She would ease your suffering."

Sancha frowned. "Ease my suffering?" she murmured, lifting her hands and looking at them. "No, I do not think she would be able to do that." Her eyes welled with tears. "My Library is burned. What ease is there for that loss?"

"And yet we live," Cordelia reminded her. "And while we live, we have the hope of revenge."

"Tania, show Sancha the pages you tore from Oberon's book," Titania said.

Tania took out the few pages and pushed them across to her sister. Sancha spread them out, leaning over them, her fingertips on the blank ivory-colored paper.

"Sun, moon, and stars," she murmured. "This goes beyond luck." She lifted her head and looked at Tania. "This is the spirits of fortune working for our aid—it can be nothing other."

"You can read them, then?" Tania asked.

"Indeed I can," Sancha said. "Listen, and learn of the fate of our dear father." She began to read, her fingers following the lines of script that only she could see.

"In his slumber was King Oberon taken and overthrown by the Sorcerer King of Lyonesse. And bound he was in the unbreakable circle of an Amber Prison, yet fearful still was the Serpent of Lyonesse that Oberon's power would see him burst forth from his entrapment. And so the Sorcerer King wove evil enchantments about the Amber Prison, bending to his will the Isenmort sword which the Princess Rathina had used to free him, and forging from it straps and bonds of Isenmort to enwrap the Amber Prison so that all the strength of the sun could not break the seal that lay upon Oberon's jail."

Sancha's voice shook as she read. No one spoke as her fingers turned the page over. Tania was hardly even breathing.

"And then did the Sorcerer King taunt Oberon with foul words and curses, lamenting that he could not entirely destroy his prisoner, but speaking of the joy he would take in the slaughter of Oberon's children. And were this not enough to fill Oberon's heart with darkness, the Sorcerer spoke of his plan to overwhelm

Faerie with the armies of Lyonesse, and of how
his Queen, the lady Lamia, had long returned to
Bale Fole, to the great fortress of Lyonesse, and
how she had been amassing in secret a mighty
armada which would fall upon Faerie as an
ocean wave falls upon a child's castle of sand."

"Then the armada already exists," said Titania.
"That is bad news. I had hoped we would have a few
weeks or even months before reinforcements arrived
from Lyonesse."

"Even if the hag Queen of Lyonesse let loose her
ships upon the same eve as the Sorcerer was freed,
still we have several days ere the red sails will come
into sight," Eden pointed out.

"'Tis too short a time," Cordelia said. "Days? Is
that sufficient time to put a ring of bright Faerie
swords around the Sorcerer King?"

"'Twill need to suffice," Zara said. "'Tis that or surrender our land to the blight of Lyonesse."

"There are people here who can be sent to all the
corners of Faerie," Rafe Hawthorne added. "They will
tell of our plight and ask for aid as swift as may be."

Their debate was interrupted by a low cry from
Sancha, who was still reading the pages from
Oberon's Soul Book. "I know where father has been
taken," she said. "Listen.

"Thus spake the Sorcerer King to downfallen
Oberon: 'Know you that my first desire when my
armies conquer Faerie will be to seek the mine of

Tasha Dhul, for I would have the black amber to my hand, and with it will I furnish an army of tens of thousands that I will send into the Mortal World. And lest you deceive yourself with the false hope of rescue or escape, know this: You shall I banish to the uttermost margins of your Realm. To Ynis Maw shall I send you, Oberon Aurealis that once were King, to the Island of No Return!' And thus speaking, the Sorcerer King summoned up a great enchantment of storm and hurricane and upon the breast of a tornado was Oberon swept away to the Island of Banishment."

Ynis Maw! Tania had never been to the desolate island, but she had seen it many times in dreams sent to her by Gabriel Drake. It was a bleak fist of rock jutting from stormy seas off the northern coast of Faerie, a place where only the worst traitors were sent.

Tania looked around the table. "So, how do we get him back from there?"

"We don't," Edric said bleakly. "There's no way."

"There has to be," Tania insisted. "Eden, you've got all that Mystic Arts stuff going for you. You *must* know a way of getting him back."

Eden shook her head. "That were an enchantment far beyond my skill, Tania. You'd as well ask me to draw down the moon for a royal chariot."

"There is only one way," said Titania, and her voice was firm and steady. "We will have to go to Ynis Maw."

"How far is it?" Tania asked.

"Nearly two hundred leagues," said Cordelia. "We would need horses—and the fortune to outwit Lyonesse's guards. Nonetheless, 'tis not an impossible journey. But even should we reach the island and find our father, how would we break the bonds of Isenmort set around his prison?"

"Black amber will sever the Isenmort bonds," Eden said. "Were we able to lay stones of black amber upon them, the Isenmort bands would be burned away to nothing."

"You mean black amber can dissolve metal?" Tania asked. "I didn't know that."

"In the Mortal World it is not so," Sancha said. "But here in Faerie, Isenmort cannot endure the touch of black amber."

"So, how much black amber have we got between us right now?" asked Tania.

They all still had the black amber stones that they had been wearing to protect themselves in the Mortal World: There were five jewels in all.

"That may be enough to sever the bonds of Isenmort," Eden said. "But only Isenmort itself can break the Amber Prison that holds our father."

"Can't the bands themselves be used?" Edric asked.

"No, they will be turned to vapor by the touch of black amber."

"Then I'll have to go back into the Mortal World," Tania said. "I'll bring something metal through into Faerie."

"Even if the black amber we have here were enough to allow you to cut your way into the Mortal World, how would you return?" Eden asked. "Experience shows us that any weapon that breaches the Sorcerer King's barrier is destroyed. Even if you gathered a mountain of Isenmort, you would be unable to return to us with it."

"And we would have no black amber to break our father's bonds," Cordelia added. "No, Tania. It is bravely said, but it will not work."

Another idea formed in Tania's mind. "We're all still wearing the clothes we had on back in London," she said. "There has to be some metal in them: zippers and studs and so on. Couldn't we use that?"

Edric nodded. "And I've got house keys and some coins on me."

Tania had noticed that the Queen had been lost in deep thought all through the conversation about the black amber, but now she spoke. "My clothes have metal catches and a zip fastener," she said. "That was a good thought, Tania."

Tania looked at Eden. "How much metal would it take to wreck an Amber Prison?"

"Enough to fill the palm of a hand would suffice," Eden said.

"Then we're okay," Tania said. "We must have that much between us." She looked around the table. "So, what else do we need?"

"Princess Cordelia mentioned horses earlier," Edric said.

"Indeed, I did," Cordelia said. "Many of the Palace

horses fled into the forest when the Gray Knights awoke. I saw traces of their passing as we came to this place. I will be able to track them—then shall we have noble steeds to bear us to Fidach Ren."

"And at journey's end we will be able to deliver the King from his prison," Sancha said. "Then let Lyonesse beware!"

Tania caught Edric's eye across the table and grinned. Things were looking up: They had black amber and they had Isenmort to break Oberon's bonds. There was hope now that the Sorcerer King could be thwarted.

"We cannot all go to Ynis Maw," Titania said. She looked at Sancha. "You are certainly not well enough, my dear child. You must stay here and recover."

"And I cannot stray from this place," said Eden. "I cannot protect this house from the hounds and the Gray Knights unless I am here. I would not risk all these people being hunted down and killed." She looked at Titania. "I do not think you should go, Mother," she said. "The journey will have many perils, and I would have you safe at my side where no harm can come to you. For without you, our father will not have the strength to defeat the Sorcerer King."

Titania frowned at her. "You're asking me to remain in hiding once more while I send my daughters out into danger," she said. "I cannot do that."

"While Lyonesse threatens the Realm, Your Grace, your people will be heartened to know that you at least are kept in safety," said Rafe Hawthorne.

"My husband needs my help, Master Hawthorne."

Titania's eyes flashed. "I did not return to Faerie only to hide away when I am needed most."

"You will be needed *most* once Oberon is free," Eden reminded her. "By protecting yourself now, you will better be able to defy the Sorcerer when the time comes."

"Your people will bless you for it," said Rafe Hawthorne. "Do it for them, Your Grace."

For a few moments Tania saw indecision flickering in the Queen's eyes, then Titania sighed. "Perhaps you are right," she said. "And if Master Hawthorne will pour a bowl of clear water for me to look into, I shall at least be able to watch over you in your travels."

"Then it is settled," said Cordelia. "Tania and Zara and I shall go."

"And me," Edric added. "There's no way I'm staying behind."

Tania smiled at him; she had already known he would insist on going with them. "Then, it's the four of us," she said. "But how soon should we get going? Right now?"

"None of you have slept for two days," Titania said. "You must rest first, otherwise you will be fit for nothing."

"So be it," Cordelia said. "A few hours abed and then we will rise dew-fresh in the dawn. I will find us mettlesome steeds, and may the long miles to Prydein flow away under us and may the sun shine bright upon our venture! To the farmost north—and to the rescue of the King!"

IX

It was shortly after sunup the next day, and the four travelers were standing at the edge of the jade barrier. The forest beyond was still shrouded in a heavy, dark green gloom, but the curved roof of the dome shone with a glow that was like sunlight through fresh spring leaves.

Eden and Titania and Sancha were with them, and many eyes watched from outside the Hunting Lodge and from the thrown-open windows. The four of them were no longer wearing their mortal clothes. Mistress Mirrlees had used her Arts to create new garments for all of them. They were dressed in simple tunics and leggings of brown and green and shoes of supple tan leather. They each wore a crystal sword at one hip and carried a stoppered water-pouch and a small bag of food at the other. Even Zara had not objected this time to looking more like a peasant than a princess—she knew as well as the others that they would need practical clothes for their long journey up the length of Faerie.

Tania was carrying all the black amber jewels to protect her from the poisonous bite of the Isenmort that she had stripped from their mortal clothes. Everything metal—keys, coins, zipper teeth, hooks and eyes, and studs—was gathered in a cloth bag hidden inside her tunic.

"I can do little to aid you on your journey," Eden said as they were preparing to make their way through the barrier and out into the dangers of the forest. "But take this." She handed Tania a small blue-green ball, about an inch in diameter. It felt warm in Tania's open palm, the shining surface moving constantly as the colors merged and flowed together like oil on water.

"It is a wishpearl," Eden explained. "A simple glamour that I managed to save from the ruin of my sanctum."

"How does it work?" Tania asked, gazing in delight at the sliding colors of the small ball.

"If you find yourself in harm's way, take it in your palm and wish for what you need," said Eden. "Then smash the wishpearl upon the ground and your desire will be revealed to you. But be sure to use it wisely, for it can be called upon only once."

Tania looked wide-eyed at her. "You mean, I could wish for a helicopter? That would be so cool."

Eden smiled gently. "I do not know what a *helicopter* may be," she said. "But you must understand that the wishpearl can only create illusions. Were you to be assailed by Gray Knights, you could wish for a griffin to appear to frighten their horses and give you time to escape. But the griffin will not be real, it will not be able to harm your enemies, and that for which you wish will only exist for a few moments."

"Long enough for us to escape," Zara said. "Most excellent! Keep it safe, Tania."

Tania slipped the wishpearl into an inner pocket. She turned to her Faerie mother. "Keep everyone safe," she said, looking over Titania's shoulder at the people watching them from the Lodge.

Titania stepped forward and they embraced. "I will," she promised. "And don't you take any unnecessary risks, either. Keep away from any signs of habitations: farms and villages and hamlets. Try not to let anyone see you."

"That is wise advice," Eden added. "The people of Faerie are good and true, but I would not wish their loyalty tested at sword-point if the Gray Knights are on your track. Keep to the wild places—eat what you find growing on your travels. The trees and fields and hedgerows of Faerie will supply all your needs. Fill your water-pouches from streams and brooks and always keep one pair of eyes open when you sleep."

Tania nodded. Despite the danger and desperation of their plight, she felt a sense of excitement and curiosity growing in her; they would be journeying into regions of Faerie of which she had no memory at all, so for her part of the quest would be a rediscovery of her homeland.

"Once you pass from the forest, head to the north-west," Sancha said. "You should travel through Passion Meadows and thence up to the foothills of Sinadon. Pass the mountains to the west, but avoid the walled city of Caer Regnar Naal. Edric was born and bred in the north, and he will be your guide once you enter the wilds of Weir—but stray not too near the high castle of Duke Aldritch. Once across the bleak River Lych, you will be in the wilderness of Prydein. There you must never let your guard down. Many strange beasts dwell in those parts; they are savage and have little love for Faerie folk."

Titania looked gravely at Edric. "I give my daughters into your hands, Master Chanticleer," she said. She smiled. "And you into theirs." She rested her hand on his shoulder. "Come back safely, Edric," she said. "And bring the princesses and the King back to me."

"I will, Your Grace," Edric said, dropping to one knee.

Eden was staring into the forest darkness beyond the emerald wall. "Be most careful upon emerging from the enchantment. The hounds may be close by."

"Don't worry, we will," Tania said. She looked at the others. "Ready?"

Cordelia unsheathed her sword and without another backward glance, stepped into the shimmering barrier. For a split second, she was lit by a glorious green glow—then she was gone. Drawing their own swords, Tania and Edric and Zara followed her.

Tania's eyes filled with blinding green light as she walked into the barrier. A sensation like a mild electric shock tingled over her skin, and then she was through and standing in the forest with Cordelia and Edric and Zara close by. She turned. There was no sign of the barrier behind her, just an endless procession of trees bathed in early light marching off into the distance. It was hard to believe that Eden and Titania and all the others were standing only a few feet away.

"What would happen if someone accidentally hit the barrier?" she asked.

"They would see nothing," Cordelia told her. "They would pass through to the other side and be none the wiser. Do not fear, Tania; they are safe."

"Aye, far more safe than are we," Zara muttered, peering into the trees. "Do you hear that?"

"What?" Tania asked.

"Listen!" Zara hissed.

A long, eerie howl floated toward them.

"The Morrigan hounds," Cordelia said. "And not far enough away. But I must find the trail left by the horses or we shall not get out of Esgarth alive. Follow me, and be as silent as you can." She turned this way and that, sniffing the air and staring through the trees. Then she took off at a low, loping pace, her head down, eyes scanning the ground. The others followed close, Tania first, then Zara, and Edric at the rear.

Even if Tania had known where they were when they had started, she would quickly have lost all sense of direction. Cordelia led them up mossy slopes of berry red rowan and down stony hillsides where gnarled trees clung at hazardous angles with their roots standing proud of the earth. They jumped pebbled brooks and clambered up tussocked mounds, sometimes coming out into a small glade where they could see the sky yellow with dawn above their heads, sometimes plunging into deep willow-clad ravines where the night still brooded under the dense roof of branches.

A howl sounded, uncomfortably close by. Cordelia stopped and sniffed. "I smell dead things," she whispered. "There are Gray Knights close by. But I have found the trail of some living horses. At least five horses galloped this way not many days ago, afraid and running swift. If I am leading us true, then I think I know where they may be." She pointed into the trees. "Yonder lies a fold in the land, no more than ten furlongs from here—a place called Deepdene. The Wyvern stream runs through it as it makes its way down through the forest to join the Tamesis. There is lush grass there. It would be a good place for horses to find rest and comfort."

"Let's hope so," Tania said. The cries of the Morrigan hounds were making her skin crawl.

Cordelia was quickly on the move again; they followed hard at her heels as she ran like a gazelle through the trees, her head up now that she was sure of where they were going.

The hound came on them seemingly out of

nowhere. The first Tania knew of it was a blur of darkness that came hurtling down from a high rock. It crashed into Cordelia, sending her tumbling to the ground, her sword slipping from her grasp. Tania saw Cordelia twist under the huge dog, turning onto her back, her teeth gritted as she thrust her arm between the slavering jaws and forced the great ugly head back while she felt blindly for her sword with her free hand.

Tania flung herself forward, gripping her sword hilt tightly as she drove the white blade into the beast's side. There was a horrible yelping scream as the creature writhed in its death agonies. She heard a commotion behind her. Edric was shouting. There was a growl—cut off short. The thud of something heavy hitting the ground. A whimper. Tania turned to see a second dog lying dead, Edric standing over it with his sword lifted for another blow.

Cordelia dragged herself out from under the first hound and snatched up her sword. "Quickly now, the howls will have alerted others."

They ran like the wind, leaping fallen branches, careless of the low branches that whipped their face and tore at their hair. A dreadful baying sounded to their left. Cordelia halted for a moment then sped off to the right. But they had not gone more than ten yards before Tania heard barking from straight ahead of them. Again, Cordelia changed direction.

Tania began to see shapes moving through the trees—some way distant still but keeping pace with them, gray blurs that came and went behind the slender trunks of the birch trees through which they were running. The mounted knights of Lyonesse.

The clamor of the dogs seemed to be all around them, and Tania began to fear that they were not being chased so much as driven. Panting and stumbling over the uneven ground, she glanced to each side. Yes! She was sure of it now: Large gray shapes were shadowing them and the terrifying baying of the Morrigan hounds sounded to the left and to the right and close behind.

"They're herding us along!" Edric shouted. "We have to break out of here!"

"Should I use the wishpearl?" Tania said, gasping.

"No!" Zara panted. "It is too soon."

"And no illusion will fool the hounds!" Cordelia shouted back. "They are following the scent of the black amber that you bear, Tania. While we have it with us we cannot lose them."

"Nor outrun them for long," said Zara. "There are horsemen on our flanks. How soon ere they close in for the kill?"

"We have to get rid of the black amber," Edric called. "Throw the hounds off our trail."

"But if we do that, how are we going to rescue Oberon?" Tania panted. She stared around wildly. The gray horsemen were closing in. She could hear the thunder of hooves. She could see the glitter of blades, the worm-shine flick of a gray cloak.

"Give me the bag of black amber," Cordelia called,

her arm reaching blindly back toward Tania like a relay runner groping for the baton.

Tania managed to unlace the pouch from her belt and thrust it into Cordelia's hand. "I will lead them away," Cordelia panted. "See yonder fern-brake? Get you to ground there. I will return." She darted away to the right, leaping through the undergrowth, quickly swallowed up by the forest. Tania and the others made for the overhanging ferns. They threw themselves into cover, lying as still as they could.

Tania gulped in air, her heart hammering, her lungs burning. What had she been thinking to let Cordelia run off alone like that? "We can't leave her!" she said, scrambling to her feet.

Edric snatched at her tunic and brought her down again. She struggled against him for a few moments. Zara came squirming through the undergrowth toward them.

"Hush!" she warned Tania. "Cordelia knows what she is at. They will not catch her."

Tania forced herself to be still. It went against every instinct in her body to lie hidden while Cordelia was in danger. She could hear the baying of the hounds, but they seemed to be heading away from them. Tania held her breath for a few moments, listening for hoofbeats. She heard none.

"I think it worked," Edric said. He looked at Tania. "She'll be fine."

Tania frowned at him. "I hope you're right." An uncomfortable burning sensation inside the front of her tunic made her twist onto her side. Her skin felt as if it was being scorched under her clothes. She put her hand down inside her tunic. Her fingers touched something as hot as flame. It was the bag with the metal inside it. She let out a cry of fear and pain, her feet kicking as she struggled to pull open her tunic.

Edric tried to hold her. "What is it?"

"The metal!" Tania cried. "It's burning me!" At last she managed to pull the cloth bag from inside her tunic and hurl it away. Gasping with relief, she lifted the hem of her tunic. There was a red weal on her skin.

"Once you gave Princess Cordelia the black amber, you weren't being protected anymore," Edric said, looking anxiously at her. "Are you badly hurt?"

"No, it's not too bad," Tania replied. "But what do we do now? How are we going to carry the metal?" She crawled over to the fallen bag. She reached tentatively for it, as though extending her fingers toward a fire. There was no heat, so she touched the bag. Unseen flames blazed up her arm. She pulled back, massaging her stinging fingers. "It wasn't this bad before," she said, looking at Edric and Zara. "I didn't get burned through cloth last time I touched something metal. What's made it worse?"

"Mayhap the Faerie part of your nature grows stronger," Zara suggested. "That would make you more vulnerable to the bite of Isenmort."

Could that be it? If so, it could not have come at a worse time. Tania groaned. How could everything have gone so wrong so quickly? The black amber was gone. Cordelia was gone—perhaps already captured or dead. And now she couldn't even carry the bag of metal that they would need to break Oberon's Amber Prison.

"Shhh!" hissed Edric.

Something was approaching rapidly, pattering through the forest, breathing hard.

"Cordelia!" said Zara.

A moment later Cordelia came bursting into their ferny shelter and dropped to her knees, her head hanging, her hair matted and dripping sweat. It was several moments before she was able to speak. "That was a merry chase!" She wiped her sleeve across her forehead. "But luck was with me. I came upon a ravine and threw the bag into it." She grinned. "I saw at least two of the hounds go plunging to their deaths after it as I ran away. There will be confusion now for a time. The hounds were bred to follow the scent of black amber above all else, and the Knights will have trouble getting them away from the gulf." She looked at them, noticing their somber faces. "What is the matter?"

"Tania has been burned by the Isenmort," Edric told her. "We're trying to figure out how to carry it."

"Mayhap we can wrap it in leaves and tree bark," Zara suggested.

"And what about the black amber?" Tania asked. "What's the plan now we've lost that?"

"There may be black amber in Caer Kymry," Cordelia said. Tania gave her a puzzled look. She felt as if she had heard the name before, but where?

"It is the home of Hopie and Lord Brython," Cordelia explained. "It lies out of the straight north-ward path, but it may serve our needs to go there."

"And swiftly!" Zara broke in. "Hark!"

Hoofbeats. Tania could hear them clearly. Approaching fast. Fear welled in her, overwhelming every other thought.

"Gray Knights," Edric hissed.

Cordelia sprang to her feet, her voice harsh with alarm. "Follow."

They burst out of the undergrowth in a tumbling panic and fled through the trees. Tania glanced back in terror. She could not see their pursuers, but she knew they could not be far behind.

"We are there!" Cordelia called back, and as Tania watched, her sister suddenly plunged downward through a mass of rhododendron bushes. Parting the branches, Tania saw that the land fell away to a deep green valley through which a white stream threaded. And there, standing close together under the lee of a raw brown cliff face, were half a dozen well-bred horses.

Tania scrambled down behind her sister. She could hear Zara and Edric following, and soon they were all running across the long grass toward the horses. Cordelia outstripped them all, calling to the horses in a strange whinnying language. The horses trotted toward her, neighing and dipping their heads in greeting.

Suddenly Tania stopped in her tracks. She turned, staring in dismay at Edric and Zara. "I forgot the metal!" she cried. "It's still up there."

Zara went white. "We dare not go back."

"We have to!" Tania said. *"I'll go!"*

Edric caught hold of her arm. "No!"

She glared at him. "This is my fault," she said, shaking his hand off her. "Don't try to stop me!" But before she was able to take another step, she saw tall gray shapes appear at the cliff edge. Gray Knights upon skeletal gray steeds. At first there were only two, but moments later another appeared, and then another, until the hilltop was lined with the evil creatures.

One of them let out an ululating cry. The others joined in, lifting their swords high into the air. The first spurred his horse on down the slope, and soon the others were following.

Returning for the metal wasn't an option. Edric grasped Tania's hand and ran with her to where Cordelia was waiting with the horses. Tania hardly knew what was happening as she was pushed up onto the back of one of the horses. Cordelia said something to it and gave its rump a slap.

"Cling to the mane!" she shouted to Tania. "Grip with your legs."

In a daze Tania saw Edric and Zara and Cordelia leap onto other horses, and then the world blurred around her as her own horse began to gallop at full speed along the valley. She was vaguely aware of the piercing howls of the Gray Knights at their backs. The wind stung her eyes as she crouched low over the horse's neck, her fingers tangled in the flying mane, her legs clenched to the creature's body.

She was terrified of falling off, but she managed to cling on grimly as the chilling cries of the Gray Knights faded behind them. Tania risked a quick glance around. Cordelia was at her side, riding with easy grace. Edric was close behind her, Zara a little farther away.

"We have outrun them!" Cordelia shouted. "All is well!"

Tania stared at her in shock. *All is well?* They had lost the black amber and they had lost the Isenmort. The murderous Gray Knights of Lyonesse were close behind. And even if they were able to shake them off and make the long journey to Ynis Maw in safety, how were they going to rescue Oberon?

How were they going to save Faerie?

Part Two:

Ynis Maw

_X_

The night was full of huge Faerie stars, but their twinkling charm was paled by the unearthly glow of the towering crystal columns that surrounded the travelers as they rested after another long day on horseback. For once, Tania's aches and pains were forgotten as she gazed at the circle of crystal stones. They were massive and multifaceted, sunk deep into the earth, and jutting into the sky at odd, irregular angles. They soared high above their heads—fifteen to twenty feet tall, several feet thick, their myriad planes smooth and sharp-edged, glowing and sparkling with a weird, blue-white light that threw a bewildering network of shadows over the grassy hilltop.

Tania had first caught sight of them about two hours ago: a distant flashing of mysterious sapphire light on the horizon against the purple evening sky. It had looked to her as though someone had thrown down a handful of long, slender jewels onto the summit of a solitary hill.

"Crystalhenge, at last," Cordelia had said. "We will rest there till morning."

It was not until they had ridden their horses up the gentle slope and moved among the immense crystals that Tania had got any real impression of the size of the monoliths.

Their horses grazed at ease in the sheltering lee of the hill. The travelers were two days' ride from Esgarth Forest, and there had been no visible sign of pursuit so far. The first day of riding bareback had been an absolute torment for Tania. Cordelia had kept them galloping until Tania had been driven almost beyond endurance, her thighs burning from gripping the horse's sides, her fingers numbed where she had hung on desperately to the flying mane, her whole body one big howling bruise.

They had halted after what felt like an eternity of agony; Tania had slid from the horse's back and lay gasping for breath on the ground, hardly aware of their surroundings. Edric had gently massaged her knotted muscles while her sisters had gathered reeds from a nearby lakeside. Cordelia had twisted and tied them skilfully together to create makeshift bridles and reins.

And then, far too soon for Tania, they had to carry on their journey. Being able to hold the reins made things a little easier, and now Cordelia allowed them to move at a gentle trot. Tania was too exhausted and in too much pain to pay attention to the land through which they were passing as she was bounced up and down on the horse's broad back, but as the day waned, she was aware that the sun was in her eyes, meaning they were traveling west.

They had slept the first night in a copse of oak trees. Tania had slipped gratefully to the ground, and despite all her aches she had fallen into an almost instant sleep. She had awoken ravenously hungry, and in less pain than she had expected. That morning had been less unbearable, and gradually through the long day the discomfort had ebbed, almost as if her muscles were remembering their old strength and some long-lost memory of how to ride was awakening inside her.

Tania stretched out in the grass, her head pillowed on her arms and her mind wandering as she gazed up through the haze of blue-white light into the velvet sky. The others were talking softly.

"How long to Caer Kymry?" she heard Zara ask.

"Three more days," Cordelia replied. "We've done well thus far, and I would say we are almost halfway there, but the land will become more challenging the farther west we ride. We can ford the River Churn at Elfindale, and thence through Holmdene Forest and Fawnbreak Vale to Oakbank Ridge and up into the Kestrel Mountains that lie on the eastern edge of Talebolion. Then we must travel northwest by Ferndene Deeps and Woodfarrs Edge and follow the River Hollingbourne until we reach Half Moon Peak. From the shoulders of the mountain we shall be able to look down upon Caer Kymry and

Ynis Tal and the Great Western Ocean."

Tania loved the sound of the poetic names. She sat up, seeing how the flickering blue light of the rearing crystal monoliths washed over her three companions. "Is everything in Faerie as beautiful as this?" she asked drowsily. "It's like being in a dream."

"Faerie contains many marvels and fair sights," Zara said. "I love most the far valley of Leiderdale, in Dinsel. There is a stone there, tall and flat-topped—the High Chantrelle, it is called—and if you stand upon it and face west and sing, the valley walls will send your songs back to you in a thousand delightful harmonies."

"Do you have a favorite place, Edric?"

"I was brought up in Weir," he said. "My best childhood memories are of being taken to the upper reaches of the River Lych, to a place called Reganfal. It's a wild, rugged land where the river makes its way down a whole series of waterfalls. In high summer, when the salmon are leaping and the air is filled with rainbows, there's nowhere I'd rather be."

Tania found herself hoping that one day she would be able to stand with him and watch the rainbows and the salmon. One day.

"If I had to choose," Cordelia said, "then I would say that Passion Meadows gives me more heart's-ease than any other place." She looked at Tania. "We would have passed through the meadows had our journey taken us directly to the north. It is a beautiful place, Tania—mile after mile of rolling fields as far as the eye can see, all covered in a blanket of poppies. They are blossoms that grow nowhere else in the Realm, for they constantly change color as the wind blows across them." Cordelia sighed. "It is something to marvel at, indeed."

"I hope I get to see all those places," Tania said.

"You shall," Zara said. "I have faith that you shall."

"But now we should take solace in sleep," Cordelia said. "A hard road lies before us and I would have us safe within the walls of Caer Kymry ere the sun sets three nights hence. I will take first watch."

"Do you think they're still following us?" said Tania.

Cordelia frowned. "I have led us on a crooked path in the hope of throwing pursuit off, and I have seen no sign that Lyonesse is close on our trail. Yet ever the birds fly north and west away, and the animals are fearful in their dens." She shivered, staring back into the east. "The land is uneasy. I hear it in the trembling of the leaves, and in the whispering of the grass, and the murmur of running water." She looked at Tania. "Evil haunts us, sweet sister. I feel its breath upon my neck as we ride." She stood up and walked to the edge of the crystal ring, sitting with her back to one of the huge stones, gazing into the night with her sword ready at her side.

"And there's a comforting thought to sleep upon, forsooth," Zara remarked with a wry smile. She lay down, curling up on the grass and becoming still almost at once.

Edric and Tania lay near each other. Tania liked to have him close by, to be able to hear his breathing in the night and to know she could just reach out and touch him.

"Tired?" he asked.

"Yes. But not as achy as before."

"Good. You were in a bad way when we first set off. I was worried that you might not be able to keep going."

"Tell me about it!" They were lying on their backs now, holding hands. Tania stared sleepily into the sky. "Do the constellations have names here?" She yawned.

"Yes, they do." Edric pointed. "Do you see those three stars in a row with the two stars going off to the left? That's called the Starved Fool. And those five stars in the *W* shape is the Girl in Violet." His pointing finger slid across the sky. "That's the Phoenix, and next to it is the Singing Dragon."

"How is it a dragon?" Tania murmured, her eyelids drooping. "It doesn't look anything like a dragon."

"You have to use your imagination," Edric said. "Would you like to hear the story of the Phoenix and the Singing Dragon?"

Her eyes closed. "Yes, please."

"A long time ago," Edric began, "there were three young minstrels who lived in a place called Heron Hill. . . ." But within a few seconds of beginning the story, the words Edric was speaking stopped making sense to Tania and his voice became no more than a warm and comforting murmur as she fell asleep.

"No! No! No!"

"Tania! Wake up. It's okay!" Edric's urgent voice pulled Tania out of the nightmare. She opened her eyes to see him kneeling over her, his face anxious.

"Oh! That was so horrible!" She stared up at him; beyond his crystal-lit face, the starry night still lay deep over Faerie.

"It was only a dream."

"It felt so real." She shuddered. "And it's not the first time I've dreamed it." She clutched his hand. "We were on Ynis Maw," she began falteringly. "It was dark. There was a storm and it was raining really hard. We were together, you and me. At the start we were running through a lot of rocks. Then we were climbing a steep hillside. And there was something chasing us—some kind of monster with red eyes." She shivered at the memory. "You went ahead and then you reached down for me, but when I took hold of your hand, it wasn't *you* anymore. You'd changed into"—she swallowed—"into Gabriel Drake. And he had hold of me and I couldn't get loose."

Edric looked down at her. "That sounds dreadful," he said. "But I'm here now, and I'm not going to change into anyone."

"Promise!"

He smiled. "Promise." He leaned forward and gently kissed her. "Go back to sleep," he whispered, his breath warm on her cheek. "We've got a hard day ahead of us."

"Okay. I'll try." She lifted his hand to her lips and kissed it. "Stay close till I fall asleep."

He nodded. "You bet."

She closed her eyes, comforted by the feel of his hand in hers. Shreds of the dream came drifting back like a dark mist. She opened her eyes and saw his face smiling down at her.

Reassured, she closed her eyes again and drifted into a deep and blessedly dreamless sleep.

XI

It was late in the afternoon, three days on from Crystalhenge. Tania and the others were lying on their fronts to peer over the edge of a high, rocky cliff overlooking a broad ocean bay. The sun was low on the horizon, washing the white expanse of the bay with soft, hazy light. A salty tang filled the air.

The crag was an outcrop of the brown bulk of Half Moon Peak that towered at their backs. When they had come to the crag's eastern flank, Cordelia had gone ahead on foot to scout the land. She had come back quickly, asking the horses to wait, then leading Tania and the others to this lofty place; telling them to keep low, warning them that evil was afoot in Kymry Bay.

For the past two days they had been riding through a land of steep, rocky valleys and high mountains, forest-clad and with great broken-toothed peaks of bare brown stone. They had forded noisy, rushing streams and ridden through dense woodlands of cypress and ancient fir. In several places they had been forced to dismount and lead their horses up steep slopes where loose stones rolled under foot and hoof. At other times they had ridden to an impassable ravine or an unassailable cliff face that made them retrace their steps and find another way—but all the time Cordelia was leading them northwest toward Caer Kymry, the sea-washed fortress of Talebolion where Hopie lived with her husband, Lord Brython.

Finally, they had come to the coastline of that mountainous land—and they had found Caer Kymry under attack.

Kymry Bay was a wide crescent of white beaches and ivory-colored outcrops of rock lashed by the waves. On a high promontory in the middle of the bay stood a white castle, joined to the land by a narrow causeway and glowing with a pearly light. Tania had never seen such a strange structure before; it looked like something that had been created and shaped beneath the waves. It had tall curved, fluted, and ribbed walls crowned with knobbed battlements from which spiraling turrets and twisting steeples coiled upward like the spikes and barbs that grow on seashells.

As Tania stared down into the bay a knot of fear tightened in her stomach. Drawn up onto the beach a little way off from the castle were two ships. They were wood-built, long and low and broad across the beam with a single mast from which hung a great square, red sail. The prows of both ships were carved into the heads of snakes with forked black tongues.

A host of Gray Knights was gathered on the causeway that led to the high-arched gateway of the castle. Tania watched with narrowed eyes as a fierce yellow light flamed upward; some kind of cart or wagon had been set alight. As the knights began to push it along the causeway toward the gates, spears and rocks and arrows rained down on them from the castle walls. Many knights fell, turning to ash; others returned arrow fire, but still the flaming wagon drew closer to the castle gates.

"They will burn the gate," Cordelia groaned. "The fortress will be taken."

"No, look," said Edric. "They're coming out."

Just as the burning wagon was about to strike the gates they were opened from within. Moments later a company of horsemen came cantering out onto the path, dividing to avoid the flames and coming at the Gray Knights with swords and spears that glinted in the sunlight. Even from this distance, Tania could see that the armor of the mounted Faerie knights was as extraordinary as the castle from which they came. Their breastplates and shields could have been the shells of crabs; their spiraling helmets were like conches, curling upward to points.

At first the mounted Faeries pushed the attacking knights back, but more Gray Knights began to press forward, bringing the charge to a sudden, chaotic halt.

"We must give them aid!" snarled Cordelia,

scrambling to her feet. She stood on the clifftop, turning away from the battle and whistling shrilly. Moments later their four horses came heaving and scrabbling up the hillside. Brandishing her sword and shouting challenges down to the Gray Knights, Cordelia leaped astride her horse.

Tania stood up and took the reins of her own horse, aware that Edric and Zara were also on their feet. She flexed her knees and sprang up, using her hands to boost her onto the horse's back. A few moments later all four of them were mounted. Tania saw Edric and Zara draw their swords; gripping the makeshift reins in one fist, she pulled her own sword from her belt. She glanced sideways at her companions, seeing the fierce bravery in their faces as they prepared to ride into battle. Her own courage seemed to have deserted her.

We are so dead! It would take hundreds of us to beat them!

Then she heard Eden's voice in her head. *It is a wishpearl. If you find yourself in harm's way, take it in your palm and wish for what you need.*

Would the wishpearl be powerful enough to conjure an army? Tania imagined how a mounted tide of Faerie knights might go thundering down the slope of the cliff and sweep the Gray Knights into the sea. It had to be worth trying.

"Wait!" she shouted. "There's another way!" She fumbled in her clothing for the wishpearl and drew it out, warm in her closed hand. "I wish for a Faerie army," she said loudly. "I wish for them to appear up here on the cliff and for them to charge down at the Gray Knights." She brought her arm down, releasing the wishpearl so that it was dashed to the stones beneath her horse's hooves.

It broke into a thousand tiny fragments. There was a weird sound like the faint laughter of many small voices and a wisp of blue-green smoke curled upward. Then there was a rushing noise like a hurricane. Tania felt her clothes snapping against her body; her hair whipped across her face. She was almost torn from her horse's back as it shifted under her, its mane flying, its hooves seeking firmer purchase on the rocks.

And then, from out of nowhere, they were surrounded by a host of Faerie knights on horseback. They were wearing the same seashell armor as the knights of Caer Kymry, and each of them brandished a sword or spear.

Tania felt a wild exhilaration as the horsemen began to move forward, urging their mounts over the lip of the ridge and down the precipitous slope that led to the bay.

"We must ride with them!" Cordelia cried. "Battle is joined."

But Zara caught her arm. "No! Wait! Let them rout the filth of Lyonesse ere we risk our lives."

They watched from the clifftop as the Faerie army went galloping across the stony ground toward the castle. It was hard for Tania to accept that they were an illusion—they looked so solid and real, with the rumble of hooves and the clatter of their armor and their war cries ringing out across the bay. Tania wondered how many knights the wishpearl had conjured. Five hundred? More? It was hard to tell. But one thing was certain: The charging army far outnumbered the Gray Knights.

Seeing the Faerie horsemen thundering toward them, the Gray Knights at the landward end of the causeway broke off the fight with the knights of Caer Kymry and fled toward their ships. The rest of the Gray Knights went streaming back after them, many leaping or wading into the sea, none of them daring to stand up to the tide of oncoming horsemen.

Tania saw one Caer Kymry knight stand tall in the stirrups brandishing a barbed sword and rallying the others to give chase to the fleeing enemy. More Faerie knights poured out of the gates of the castle, galloping along the causeway and throwing themselves on the creatures of Lyonesse as they ran. Flaming arrows were fired toward the ships. Some fell short, but others found their mark.

"It is a rout!" Cordelia declared, her eyes shining. "Come, let us join with them." This time no one stopped her as she urged her horse down the steep slope. Tania, Edric, and Zara followed close behind, the salt-wind in their faces as their horses galloped sure-footed over the rocks.

But before they reached the battlefield, Tania saw that the mystical Faerie army was faltering and wavering, so that now she could see the beach and sea through their fading forms. She watched in dismay as the entire host dissolved away into mist.

"No! Come back!" she shouted, afraid that the Gray Knights would take new heart and turn to fight again. But it was too late for the knights of Lyonesse to recover. One of their ships was already burning fiercely. The knights of Caer Kymry had destroyed the majority of the undead creatures of Lyonesse, catching them as they struggled through waist-deep waves, and were busy turning the remainder back to the dust that had spawned them.

The Faerie knight that Tania had seen rallying the troops had come to a halt on a sea-lapped boulder and was staring out over the scene of the battle. Tania assumed at first that it must be some brave captain, but when she looked closer, she saw that long dark brown hair hung from the helmet almost to the knight's waist. And at that moment the knight turned toward them and Tania realized that it was her sister Princess Hopie.

Seeing them for the first time, Hopie let out a shout of joy and sprang from her horse, running toward them with her arms outspread. Tania and her sisters met her on the white sands, Zara dancing up and down in excitement and Cordelia letting out high-pitched whoops of joy. Even Hopie's usually solemn face was wreathed in smiles.

"Now I understand the appearance of the phantom army," she said with a laugh. "It was one of Eden's glamours, was it not? Is she with you?"

"No, but she's safe," Tania said. "She's in Esgarth Forest with Titania."

Hopie's eyes shone. "The Queen is in Faerie! That is good news, indeed."

Another rider came cantering up to them: a tall, broad-set man with deep dark eyes and a brown beard. It was Hopie's husband, Lord Brython. He leaned on the pommel of his saddle, smiling at the princesses. "Well met, sisters-in-law," he said. "This battle is over, at least. What news from the south?"

"There's a lot to tell you, my lord," said Edric.

"Then the Princess and I offer you our hospitality," he said. "You look as if you have spent many a night in the wilds. Come, mount again and follow me—you shall tell us your tales within the steadfast walls of Caer Kymry."

XII

Caer Kymry looked to Tania as extraordinary on the interior as it had from the outside. She gazed around in amazement as they walked along a curved, winding corridor with rounded, rippling walls that shimmered with a mother-of-pearl radiance. Seashell torches lit the way, filling the air with a diffused light that played over carvings of crabs and seahorses and painted shoals of multicolored fish that coiled up the walls and over the ceiling and down underfoot in a rush of dazzling iridescence.

A long winding stair took them to a high turret room with windows that overlooked the ocean. The room reminded Tania of the inside of a sea urchin shell, segmented and hollowed with ribbed growth patterns that corkscrewed to the pointed ceiling. The walls were decorated with things taken from the sea— brightly colored shells of all shapes and sizes: periwinkles, whelks, murices, and conchs, mussels and cockles and clams. There were dried starfish and curiously shaped pieces of coral and ocean-smoothed stone displayed on the windowsills, and the coverings on the seats were decorated with pictures of sea creatures and twining seaweed.

They rested on couches while servants brought them food and drink. Once they had eaten there was the promise of hot baths and soft beds—but first Lord Brython and Hopie shed their armor and sat with them, dressed now in simple clothes of brown silk. Brython told them how the two Serpent ships had arrived with the dawn and how the Gray Knights had attacked the castle, losing many of their number in fruitless assaults on the walls, before withdrawing and planning the fiery attack that Tania's wishpearl army had thwarted.

"Why were there only two ships, my lord?" Edric asked. "The news we had was that there was a whole armada on its way."

"I would guess that these were but scout ships, sent to test our resolve," Brython said. "If the armada is on the move, as you say, then I do not believe it will make landfall in these parts. It will sail along the south coast and the armies of Lyonesse will disembark at Caer Marisoc, and make their way across Udwold to join up with the Sorcerer."

"Or they may round Rhye Beacon and enter the estuary of the Tamesis," said Hopie. "There is deepwater at Fortrenn Quay, sufficient to harbor a hundred ships."

Now it was time for the travelers to tell the princess and her husband all that had happened over the past few days, both in the Mortal World and in the palace.

"We had to get rid of the black amber, or the dogs would've caught us," Tania explained at the end. "And then I freaked out and totally forgot the bag we had the metal in—the Isenmort, I mean." She looked despairingly at Hopie. "The whole idea was to use the black amber and the Isenmort to rescue the King. But that plan's pretty much wrecked now."

"I brought them here in the hope that you would have some small store of black amber," Cordelia said. "Legends say it was once so."

"Alas, we have none," Brython said. "It is true that the great castles of Faerie once held such treasure under lock and key, but it is long now since all the black amber was removed. Did you not know? It was the black amber of the ten Caers that was used to decorate the crowns of Oberon and Titania."

"No, I did not know that," Cordelia said with a grimace. "I have led us on a fool's errand."

"I think not," Hopie said. "Do not forget, dear sister, had you not come here when you did, then the filth of Lyonesse might be feasting even now in these chambers." She smiled. "The fates weave their webs in contrary ways, their subtle ends to perform."

"You speak as might Sancha were she here," said Zara. "And you are right: Eden's wishpearl did indeed save Caer Kymry and all within, but that gets us no closer to fulfilling our task. How are we to rescue our father from Ynis Maw?"

Hopie frowned, and sat in thoughtful silence for a

few moments. "The Tapestry of Fidach Ren may hold the answer," she said at last. "Come, I will show you."

They followed Hopie and her husband to another chamber. It was smaller than the first, and window-less, the pearly walls lit only by candles. A tapestry hung on one wall. Tania was intrigued by it—she knew that Faerie was a timeless place, and she took it for granted that she was constantly surrounded by people and things that had existed for thousands of years, but this tapestry was the first thing she had seen in the Immortal Realm that looked truly ancient.

It was threadbare and frayed at the edges, its colors faded to dull brownish hues, so that it was quite tricky at first to make out the picture. But after a few moments, Tania realized that she was looking at a very stylized depiction of a landscape—or, rather, at a long finger of rocky land that jutted out into a green sea. On the vague horizon she could just make out a dark shape like a sharp-edged mountaintop pushing up out of the water. But something else caught her atten-tion. There were things in the air above the land. Things with wings. She moved closer, narrowing her eyes to try and make sense of the flying shapes. Insects, like large dragonflies, perhaps? No, the shapes were all wrong for that.

She let out a gasp. They were slender flying *people*. Not Faerie children but full-grown people with gos-samer wings sprouting from their backs. Tania vividly remembered the wings that had grown from her own shoulder blades; she had never forgotten the wonder and joy of flying. Looking at the winged folk in the tapestry brought the experience back to her with a pang of intense loss.

"This tapestry is ancient beyond all understanding," Hopie began, and her voice was no more than a reverent whisper. "The land it shows is Fidach Ren in the far north of Prydein, and the sea-girt island is Ynis Maw."

"Ynis Maw?" Tania echoed. "That's the place where Oberon is being held."

"What are these flying creatures?" asked Zara.

"There is a script that runs around the tapestry," Hopie said. "It is in a very old language, but much of it can still be read. It tells of an elder race that dwells in the wild land of Fidach Ren, and refers to them as the Karken En Ynis Maw."

"What does that mean?" Tania asked.

"It means the Keepers of the Black Isle," replied Hopie.

"Legend suggests that these creatures have some ancient bond that links them to Ynis Maw," Brython added. "And also that they are the custodians of an arcane and secret knowledge."

Hopie looked at them. "If anyone in Faerie can aid you in your quest to free our father, then I believe these wild folk may hold the key, although they are said to be a strange and dangerous people."

Zara peered more closely at the tapestry. "But can they be real? And if ever they *were* real, is it possible that their race lingers on in the wild north?"

"There are a lot of strange creatures in the mountains of Prydein," Edric said. "The people of Weir hardly ever travel north of the River Lych, and even the folk who live in Caer Circinn in Minnith Bannwg keep to the eastern shores."

"Twenty-five leagues of mountain-land lie between us and the straight road north," Cordelia said. "And from there Fidach Ren lies over a hundred leagues hence." She looked at Hopie. "We must leave *now* if we are to stand any chance of success. Can you give us food and water and blankets for the journey, and mayhap fresh horses?"

"You cannot leave without rest," Hopie said.

"And why take the arduous path by land at all?" said Brython. "One of the Serpent boats still lies on the beach—mayhap you could sail it north along the coast? We can supply you with trusted mariners to guide your way."

Zara smiled, and Tania noticed there was a gleam in her blue eyes. "Mariners, you say? Nay, brother-in-law, we shall need no mariners. Give me but a tall sea-facing rock to stand upon and I will sing up a whale to speed our northward passage."

Cordelia nodded eagerly. "And I shall impart the urgency of our cause to it," she said. "The whales of these waters are noble beasts—I doubt not that one of their number will aid us. Northward, ho!" she exclaimed.

"But even the greatest necessity must wait on fatigue," said Brython. "You will bathe and sleep one night in Caer Kymry before you set sail."

"Very well," said Cordelia, her eyes shining. "But we depart at dawn!"

XIII

Tania was awoken by Edric's voice. He was leaning over her, his face lit by a candle that shone through a lantern made from translucent shell. Beyond the sphere of candlelight the room was dark, the air sibilant with the murmur of the sea.

"What time is it?" she murmured. "Is it morning yet?"

"It'll be dawn soon," he told her.

She sat up, rubbing her eyes. "Give me a couple of minutes."

He waited outside the chamber while she splashed some water on her face from a clamshell bowl and then got dressed. She was surprised and pleased to find that her traveling clothes had been cleaned and dried overnight.

"Did you sleep well?" Edric asked as they made their way down a long twisting stairway.

"Like a log," she said, taking his hand. "You?"

He nodded. "It was odd waking up and you not

being the first thing I saw, though," he said. He gave a wry smile. "I sort of got used to that."

She paused on the stairs and met his gaze. "Me, too." She reached out and took his hand, looking deep into his warm brown eyes. "I wish . . ."

"What do you wish?" he asked softly, moving closer.

"I wish we could have had more time together before this had to happen." She frowned. "It feels like we haven't had a moment to . . . to . . . *enjoy* each other, you know? But that's typical me: I fall in love and—bam!—it's the end of the world!"

"It's nothing like the end of the world," Edric said, grinning suddenly and lifting his hand to stroke her hair. "I don't rate the Sorcerer King's chances much—not up against the two of us and your sisters and the Queen and King Oberon and the whole of Faerie." He shook his head. "He's toast!"

Tania laughed and squeezed his hand. "You bet he is!"

They kissed, and for a few precious moments Tania was almost able to fool herself into believing it could be true.

"I love you so much," Edric whispered. "The Sorcerer King isn't stronger than that. *Nothing* is stronger than that."

She held his gaze, biting her lip to stop herself from telling him how terrified she was that all the love in the universe wouldn't be enough to hold back the Sorcerer King's ruinous hatred.

She took a long, slow, calming breath. "Are the others up yet?" she asked, turning and continuing down the spiral stairs.

"Yes. As far as I can tell, Cordelia's been up for hours." He looked uneasily at her. "There's some news: Zara isn't coming with us."

Tania stared at him in alarm. "Why not? Is there something wrong with her?"

"No, it's nothing like that. She'll explain."

Lord Brython and the three princesses were waiting for them on a balcony that looked out over the western ocean. It was still dark, and to the east, the great hump of Half Moon Peak filled half the sky. A table was set for breakfast, a meal of fish and cheese and new-baked bread.

Tania sat opposite Zara. "Edric says you're not coming with us."

"No, indeed," Zara replied. "Hopie awoke me early and I have spoken long with her and Brython. I have a new duty to attend."

"If we are to hold Faerie against the coming of the ships of Lyonesse, we will need to gather all our forces together," Brython said. "Princess Zara has agreed to travel south into Mynwy Clun with a few of my trusted knights, where she will make contact with Earl Valentyne and ask for his aid."

"Eden's husband?" Tania said. "But why does Zara have to go? Can't you send someone else?"

"Brython and I cannot be spared," Hopie said. "We do not know whether more serpent ships will come, and we cannot leave Caer Kymry without leadership. But if we are to solicit Valentyne's aid, we must send an emissary of high rank. A member of the Royal Family."

"Earl Valentyne is the head of an ancient and noble Faerie house," Brython explained. "When the Great Twilight came and Eden retreated into her solitary tower, he quit the Court and returned to Caer Mynwy. He has dwelt there ever since, refusing all contact with the outside world."

"He will make a great ally in our fight against Lyonesse," said Zara. "He commands a loyal army. I must go and speak with him to ensure he joins us to defend his King." She rested her hand on Tania's. "Be not sad at this parting; we will meet again soon in merrier times." She squeezed Tania's fingers. "We shall defeat this evil, Tania—I know we shall. And you and I will dance again in the Great Hall of the palace and play duets upon the spinetta and the lute once more." Her eyes glowed. "This I promise!"

Tania took a long breath. "Yes," she said. "Of course we will."

The sun was still hidden behind the mountain, but Half Moon Peak was edged with light, and the eastern sky was glowing with the dawn as Zara stood on a tall, smooth-topped rock outside the castle and began her song. Tania had heard her sister sing many times, even a song that had caused fish and dolphins to dance in the sea, but she had never heard such strange and uncanny sounds come from Zara's throat before.

Zara faced the ocean with her arms outstretched, her voice soaring and swooping, sometimes singing a high, keening melody that was like the crying of seagulls, sometimes descending to a low-pitched note that seemed to make the rocks tremble beneath their feet. While she sang the daylight grew and color began to seep back into the world. The gray sky blushed with a clear, bright morning blue, darkly mirrored by the rolling sea.

Tania saw shadows go leaping westward and felt a sudden warmth on her back. She glanced around and saw that the sun had rounded the shoulder of the mountain and was throwing out a diamond white light, so bright that it made her eyes water.

Suddenly, she felt Edric's hand in hers. "Look!" he murmured, pointing. "Can you see it?"

The sunlight was dancing dazzlingly bright on the waves, but she could just make something out—a movement too solid for waves, far, far out to sea.

"They come," Cordelia whispered, standing beside her. "Oh, merciful spirits of water, look how they come to her!"

The disturbance on the face of the ocean began to draw slowly nearer.

"Our sister has a powerful gift, indeed," Hopie agreed.

Tania saw two dark shapes racing landward in a fury of white foam. When they were some twenty yards from the shore, they came to a long, curving halt. Now Tania could see two smooth gray-blue mounds, each with a single dorsal fin cleaving the water.

She gripped Edric's hand. "They're humpback whales!"

One of the whales lifted its long barnacled head clear of the water, showing them its wrinkled white throat. The other dove, the great fan-shaped fluke rising high before slapping the surface of the ocean, sending up a spout of spray. A few glorious moments later the whale breached, surging out of the waves, its huge gray body more massive and wonderful than Tania could ever have imagined. It came almost clear of the water, curving and turning onto its side and then crashing down, so that the sky was suddenly full of white water.

Zara's song ended and Cordelia went bounding up the rocks to stand at her side. The whales moved closer to shore now, their heads lifted above the waves. Tania was fascinated by their eyes, strangely small in their great heads but filled with intelligence.

"Hail to thee, wise wanderers," Cordelia called. "Deep drinkers, great hearts, warm-blood brethren, we crave a boon of thee."

Tania glanced at Hopie. "Do you think they'll help us?"

Hopie nodded. "Yes," she said. "They will help us."

* * *

Tania gasped. "I didn't know whales could swim so fast!"

She and Edric were at the prow of the Serpent ship, clinging tightly to the spars, the wind and spray fierce in their faces and the boards thrumming beneath their feet.

"I told them that speed was of the essence," Cordelia shouted down from her perch on the sinuous neck of the snake figurehead. "This journey would have taken us ten or twelve days by horse but while we have these Vahlkin lords at our service, my hope is to see the Black Isle three days hence!"

It had taken Cordelia only a short time to get the humpback whales to agree to aid them. In fact, from the way the two enormous animals had cavorted in the water, splashing with their flukes and sending fountains shooting from their blowholes, Tania got the impression that they were glad to be asked to help against the evil of Lyonesse.

It took a little while for strong ropes to be found and tied together so they would be long enough to form a makeshift harness. Then Cordelia had stripped off her outer clothes and had performed a perfect swallow dive off the rocks, swimming with the whales and helping others in rowboats to secure the ropes around their huge bodies. The ropes were tied to the front of the remaining Serpent ship and the whales hauled it effortlessly off the beach.

Then it was time for parting. Tania found it hard to say good-bye to Zara—of all her sisters, it was lighthearted Zara who was most able to lift her spirits. The thought of journeying on without her was a gloomy one and it was with a heavy heart that she gave a final wave to those left on the rocks when the whales pulled tight on the ropes and towed the ship out of the bay.

They had traveled west for a while, skirting the forested island of Ynis Tal with the open ocean to their left. But all sight of land had been left far behind them now, and they were speeding north on a feature-less expanse of empty blue water.

"We are on the Bight of Damask," Cordelia called. "By the time the sun is at its zenith we shall see on the horizon the great island of Chalcedony. Beyond that is the coastline of Weir, where three-hundred-foot cliffs plunge sheer into treacherous waters."

"And then?" asked Tania.

"After that, there's a long inlet called Beroald Sound," Edric told her. "It's the north coast of Weir, and if we followed the coastland east, it would take us to the mouth of the River Lych and close to Caer Liel itself. But we'll cross the mouth of the sound to Gallowshead."

"Aye, Gallowshead, indeed," Cordelia said, climb-ing down to where they were standing. "Prydein's southernmost promontory. Beyond that is Hob's Tongue and the barren wastes of Highmost Voltar and Rhoth. And beyond Rhoth is the long black coast of Fidach Ren." She wiped the fine spray off her face. "I am famished; this sea air hollows me out like a gourd." She strode sure-footedly along the deck to a chest that had been filled with provisions for their voyage.

Edric peered northward with narrowed eyes. "I don't like the look of that sky," he said.

Tania followed his gaze over the prow of the ship. The horizon was filling with layers of thick dark gray cloud, like a grim barrier stretching across the sea. "Is it a storm?"

"Yes. And it looks like a bad one."

For some time they watched the storm clouds gathering ahead of them while the notched coastline of Weir slid cheerlessly by on their starboard flank. As the afternoon progressed the sky turned slate gray above them and the sun became at first a watery disk, and then a foggy smear, before finally being swallowed by the rearing clouds. A chill air hissed in the rigging and icy raindrops needled their skin.

"There are havens along the north coast of Weir," Edric said. "If we follow the coast to the east, we may find shelter."

Cordelia gave a curt nod and climbed onto the neck of the snake figurehead to call out new instructions to the whales.

They had been moving steadily eastward along the harsh coastline for some time, and it was clear now that the storm had no intention of allowing them to escape. They found no chance of shelter in the brutal saw-toothed line of cliffs; all they had encountered so far were black rocks that lifted out of the sea like fangs and claws. Tania stared into the dark throat of the approaching clouds. Gray veils hung over the somber sea, curtains of slanting rain that fell as thick as fog. The sea became choppy, white spume capping the rising waves. The ship began to lift and fall, the towropes sometimes stretching taut and at other times hanging loose as the whales fought the swell. Suddenly a wall of white water reared over the prow; Tania had no time to react as several tons of icy water crashed down on her.

She fell, slithering across the deck, scrabbling wildly for a hand or foothold. She hit blindly against something solid and managed to catch hold of it as the water flooded around her.

"Tania!" She heard Edric shout above the growing noise.

"Here!" she yelled back, shaking her head frantically to get her saturated hair out of her eyes. She had slipped half away down the ship and was clinging to the mast. Edric was crawling along the deck toward her while at the prow; Cordelia was hanging on to the knotted ends of the towropes.

"Are you hurt?" Edric called.

"No." The ship ploughed into another huge wave, and the deck plunged away. As the vessel stood on its nose all Tania could see was a maelstrom of turbulent green water rearing up in front of her.

The ship rose again with a sickening lurch, water swirling over the deck. Moments later, the full wrath of the storm struck them, howling across the sea like a furious demon. The wind screamed and the rain lashed them like whips, buffeting the ship. Coughing up sharp seawater, Tania saw Cordelia, her face twisted with terror as she clung on at the prow.

"Hold on!" Edric shouted. "I'm coming!"

The deck pitched downward. Behind Edric a solid wall of water came thundering over the prow with a noise like an avalanche. When the wave broke apart Tania saw with a jolt of horror that Cordelia was no longer there. The wave had ripped away a whole section of the prow—and the princess had been swept away with it.

XIV

"Cordelia!" Tania screamed. Panic sent her staggering across the flooded deck, crawling on hands and knees to get to the place where she had last seen her sister.

"Tania, no!" She heard Edric's voice above the roar of the storm, but it didn't stop her. She snatched at a broken end of timber—a remnant of the gunwale that had circled the prow. The whole of the serpent figurehead was gone, broken off low on the keel. Lost also were the towropes and the forespar.

Tania stared into the cauldron of the sea. *Cordelia!* The tempest threw her scream back into her throat. Cold water dashed in her face and the deck heaved.

She felt Edric's arm clamping around her waist. "We have . . . to get away . . . from here. . . ." He clung on to her. "Too . . . dangerous . . ."

She looked into his white face. "Cordelia!"

"I know. There's nothing . . . we . . . can do. . . ."

He kept one arm coiled around her as he began to

edge away from the broken prow. The ship pitched again and suddenly they were in water up to their chests. The sudden knowledge that they could die cleared Tania's mind. She hung on to the ship's side, fighting the sea as it tried to sweep her from the deck. A deep, stomach-churning groan filled the air. The ship was dragged to one side, the deck tipping. There was the noise of splintering timbers and the whole ship shuddered.

Tania saw rocks like huge black teeth rear up through the rain. A gush of white water blinded her. The deck shook. Edric's arm slipped away and she heard him shout. The piece of wood to which she was clinging came loose in her arms. She felt herself falling in a vortex of white water and suddenly realized that she was under the surface of the sea, being tossed about like a rag doll beneath the waves. She let go of the timber and tried to swim, holding her breath, her eyes full of rushing bubbles.

She was thrown against something hard and sharp. It was rock. She tried to snatch at it, but the sea tore her away. The noise of the foundering ship beat at her ears, magnified almost beyond endurance by the pounding water.

I'm going to drown. . . .

Something bumped against her back. *More rock,* she thought hopelessly; she might as well have her brains dashed out by a rock as anything else. There was no point in fighting it. Everything was wrong and broken and impossible.

The thing bumped her back again—harder this time, pushing her forward and upward until she became aware of a greenish light above her head. A new hope stirred in her and she kicked and swam for the surface. With a gasp she broke through the skin of the sea, filling her lungs with air. Mountainous waves seethed all around her, the air full of teeming rain and whirling spindrift.

There was nowhere for her to go. She was alone in the storm and her strength was failing.

She felt something brush against her legs. A broad, triangular shape clove the water. She grabbed at it and found herself being hauled along in a fume of white water. She would have laughed with relief if she'd had the strength. She was being dragged through the water by one of the whales.

It was too dark for her to have any clear idea of where she was being taken, but in flashes of lightning she got an impression of tall black cliffs looming to her right. Suddenly the whale slid away from under her, leaving her treading water and gasping for breath. A great blunt snout nudged her, pushing her toward the rearing cliffs. *It's too far!* she wanted to scream. But the snout nudged her again, and she began to swim.

She felt something solid under her feet. The waves slapped at her as she scrabbled over a smooth, slippery surface. The surf rolled her over and over. She dragged herself out of the sea, and lay gasping for breath on a shining spit of black rock.

Gathering her remaining strength, she stumbled

to her feet and staggered up the slippery rocks to a vertical cliff face. Here at least there was some respite from the rain and the biting wind. Tania sat with her back to a rock, her knees drawn up, her arms around herself. The euphoria of her miraculous escape quickly evaporated. Her sword was gone. The ship was gone. Cordelia was gone. She was alone and defeated on an unfriendly coastline— and Edric was . . . No, no!

Don't think about that. It's too much.

Perhaps it would have been better for her to have drowned after all.

But even as despair threatened to overwhelm her, she saw two dark shapes moving toward her through the rain.

"Tania!" One of the shapes called out to her—and it had Cordelia's voice.

Tania got to her feet with a shout of joy as a flash of lightning revealed Cordelia and Edric. The three of them fell into one another's arms. Tania clung to both of them, burying her head in Edric's shoulders. "I thought you were dead!"

"A whale brought me safe to land," said Cordelia, hugging her tightly. "Did I not say they are noble beasts?"

"They saved me, too," Edric said. "Then they saved all of us." He stared out at the tumbling sea. "I hope they're all right."

"They will not be harmed," said Cordelia. "They will seek deeper water now." She frowned up at the sheer cliff. "But what of we three? This quest is dogged by ill luck."

"We need to get off the beach," said Edric. "This isn't the wilderness of Prydein. We're on the coast of Weir. There will be roads and villages and hill farms. Someone will help us."

"And yet the Queen warned us against hoping for aid from Drake's father, the lord Aldritch," Cordelia reminded him. "Will two princesses of Faerie find sanctuary in this place at such a time?"

"They will if no one knows who they are," Edric replied. "If asked, we'll say that I'm Edwin Poladore, and that you're my sisters, Dorimar and Brosie. We can say we come from the south and that we're refugees escaping from the horrors of Lyonesse. But don't mention the ship. Say our wagon lost a wheel and the horses bolted. Say that we're making for the village of Lud."

"Is that a real place?" Tania asked.

"Yes, it's a remote hamlet up in the hills near the rising of the River Lych," Edric said. "We can say we have distant relations there." He shielded his eyes from the rain as he studied the cliff face. "But first of all, we need to get off the shore—and that's going to be enough of a challenge."

In the event, the climb wasn't as difficult as Edric had feared. They quickly found a place where the black rock face was broken apart and crumbling to scaleable rubble. It was a steep climb, but they were soon making steady progress through a rugged landscape of rain-wet boulders and water-filled gullies and wind-whipped scrub.

Tania was chilled to the bone. She walked along with her eyes screwed to thin slits, her arm linked with Edric's. Cordelia walked slightly ahead of them, her shoulders hunched against the weather. Suddenly Tania was aware that the ground beneath her feet had become smoother—hard and solid and no longer scattered with ankle-twisting stones. She forced her eyes wider. They were on a roadway that wound through the hills, a simple rutted earth track bubbling with rain, but it was the first sign of habitation that they had seen.

Cordelia looked at Edric. "Which way will lead to our respite, think you?"

"I don't know, my lady," he admitted.

There was a pause.

"This way," Tania decided, heading off to the left and pulling him with her.

"Why?"

"It's downhill."

"Harken!" Cordelia's sharp command was the first word that had been spoken between them for a long time. The relief of finding the road had faded as it had led them on and on through featureless hills for what seemed to Tania like hours.

They stopped. Tania tried to listen for any sound above the whine of the wind and the hiss of the rain. "What?" she said.

"Hooves," Cordelia replied. "And wheels. And *song*. On the road behind us."

They turned and stared back the way they had come. After a few moments a pair of harnessed horses came around a shoulder of the hill, heads down as they pulled a wagon along the road. It had high wooden sides and a stretched tarpaulin for a roof—and seated in the front was a man in a heavy oilskin cloak who sat spread-legged and sang raucously as he flicked the reins.

> *"The man in the moon took off his gown,*
> *blew his candle out, took his lantern down,*
> *put on his very best robes he did,*
> *to merry-make till dawn, till dawn,*
> *to merry-make till dawn . . ."*

They moved to the side of the road as the wagon approached. "Don't speak unless you have to," Edric warned Tania. "He'll be suspicious of the way you talk." He stepped forward with his arms raised. "Hail!" he called. "Three lost wayfarers seek aid this stormy night!"

The driver yanked on the reins and the horses came to a halt. "What is this, by the rood! Lost way-farers? Surely 'tis madness to be abroad on such a night! Nay, do not trouble yourself to answer, climb up into my wagon, there is room and to spare. I carry provisions—you will find cloaks. Wrap yourselves and be at ease. And then you shall tell me how three such draggled wretches as yourselves happen to be upon Cock o' the Walk Road in such weather."

It was a relief to be out of the rain and the wind. The wagon was filled with grain sacks and boxes of fruit and vegetables, as well as tied bundles that included warm woolen cloaks with deep hoods. They swaddled themselves in cloaks and Edric told the friendly driver the story they had concocted. He seemed to accept it without question. Word had already reached Weir of the troubles in the south, and he understood their wish to get away from danger.

"But whither do you go?" he asked. "In these times, travelers from the south may not always expect a friendly greeting in Weir, not since the King dishonored the Court by banishing our lord Gabriel."

A knot of fear tightened in Tania's stomach. "You know about that?" she burst out. Edric glanced at her in alarm, but the driver answered her without suspicion.

"Aye, lass," he said. "'Tis said Lord Gabriel fell foul of the schemes and devices of the Royal Court, through no fault of his own." He shook his head. "They are a devious breed, the House of Oberon Aurealis."

Tania saw Cordelia's eyes blaze, but Edric managed to snatch hold of her arm and stop her from pouncing on the man's back. She subsided, glaring at him but saying nothing.

"We heard a different tale," Edric said cautiously. "We heard that Gabriel Drake's punishment was warranted."

"I dare say they speak differently of the matter in the south," he said. "But I would keep such counsel to yourself while you travel through Weir, lest your tongues betray you and you find you have escaped one peril only to fall foul of another." He flicked the reins. "And be especially prudent with your words when we come to journey's end this night."

"Why?" Tania asked. "Where are we going?"

"Why, to Caer Liel, lass," said the man. "And look you now—there it lies!"

Tania got to her knees and peered over the driver's shoulder. They had just rounded a hump of rock and there, at the end of a long, steep valley, perched high on the shoulders of a great black mountain, she saw the high bleak walls and leaping red watch-lights of the fortress of the House of Weir—birthplace of the man she dreaded above all others, ancestral home to the family of Gabriel Drake.

XV

Tania gripped Edric's hand, filled with foreboding as the wagon came to the top of the long zigzag path that led to the castle gatehouse. *We shouldn't be here!* The towers of Weir reached into the stormy sky like crooked, grasping fingers. Banners cracked in the wind and rain poured in cataracts off the battlements. A cloaked man stepped from a postern gate and spoke briefly with their driver before disappearing into shadow again. The huge wooden doors, studded with black stone, swung slowly open. The driver gave a word of command to the horses and the wagon rumbled forward under the dark echoing gatehouse and into a cobbled courtyard.

"I bid you farewell," said the driver. "I must away to the stables, but you will need to present yourself to the captain of the guard. Fear not: He will not turn you away. And you are welcome besides to take the cloaks I loaned you."

"That is most kind," said Edric.

"Nay, lad, 'tis said that a generous heart is its own reward, and mayhap the spirits of fortune will grant me good grace for my deeds."

Tania and Cordelia and Edric climbed down from the wagon and watched as it rolled away between the tall stone towers.

"Remember what he said," Edric cautioned. "Don't speak more than you have to, and don't say anything that would give away where we've come from."

"I shall speak no falsehoods, Master Chanticleer," said Cordelia. "If asked, I shall announce myself as a princess of the Realm."

Tania put her hand on her sister's arm. "Cordie," she begged, "just this once, forget who you are, please."

Cordelia made a disgusted noise in her throat. "I will not lie."

"Then try not to say anything, my lady," Edric said.

A door opened and a cheerful red light led them into a simple guardroom.

"I am Nathaniel Ambrose, captain of the Lord Aldritch's guard," said a tall dark-eyed man in a black uniform. He slammed the door behind them on the tempestuous night. "State your names and your business in Caer Liel, and if you be good and honest folk, such hospitality as we have shall be offered to you." He gestured to a stone fireplace where rosy flames danced. "Warm yourselves," he said. "Food and drink shall be brought while you tell your tale."

A soldier brought them bread and cheese and a

pitcher of water and they sat on stools around the fire while Edric told the captain their concocted story. The captain listened expressionlessly as Edric explained how their wagon had broken a wheel on the stones and how their horses had bolted in the storm. At first, Tania was afraid they would be recognized, but even when they were told to take off their cloaks so that they could dry themselves properly, the captain showed no sign of knowing who they were. With their drenched hair and their simple peasant clothes, she guessed that she and Cordelia would hardly be taken for princesses, and it was a long, long time since Edric had last been here as a servant to Gabriel Drake.

"Where are you bound?" the captain asked.

"We have distant cousins in the village of Lud," Edric replied. "I hoped we would find shelter there."

The captain nodded. "Very well. You shall have bed and board for the night. I will make inquiries as to whether any horses may be made available to you on the morrow to continue your journey. Else, you will need to wait upon some journeyman heading north who will be prepared to take you as passengers." He called out and a soldier appeared at the door. "Quarter these folk in the upper rooms of the gatehouse." He turned back to them. "They are but simple cells, to tell the truth, but they are proof against wind and rain and will suffice for your needs."

"Thank you, sir," Tania said quietly. "It is very kind of you to help us in this way."

He gave a brief bow. "Nay, lass, it is but simple

courtesy. I would not leave a dog out on such a night. Get you away to your rooms and sleep well. No foe has ever breached these walls, and even were the Dark Sorcerer himself to bend his will upon us, I trow these old stones would hold him at bay."

The soldier took them by candlelight up a narrow turret-stair to small bare stone chambers that held single beds and little else. Tania said good night to Cordelia and Edric as they were ushered into rooms along the corridor. For a moment she feared that they were being separated for some sinister reason, but then she thought of the warmth and kindness shown to them by the wagon driver and the captain. There was no reason to mistrust everyone in Weir just because of Gabriel Drake; after all, Edric came from here. She thought it must be strange and sad for him to have to return in disguise and afraid for his safety to the place that had been his childhood home.

Alone in her own room, Tania shed her outer clothes and slid between the blankets of the small bed. It was unexpectedly comfortable and she was soon feeling warm and drowsy. She glanced at the tall, narrow window that cut through the thick stone walls. The rain was snaking down the glass and she couldn't see anything but black night out there, but she could still hear the storm raging away in the mountains. She blew out the candle and curled up under the blankets.

The last image that went through her mind before sleep took her was of Gabriel Drake's silvery eyes in the darkness moving restlessly as though seeking her out. And then the eyes became still, staring straight at her, and he let out a mocking laugh.

Tania was standing at the window. Threads of rain still spun down the glass, and she had to lean far over the thick stone sill to see down to the path that zigzagged up the mountainside. A troop of soldiers holding red torches lined the upper reaches of the path; between them, a solitary horseman rode up the sloping roadway, wrapped against the storm in a heavy black cloak, his head lost in a cavernous hood. The horseman came to a halt where the path leveled out in front of the gatehouse.

The captain of the guard appeared from under the walls. "Greetings, my lord," he said. "Welcome home."

"It is good to be home, even on such a night as this," said the rider, and Tania felt a shiver of fear at the sound of that familiar voice.

The rider raised his arms and pushed his hood back, and Tania found herself staring down at the handsome face of Gabriel Drake.

Tania awoke with a start. The first thing she saw was a long narrow window set into a bare stone wall. For a few moments she couldn't work out where she was.

"Castle Weir!" she whispered as memory flooded back. It was hardly surprising that being in this place had given her bad dreams. She reminded herself that everything was all right; they hadn't been recognized by Drake's people and Gabriel was far, far away in the south. In the morning they would be allowed to continue their journey.

The room was silent and still, and there was no longer the sound of rain and wind. Tania lifted her head, peering at the window. It was still dark outside, but there was an odd reddish glow on the uppermost stones of the frame. She slipped out of bed and padded across the bare wooden floor. The wall was so thick that she had to lean far forward to grasp the latch and push the window open into the night. Her feet were almost clear of the floor as she stretched to look down. Below her the gray stone walls of the gatehouse plummeted sheer to the winding mountain pathway.

She gave a start of alarm as she saw the source of the red light. Two rows of soldiers lined the roadway—and a lone horseman was riding slowly between them up to the gate. Tania stopped breathing, her fingers freezing into the cold stonework as she stared down at the torch-lit scene. The rider was wrapped in a black cloak, but this time there was no hood.

"No . . ." she whispered. "Please . . . no. . . ."

The captain of the guard stepped out of shadows.

"Captain Ambrose." Gabriel's velvet voice drifted up to her through the cold air. "Wake my father. I would speak with him in the Obsidian Hall."

"Yes, my lord."

Gabriel spurred his horse on and vanished under the walls, the torchbearers breaking off and following him in. There was a deep booming clang as the gate was closed. Tania slid shivering to the floor. It couldn't be a coincidence that Gabriel should arrive at the castle on the very same night as they had. Somehow, he must know she was here. She remembered the words that haunted her: *You will never be free of me! Did you not know? We are bonded for all time!*

She stared at the door to her chamber, expecting at any moment for the sable-clad soldiers of Weir to burst in and to drag her away to where Gabriel was waiting with spider patience and infinite malice. But there was no sound of booted feet on the stairs. No fist hammered on the wooden panels.

She inched herself to her feet, her courage returning. She ran to the bed and quickly pulled on her clothes. She opened the door onto the bare stone, torch-lit landing. She glanced at the closed doors of Cordelia and Edric's rooms. Should she wake them? No, not yet. Not until she had a clearer idea of why Gabriel Drake was here. One person creeping around the castle at dead of night was less likely to be seen than three.

She tiptoed down the spiral stairs. She could hear the soldiers talking in the guardroom beyond the door. Their words were muffled but she was sure she heard the phrase "back from the dead."

They were talking about Gabriel. Banishment to Ynis Maw was usually a one-way trip—they must have been astounded to see him come riding up to the gate like that.

There was another door, facing the one that led to the guardroom. Tania opened it cautiously. It led to a long corridor with windows on one side that over-looked the courtyard. The mounted heads of uni-corns ran the length of the other wall. Trying not to look at the unpleasant trophies, Tania slipped silently along the corridor and out through another door. Gabriel had said he wanted to meet his father in the Obsidian Hall. But where was that? Caer Liel was immense; it was crazy to think she'd be able to find one particular hall. But some inner voice was driving her on. She crossed a wide tiled entrance lobby. There were tall black doors in one wall. Stone staircases led upward to a balcony.

Climb the stairs—you will find him.

How?

The bond that links you will take you to him.

Tania climbed the stairs. The same sense that had made her dream of his arrival was leading her now. A thick black curtain covered an archway directly in front of her. She knew she would find Gabriel if she went through that archway.

She pushed through the curtain and came out onto a high gallery above a long, lofty-ceilinged room of black stone. Torches lined the walls, throwing out thousand shards of light. Tania kept to the shadows, peering over the balustrade. The walls of the room were lined with tablets of highly polished black stone set at varying angles so that reflections and the reflec-tions of reflections bounced back and forth until it seemed that there were a hundred fractured halls and a hundred thousand torches stretching off on all sides.

Two men were in the hall. One sat on a bulky throne of black stone; the other was down on one knee in front of him. The seated man was wrapped in a thick cloak of black fur. He had a stern and austere face with thin, smoke gray hair and cavernous eyes. The duke Aldritch, Tania assumed. The other man was Gabriel Drake. Their voices drifted up to her.

"My joy at your return from Maw is tempered, my son, by the means by which it was accomplished." The Duke of Weir's voice was low and dark and powerful. "We do not ally ourselves with Lyonesse," he went on. "That were wickedness enough to shake the very foundations of Liel and send the tombs of our ancestors tumbling."

"But they are not my allies," Gabriel replied, his voice velvet soft and persuasive. "Listen to me, my lord. Oberon is a prisoner of the Sorcerer King and the House of Aurealis is broken forever. The Sorcerer sits on the throne of Faerie and all others have fled. A mighty armada sails from Lyonesse and will make landfall within days. Then will the armies of the Sorcerer King sweep across Faerie, destroying all in their path." Gabriel lifted his head and looked into his father's eyes. "They will obliterate all those who remain loyal to Oberon. I do not ask that Weir make alliances with Lyonesse, but I must return south with your promise that Weir will not wage war against the

Sorcerer." His hand touched the duke's knee. "I wish only to save our House, Father. The Sorcerer King will conquer Faerie, have no doubt of that."

"You bring dark and treacherous tidings, my son," said the duke. "And I am not convinced. Always we have stood shoulder to shoulder with Aurealis and the other great Houses of Faerie in the long wars against Lyonesse. Yet you say I should bow to the Sorcerer King and do nothing to hinder his armies?"

"Do not oppose him openly now, Father," Gabriel warned. "A time will come when we will find ways to defeat him. But to act against him now is to die." He stood. "His enemies flee before him, and the hunt is up for the members of the Royal Family who are in hiding. Even as we speak, Caer Kymry is under attack and will soon fall."

Tania gave a grim smile—Gabriel was a bit out of date with that information, at least.

"Princess Rathina has abandoned her family and sits with the Sorcerer in the Great Hall of the palace," Gabriel continued. "Titania and the other princesses are on the run and will soon be captured. I have been allowed to come here to urge you not to fight against Lyonesse. The Sorcerer has pledged that if you offer no threat, then Weir shall remain free."

The duke frowned. "Princess Rathina has turned traitor, say you?"

"Truly, she has."

"Then the Power of Seven can never be invoked," said the Duke. He nodded, his face deep in thought.

"If this threat to the enemies of Faerie has been lost, you may take back to the Sorcerer King my solemn word that Weir will not take arms against him."

Tania had no idea what the duke meant by the Power of Seven, but it seemed clear that the news of Rathina's treachery had helped him to make up his mind.

"You say that Titania has returned to Faerie," the duke said, leaning forward and looking piercingly at his son. "Yet you are certain that she can do nothing to hold back the Sorcerer's might. Are you so sure of her powerlessness?"

"She is in hiding in Esgarth," Gabriel replied. "It is only a matter of time before she is found. Some of her daughters fled the forest but they will be hunted down and killed ere long."

"Is the Princess Tania among them?"

Tania felt a shiver down her spine.

"Indeed," said Gabriel, and now his voice faltered a little. "It is strange. I almost feel that I sense her presence. I have felt it since I neared Caer Liel. But she cannot be close by; they would remain in the south to be near their mother, and of all places surely she would avoid Weir." He narrowed his eyes. "Have any travelers come here in the past few days?"

"I know not," said the duke. "Captain Ambrose would have that knowledge. Shall I summon him?"

"No," Gabriel said. "She is not here. She cannot be." Tania let out a silent breath of relief. But then Gabriel turned to his father. "Yes. Yes, summon him.

Her image burns in my mind." He held out a grasping hand. "I almost feel that I could reach out and touch her."

"So be it," said the duke. He called and a servant appeared. "Fetch Captain Ambrose," he ordered.

Tania backed away from the edge of the parapet. Just as she had sensed Drake's presence, so he could sense hers. He wasn't certain yet, but he would be once he had spoken to the captain of the guard and learned that three travelers had arrived that night. They had to leave, *now*. Tania pushed through the black curtain. She paused for a moment on the balcony, watching as the servant made his way across the lobby and out through a door. Then she raced down the stairs and made her way at a run back to the gatehouse cells. She pushed her way into Edric's cell, leaning over him and shaking him awake.

"Tania? What's wrong?"

"We have to get out of here," she said. "Drake has arrived."

"What?"

"There isn't time to explain, but we have to go right now."

Edric threw on his clothes and it wasn't long before Cordelia was also up and dressed and the three of them were on the landing outside the cells.

"There's only one gateway out of the castle," Edric told them. "It'll be barred and guarded. We'll never get out that way."

"Then we must find weapons," said Cordelia.

"Fight our way out!"

"Against all of them?" Tania said. "I don't think so. Maybe we could knot our bedsheets together and climb out of a window."

"It's too high," Edric said. "But I saw something that might help. Quickly, follow me." He led them down the stairs. On a lower landing he pushed open a door.

"This was open when we were brought up here," he said. "It must be some kind of storeroom. I saw rope." Sure enough, several long coils of rope lay on the floor.

"There are no windows here," Cordelia said. "Come, take the rope—we will descend from above."

Each carrying a coil of rope, they went back up to Tania's room. She closed the door and they got to work tying the thick ropes together. Tania tested the knots, tugging at the rope ends.

"Will they hold?" she asked uneasily.

"We shall find the truth of that soon enough," said Cordelia.

Edric tied the rope around Cordelia's waist and she climbed onto the deep sill. She sat astride the window for a moment, then slipped out into the night. Edric and Tania took the strain, slowly letting the rope out. A long time seemed to pass before the rope loosened.

"Check she's okay," Edric said. "Then go down after her."

"How are you going to get down?"

"I'll tie the end to the bed and jam it against the wall. That should hold it."

Tania kissed him. "Be careful," she said.

"And you." He helped her onto the sill. She edged her shoulders out of the window. The drop made her head swim. She saw the brown rope snaking away from her down the shining gray stone—and there, maybe forty feet below, she could see the foreshortened figure of Cordelia looking up and beckoning. Tania slid one leg over the sill and gradually shifted her weight, holding tightly on to the rope with both hands as she climbed out of the window. She was aware of cold night air all around her and of the precipitous drop to the roadway.

Her heart was beating so loud that it sounded like drums in her ears. She gritted her teeth and struggled to catch the rope between her feet. It took her a few moments to secure it between instep and sole. Then, her heart in her mouth, she began to edge down. She felt Cordelia's hands helping her down the last couple of feet. They looked up in silence, holding hands. Edric's head was showing from the window. Tania watched as he clambered out and began to descend.

He was about fifteen feet from the ground when a new shape appeared above him at the window. A voice shouted: "Halt! Or perish!"

Cordelia gasped. "We are discovered!"

"Edric! Jump!" Tania called. She saw a flash of something white at the window and the very next moment the rope came loose and Edric dropped, the rope coiling over him as he landed between them.

He hit the ground with flexed knees, absorbing the impact and just managing to keep to his feet. "Quickly," he said. "Off the road."

He ran to a sheer edge of rock that cut sharp as the stroke of a knife across the mountainside. Beyond it Tania saw only plunging darkness. Edric looked back at them and Tania could see fear in his eyes. "It won't be easy," he warned, turning and letting himself down off the edge.

Tania heard shouting above them. It wouldn't be long now before the gates of Caer Liel would be thrown open and soldiers would come after them. She sat on the edge of the lip of stone. She could just make out Edric's shape as he climbed down the rock face. She turned, scrabbling for purchase with her feet. Cordelia crouched above her, ready to follow. Tania caught an outcrop of rock with one foot and lowered herself down. She found a handgrip. Then another. Cordelia turned, her foot groping as she came over the edge. Tania transferred her weight and began the perilous descent.

XVI

The sun rose in an eggshell blue sky, lifting above a breathtakingly beautiful landscape of rolling heather-clad hills and wide stony valleys. Tania, Edric, and Cordelia had stopped to rest by a rushing rivulet of water that tumbled down a stony gully. Tania sat with her cloak wrapped around her. The view was glorious, but the early morning was gnawingly cold. She looked nervously over her shoulder every few seconds, convinced that she would see horsemen bearing down on them, with Gabriel Drake at their head.

The tall dark mountains of Weir were at their backs now. They had made their way through the hostile night to these tumbled foothills, afraid at every step that they would be tracked down. But the only time they had seen their pursuers was at a distance: a line of horsemen bearing red torches, moving rapidly along a ridge half a mile away.

During the night, the storm clouds had crept away into the west, and now the sky was clear and bright.

Tania looked over to where Edric was standing on a raised hump of land, his arms folded against the cool wind, staring northward where the hills became blue and indistinct. Cordelia had picked up a shard of flint sometime in the night and she was now sitting at the waterside, whetting the edge of the flint on a stone. She looked up, as though sensing Tania's eyes on her.

"I will not go unarmed into the wilds," she said. She lifted the flint, gripping it like a dagger in her fist. "Let them come, sister—the first to find us will regret their impetuosity."

Edric walked back to where they were sitting.

"So, Master Chanticleer," said Cordelia, squinting up at him with her head cocked to one side. "Can you lead us true?"

"I think so, my lady," he said. He pointed into the north. "Do you see those two hills: the big one with the smaller one at its side? They are Great Erl and Lesser Erl. The Grantor Pass runs between them. If we go that way, we'll come to Whitewater Fells and Skarnside Fells and the River Lych."

"You know this landscape well," Cordelia remarked.

"Actually I don't," Edric said. "I'm much more familiar with the countryside north of the Erls. These aren't hills I know very well. As children we were always warned away from them."

"Why's that?" Tania asked.

"This is where the wild unicorns of Caer Liel roam, is it not, Master Chanticleer?" said Cordelia. "I have seen their tracks and traces aplenty."

"Wild unicorns?" Tania said. "Are they danger-ous?"

Edric nodded. "Very. They have vicious tempers and they're totally unpredictable. They attack with hooves and teeth and horns. And their horns are like skewers—they'd go right through you." He looked at Cordelia. "Have you seen signs that there are any nearby, my lady?"

Cordelia smiled grimly. "Oh yes, they are close."

Tania was beginning to feel warmer. They had been walking for some time, and the sun was high in the eastern sky. The night chills had been banished and they were moving along the bottom of a wide valley, picking their way through soft banks of moss bright-ened by yellow and white flowers. On one side the val-ley wall was of limestone cliffs and rocky outcrops; the other slope rippled with purple heather. The day was warm and still and dancing clusters of white butter-flies clouded the shimmering air. They were deliber-ately keeping to the valleys, careful to avoid the uplands and hilltops where they could be seen against the horizon. They had seen nothing to suggest that the soldiers of Weir were close on their track, but Tania was convinced that Gabriel would have emptied the castle in his desire to capture them.

The floor of the mossy valley stooped slowly down-ward, leading into a deep circular glen. A pool of water lay in the glen's center, bright as a mirror.

"We should fill our water bottles," Edric suggested. "There are a lot of rivers in these parts, but it's better to be prepared."

They began to walk toward the silvery disk of water.

"Our situation is not of the best," Cordelia commented. "Ynis Maw lies many leagues from here." She looked at Edric. "Are there no farmsteads in this region where horses could be procured?"

"There are a few farms and villages north of the Erls," Edric said. "But even if they had horses for sale, what would we use to buy them?"

"Our honest word that payment will be made in due time," Cordelia replied.

Tania gave a faint smile. "I can see that working," she said. "We'll pay you if we win the war against Lyonesse." She arched an eyebrow. "Do you think they'd go for that?"

Cordelia looked at her but didn't say anything. Tania frowned. The princess's expression had frozen on her face, her eyes fixed on something beyond Tania's shoulder. It was the look of fear in those usually fearless eyes that made Tania spin on her heel.

"I wished for steeds," Cordelia murmured. "Steeds we shall have!"

A herd of animals was coming over the hill, the soft thunder of their hooves filling the air as they galloped down the slope.

"Unicorns of Caer Liel," Edric said. "Keep absolutely still. It's too late to run."

Tania gazed at the unicorns with uneasy fascination. They were the size and shape of horses, but at the same time startlingly different. They were pale gray, and the contours of their bodies were sharp-edged and angular as if they had been roughly carved from marble. Their manes and tails were very long, colored a pale mauve. Their eyes were deep purple and full of a wild, perilous intelligence.

"Keep together," Cordelia said in an undertone.

The unicorns split into two racing streams that surrounded the travelers like pincers, cutting off any chance of escape. Tania shrank away as she found herself enclosed by a moving circle of unicorns. The animals came to a halt and turned, facing inward with their heads lowered. Tania's eyes were drawn to the white horns that jutted from their foreheads; they were about eighteen inches long, slender sharp-edged spirals that ended in vicious points. Twenty of those horns were now pointed straight at them.

"Brothers and sisters," said Cordelia, and Tania was alarmed to hear a tremble in her sister's voice. "We mean you no harm."

One of the unicorns snorted and stamped a hoof.

"We did not know that this was your water," Cordelia apologized. "We trespassed out of ignorance, not disrespect."

The unicorns stepped forward. Tania felt Edric and Cordelia pressing against her as they moved closer together. "Can't you make friends with them?" she whispered to Cordelia.

"They do not trust me and our death is in their eyes," Cordelia replied under her breath. "Listen closely. I will seek to reason with them; you must use the time to try and flee. If all fails, I have my stone knife, though I am loathe to use it."

"You'll be killed," Edric said. "And they'd still take us down. That's not a way out of this."

"Then I wait on your wisdom, Master Chanticleer," Cordelia hissed. "Mayhap an angel will swoop down and pluck us from the earth."

She had only just spoken when a high-pitched whistle rang through the air. The long, sweet-toned notes slowly changed pitch, creating a simple melody full of a strange and wistful loneliness. The unicorns backed away from the three travelers and moved off to gather together at a watchful distance.

"What was that?" Tania asked, astonished.

"I know not," Cordelia said. "But there were signals in that sound, I would swear to it."

A shape appeared on the hilltop, black and featureless against the sky. Someone on horseback, Tania thought at first, but as the rider came down the hillside she saw that it was a young man riding a unicorn. He brought his steed close then sprang lightly down into the grass.

"Do you love life so little that you would risk all to drink from Einhorn Tarn?" he demanded, walking toward them with long strides.

He was a similar age to them, very tall and slim and dressed in a simple tunic and leggings of dark brown leather. His hair was a spiky black thatch and his face long and narrow with heavy brows and dark flashing eyes.

Cordelia stepped forward, the sharpened stone in her fist. "Come no closer," she warned. "For, unicorn master or no, if you try to do us harm, I will slay you where you stand."

The young man came to an abrupt halt. A smile flickered at one corner of his mouth. "I am not the master of these beasts," he said. "I am their friend. But they will take it ill, mistress, if you murder me without cause."

Cordelia dropped the knife to her side, staring hard into the young man's face. "Who are you, unicorn-friend?"

"It becomes the strangers to name themselves first," the man said. "But I will do you a courtesy. I am Bryn, son of Baldon Lightfoot."

"My name is Edwin Poladore," Edric broke in. "These are my sisters, Brosie and Dorimar. We were on our way to visit our cousins in Lud, but our wagon broke a wheel and our horses bolted."

Bryn gave him a long, thoughtful look. "No," he said at last. "You are not." He looked at Tania and his brown-eyed gaze pierced her. "You are Princess Tania and the knife-maiden is one of your Royal sisters, I would guess, although which Princess I am threatened by I cannot say." His eyes turned to Edric. "And you are the treacherous servant to our lord Gabriel Drake." He smiled. "You three are hunted throughout the land. I am told a bag of precious jewels awaits he who brings you to the gates of Caer Liel, living or otherwise."

"Seek to earn those jewels, and you will not live to count them," Cordelia warned, lifting the stone knife again. "We will not be taken."

"Then it is good that I have no desire for such gew-gaws," Bryn said without concern. "You are lucky that you stumbled into these houseless hills. Horsemen search for you to the west and north and south, but where the wild unicorns roam, they are less apt to stray, unless they come to hunt them, and then they will only venture here in large and well-armed parties."

Hearing the cold anger in his voice as he spoke of the unicorn hunts, Tania remembered the mounted animal heads in the castle. She was aware of the uni-corns coming closer now, warily circling them, their eyes bright and curious.

"How do you know about us?" she asked.

"In these regions not a kestrel moves across the sky nor a hare through the heather but I know of it," Bryn replied. "I have spoken this morning with ravens and goshawks and with skylarks, and all tell me that a great hunt is afoot—that Gabriel Drake has returned to Weir and seeks Princess Tania and her companions who fled Caer Liel by night and are on foot in the hills." He smiled wryly again. "I fear he means them no good if he should find them." He paused, looking carefully at each of them in turn. "I can offer refuge, if you wish it," he said.

"Are you not loyal to the House of Weir?" Cordelia asked.

"I am loyal to the *Earldom* of Weir, my lady," he said. "I am loyal to the birds and the beasts and the hills and the streams. These things would I defend with my life. But I am not loyal to those who slaughter unicorns for pleasure, and I am not loyal to those whom our good King Oberon would have banished from the land, most especially when they return as a cat's-paw to the monster of Lyonesse." As he spoke one of the unicorns came up beside him. He lifted his hand to stroke the long white neck. Tania saw a protective glint in the animal's eyes as it stared at her.

"Can you help us get away from here?" she said. "We're trying to get to Ynis Maw. King Oberon is a prisoner there; we're going to try and free him."

Cordelia looked sharply at her.

"We have to trust him, Cordelia," Tania said. "Who else is there?"

Bryn's dark eyes widened. "Princess Cordelia?" he said with wonder in his voice. "I have heard of your kinship with animals, my lady. They say that you can speak with all things that walk or crawl or swim or fly."

"All save the wild unicorns, it would seem, Master Lightfoot," she said. "That is an art I would fain learn."

"In what small time we have together, I would gladly teach you something of the skill," Bryn replied. He looked at the others. "Come, I have a modest home nearby. We shall go there, if you would have my aid. There is food and drink, and we will speak of how to send you safe away from this place and speed you on your journey."

Bryn's home nestled under a limestone crag, its dry-stone walls seeming to grow out of the cliff face. The roof was covered in thick green turfs, so that from a distance the house almost looked like part of the rugged landscape.

They had to duck under the low lintel of the wooden, bark-covered door, but once inside they found themselves in a single deep and spacious room lit by rushlights. Woven reed mats covered the stone floor and hung from the walls.

A small fire flickered in a stone hearth, a brown clay cauldron hanging over it, bubbling with a thick stew. Tania breathed in the delicious smell of herbs and cooked vegetables. The dwelling was sparsely fur-nished: A narrow bed covered with woolen blankets lay against one wall, and flat-topped rocks held a few simple oddments such as knives and bowls and rush-light lamps. A hollowed-out rock held food: fruit and dried fish and meat, and on one side stone jars brimmed with clear dark water.

"Do you live on your own here?" Tania asked.

"Nay, my lady," Bryn said. "I share this valley with all the beasts and the birds." He hauled on a rope that dangled from the sloping ceiling and a section of the roof lifted to let sunlight come flooding in. He secured the rope and moved around, putting out the rush-lights. "You must be hungry and weary," he said.

"Come, eat and drink and take your rest."

They sat on the floor while Bryn ladled the stew into wooden bowls and handed one to each of them. Tania ate hungrily, more than glad of warm food after the chilly night in the hills of Weir.

"Is it normal for the folk of Weir to dwell apart from their kind as you do?" Cordelia asked curiously. "I had not heard that it was so."

Bryn sat on the edge of his bed. "I believe that I am unique in my choice of home," he told her. "I do not seek the company of people, and I have here all that I need. The unicorns protect me from unwanted visitors and the birds keep me informed of all that goes on in the outside world." He frowned. "That is how I know that the Sorcerer of Lyonesse is loose. A curlew fleeing north brought me the news some days ago—she said that the land is barren and burned where he treads, and that all life withers at his touch." A deep sadness came into his eyes. "Is that true? Does he have such domination over the land?"

"Yes, he does," said Tania. "But we're going to do something about it." She hoped she sounded more confident than she felt.

"It is seventy leagues or more to the northernmost coast of Fidach Ren," Bryn said. "You will need speedy mounts."

"Are there horses we could use?" Edric asked.

"None south of the two Erls. But I was not thinking of horses. The unicorns of Caer Liel run swifter than any horse."

Tania felt a flicker of unease. "Would they let us ride them?"

"I believe they would if I made clear to them the importance of your journey."

"But how would we control them?" Cordelia asked.

"Once they know to trust you, they will be compliant to your requests," Bryn told her. He smiled at her. "Would you like to speak with them, my lady?"

Cordelia's eyes brightened. "Indeed, I would."

"Then come," he said. "New friends shall meet with old."

They followed him outside. The herd of unicorns was grazing nearby. Bryn gave a whistle and the animals came trotting over to him. Tania found herself taking an involuntary step back as they approached. She still couldn't quite get over the strangeness of them, and those sharp-edged, spiraling horns certainly looked capable of running a person through and through.

"Brethren," said Bryn, resting his hand on the curved neck of the foremost unicorn, "these good folk are in sore need and would crave your aid." Tania felt herself scrutinized by the weird purple eyes. She tried to return their unfathomable gaze, but had to look away. The proud heads bowed and several of the animals stamped their hooves.

"To the far north, and with great haste," Bryn went on, as if in answer to an unheard question.

One of the unicorns stepped up to Cordelia and allowed her to rest her hand on its mane. "Hail to thee, child of the lone hills," Cordelia whispered, pressing her cheek to the creature's neck.

"His name is Zephyr," Bryn said.

The unicorn snorted and nodded its head.

"I never knew they could behave like this," said Edric. "I was always told they were untamable."

Bryn looked at him. "They are untamable, Edric Chanticleer. Nothing can take their wildness from them. They choose to befriend you, or they choose not to."

Another of the unicorns moved toward Tania. She swallowed hard, her eyes fixed on the needle-sharp point of the horn as it came closer. The head lifted and the wide mouth came up to her face, the nostrils snuffling.

"He is named Tanzen, my lady," Bryn told her.

The unicorn snorted and turned its head so that the curve of the neck was displayed to her. Cautiously, Tania laid her hand against the smooth gray-white coat of the animal's neck. It was warm under her fingers. Tanzen nudged up against her in an almost playful way, sending her rocking back on her heels.

"I think he likes you," Edric commented.

"Yes, I think he does," Tania agreed in surprise. She looked over Tanzen's back at Edric, who was stroking the neck of a female unicorn that Bryn said was called Drazin. "We're going to ride unicorns," she said. "How cool is that?"

It was midday and the sun was beating down on the heather-clad hills. Tania and the others sat astride the wild unicorns of Caer Liel. They had come to a halt in the valley between Great Erl and Lesser Erl. In front of them the crumpled land stretched away into a blue haze.

Bryn had come with them this far. "I will leave you now to go on alone," he said, and Tania noticed that his eyes lingered longest on Cordelia and that she met his gaze for a few moments, then blushed and looked away.

"The River Lych lies five leagues hence," he continued. "Once it is forded, you will have entered Prydein. The mountains of the north are full of dangers," he warned. "And it is said that a race of terrible creatures haunts the glens of Fidach Ren."

"Do you know if they have wings?" Tania asked, wondering whether he was speaking of the Karken En Ynis Maw, the very creatures they wished to meet.

"I know not, but they are said to be murderous and without pity," Bryn said. "Be watchful at all times."

"We'll do that," said Tania. "But we were told the same about these unicorns, so they may not be as bad as you think."

"Had I not been close by, you would have been killed," he reminded her. "Do not hope to meet friends in the north, my lady—there are none." He was about to turn his unicorn and ride back the way they had come when he paused for a moment. He reached into his tunic and brought something out, riding to Cordelia and holding out his hand. Tania saw that he was holding a curious kind of twin-bodied whistle or flute.

"The unicorns delight in music at day's end, my lady," he said.

Cordelia gave him a puzzled look. "I have not the skill," she said. "My sister Zara has the gift of music, not I."

Bryn said nothing, but continued to hold the pipes out. Frowning, Cordelia took them. "Thank you," she said.

"Farewell, then," said Bryn, breaking the odd silence. "Good fortune attend your quest, my friends. Maybe we shall meet again when all is done." He tapped his unicorn's flanks with his heels and the creature wheeled around, its forelegs striking the air, before galloping away.

Cordelia gazed after him, and there was a wistful look on her face that Tania had never seen before. Then Cordelia pushed the pipes away into her tunic and turned away.

"Come," she said. "Onward to Ynis Maw!"

They were in a place of knuckled hills that climbed and climbed into the white sky. Grasses and moss clung to ridges and banks of gray rock, leaving bare ledges that sloped inward to form a long cleft worn over the years by the gush and flood and sparkling fall of a tumbling white river. Tania sat astride her unicorn, gazing spellbound at waterfall after cascading waterfall, the spray catching the evening light and filling the hills with shimmering rainbows.

Below, the river came to a time-gnawed cauldron of turbulent water and then flowed southward through a deep-cloven valley of heather and gorse. It was there, where the land was less furrowed and bony, that they had forded the river at a wide, stony place full of the rush and scurry of the bubbling water.

"This is Reganfal," Edric said.

Tania looked at him: This was the place he had mentioned at Crystalhenge. His eyes were shining, his face spangled with fine water droplets. "It's beautiful," she said.

He smiled. "I told you it was."

Cordelia had ridden higher into the crags; she had halted on a wide flat platform of rock some twenty feet above them, gazing away to the south. She had been strangely silent all that day, answering when spoken to, but otherwise riding along with a preoccupied look on her face. Tania had a suspicion she was thinking about Bryn; of all her sisters Cordie had always seemed the least interested in people, but perhaps she had never expected to meet someone just like her, someone who loved animals as she did.

"Come on," Edric said. "I'd like us to be over the mountain by nightfall."

Tania eyed the peaks doubtfully. "Okay," she said, nudging Tanzen into movement with a touch of her heels to his flanks. "Last one at the top gets first watch."

"So be it!" called Cordelia and a moment later Zephyr was leaping up the rocks like a mountain goat.

"Hey!" Tania yelled, urging Tanzen on after her. "You won't win that easily!"

The night sky was blind with cloud. Tania was on watch. They were in a high saddle of land between two rearing peaks. She could hardly see a thing in the darkness, but she could feel the enormous presence of the mountains—and it wasn't a comfortable sensation. The farther north the three of them traveled, the more she got the feeling that the land *resented* them. It was crazy, she knew, but she couldn't shake the feeling that Prydein didn't want them there.

Before he had gone to sleep, Edric had warned her to be extra vigilant. "I've heard some strange stories about these regions," he had told her. "Stories about the Ghostlights of Prydein. People caught at night in these hills speak of vivid hallucinations—they see things that aren't really there."

"I, too, have heard of the Tricksy Spirits of Prydein," Cordelia had added. "Wicked phantoms that lure people to their deaths."

That wasn't what Tania wanted to be told just before starting her watch. But so far nothing had happened, except that she was having trouble keeping awake. She rubbed her eyes, forcing herself to stay alert. The unicorns were nearby, lying together with their legs tucked under them and their necks stretched, their heads resting on each other's backs.

Tania caught a glimpse of the moon through thinning skeins of racing cloud. She was getting used to the speed with which the weather changed here. It had been happening all day: One moment the white sun would be burning down on them and then, within moments it seemed, a cold wind would come sweeping in from the west, carrying layers of thick gray cloud on its back. Rain would spatter briefly, then the clouds would turn to rags and tatters and the sky would be blue again.

Tania's eyelids became heavy as the long night crept slowly past. Edric had told her to rouse him when she couldn't stay awake anymore, but she wanted to give him as long a sleep as possible. Her head nodded and her eyes closed. The mountains were whispering, the great dark hulks of ancient stone leaning toward her, creaking and groaning. They were going to crush her. . . .

She woke with a gasp. A misty gray figure stood in front of her. It wavered like a pale flame as it beckoned to her. "Come to me," said the man. His face was familiar somehow. "Come to me and all will be revealed."

She found herself getting to her feet. "Gabriel?"

"There is little time, my lady. You must come to me."

Tania's voice was hesitant, her head full of dark swirling clouds. "No . . . I have to keep watch. . . ." There was something dreadfully wrong about this, but she couldn't remember why she shouldn't follow the flickering silvery figure. She walked forward, holding her hands out toward Gabriel as he floated back from her.

"Just a few more steps, my lady."

"Yes."

A voice shouted behind her. *"Tania!"* Hands grabbed her, bringing her to a jerking halt.

She was at the edge of a cliff, about to stride out into nothingness.

Edric spun her around. Cordelia was running up behind him. Tania realized she was about forty yards from the camp. She blinked stupidly at Edric. He grabbed her shoulders, looking into her eyes.

"It was Gabriel," she murmured. "He wanted me to follow him."

"This is an evil turn," Cordelia said. "If the Great Traitor can enter your mind and force you to his will, how can we ever be safe from him?"

The clouds lifted from Tania's brain and fear took their place. "Does this mean he knows where we are?"

"I don't know," Edric said. "But it might not have been him. It might have been the Ghostlights I warned you about. Were you nodding off just before you saw him?"

"Yes, I was," Tania admitted. "I was having these really weird dreams about the mountains."

"The Ghostlights prey upon those who sleep," said Cordelia. "I think that Master Chanticleer is right: What you saw was but an illusion."

"I'll keep myself awake from now on," Tania said, shivering at the thought of what might have happened if Edric had not woken her. "I don't want that to happen again."

"No, you should get some sleep now," Edric told her as they walked back to their camp. "I'll keep watch for a while."

Tanzen was watching them, but he put his head down as they approached, as if reassured that everything was all right. Tania lay down, pulling her cloak over her ears. She was too tired to stay awake. As she drifted off she had the strongest feeling that, deep within the mountain, something with a cruel, cold heart was laughing at her.

It was a bright, fresh morning and Tania and her companions were galloping beside the banks of a long finger of smooth water. The silky surface of the lake reflected the scudding clouds and the distant brown mountains that rose sheer from the water's far edge. The rushing air sang in Tania's ears, blowing away all her night fears. The ground that sped away under their unicorns' hooves was tufted with tall brown grasses. Where the country lifted itself from the lake the hills were soft with pine trees. The cool air was full of their scent.

They paused for a while at the northern end of the long lake, eating a little of the food that Bryn had given them while the unicorns stepped down to the lakeside to drink. Towering white clouds edged across the sky. The pine woods had gradually moved closer to the long stretch of water, so there was now only a narrow spit of land between the trees and the lake. Heather-clad hills rose in the north, forming their next challenge.

Edric was stretched out full length in the grass, staring up at the sky. Tania and Cordelia sat close by. Cordelia was cross-legged, holding in her lap the double-bored whistle that Bryn had given her.

"Try playing it," Tania said.

"I do not have the skill."

"You just put your fingers over the holes and blow. Anyone can do that."

Cordelia didn't respond.

"Would you have liked it if Bryn had come with us?"

"Perhaps," Cordelia murmured. "He is in my thoughts, it is true." She looked at Tania. "I would like to see him again."

"I'm sure you will."

Tania got up and stretched, gazing into the pine forest. Under their green canopy the slender brown trunks of the trees reached away into deep, rich shadows. Tania frowned. She had seen a movement under the trees: shifting shapes that echoed the curving mesh of the branches but were at the same time different somehow—something that was *like* tree shadows, but not.

She walked toward the tree line, her eyes narrowed. For a few moments she lost the place where the movement had been. Then there was another stirring in the shadows and suddenly the curious lines and shapes snapped into focus and she realized that she was staring at a pair of great lordly branching antlers.

She turned to the others with a thrilled gasp. "There's a stag in there; it must be huge."

Cordelia and Edric got up and followed her. There was a brief silence while they tried to locate the sweeping antlers, then Cordelia spoke in a hushed, urgent voice. "Come away. We must go."

"Why?" Tania asked, surprised by the alarm in her sister's voice. "It won't hurt us, surely? Can't you talk to stags?"

"Indeed, I can," said Cordelia. "That thing is not a stag. Do you see any hindquarters?"

Puzzled, Tania looked into the gloom behind the antlers. Cordelia was right; the stag didn't seem to have—

"It's a man," said Edric.

"No, it can't be." At that moment the head turned and for a split second Tania found herself staring into a pair of leaf-shaped yellow eyes that burned like suns in a furred face that was half human and half animal. The wide mouth opened, the split upper lip drawing back to reveal long white teeth. A deep bellowing cry boomed out, sending birds rocketing into the sky.

They turned and ran. The unicorns were waiting, their eyes rolling and their hooves stamping the ground. Tania leaped onto Tanzen's back and he sped away, hardly giving her time to get seated before the turfs were flying in their wake. She risked one brief glance around. The antlered man-creature had stridden out of the forest and was watching them. He was broad-shouldered and deep-chested and covered in shaggy brown fur; Tania guessed that he must be at least ten feet tall. They galloped around a curve of the lake and she lost sight of him.

"What was he?" she called to Edric.

"Furlingsbarl," Edric shouted back. "A forest demon."

"This is an evil land," Cordelia called, the wind whipping her voice away. "A land where monsters breed!"

Another night had come down, this time star-filled and still. They had climbed into the mountains again and were camped on a narrow stony place from which the land rolled down to a series of slender mountain lakes linked by the white threads of winding rivers.

A soft voice and a hand shaking her shoulder woke Tania from a deep, dreamless sleep. "Is it my watch already?" she mumbled.

"No," Cordelia whispered, her face close to hers.

"But there is something I think you would wish to see."

Tania got up and followed her to the edge of the plateau. Edric was already there, crouching on his heels and staring down. She followed the line of his eyes and saw that a bonfire was burning on the slopes of the hills some half a mile away from them.

"Be still and watch," Cordelia said.

Tania hunkered down beside Edric, her hand on his shoulder. She stared at the fire. Dark shapes were moving around the flames. She could faintly hear voices, high-pitched and crackly.

"They're dancing," she said as her eyes cleared of sleep. She stared more closely. A whole group of people were leaping and prancing around the bonfire, and now she could hear the distant piping of flutes and the thud of drums.

"See anything odd about them?" Edric asked.

Tania peered more intently. He was right: There was something not quite right about the way they were moving, their dancing had a jerky, almost birdlike quality to it. "Oh!" She gave a gasp of shock as the dancing figures came sharply into focus. "Their legs bend the wrong way!"

From the waist up, the distant people seemed human enough, but it was as if their legs were fixed on backward, their knees bending back so their steps had the raking, pecking quality of large birds.

"What are they?"

"I don't know," Edric admitted.

"We should not allow ourselves to be seen," Cordelia warned. "Come away. You've witnessed another of the curiosities of this bewitched land. Now go you back to sleep."

Tania watched the strange dance for a minute or so more before crawling away from the edge and lying down again. It didn't take her long to fall asleep, but the leaping flames and the uncanny dancers haunted her dreams.

From high dark cliffs, they looked out over a great stretch of indigo blue water. Waves beat at the rocks a hundred feet below them, sending up spumes of white spray. The wind came shrieking off the sea, snapping their cloaks and sending the manes and tails of the unicorns flying. Black birds circled in the air, calling as they swooped and dived.

"If I'm right," Edric shouted over the howl of the wind, "that darkness over there is either Highmost Voltar or Rhoth."

Tania stared into the wind with narrowed eyes. A low hump of land lifted out of the dark water on the horizon. "Is that good?"

"It means we have reached Fidach Ren," Cordelia replied. "Our steeds have served us well. We have made good time, if the maps that I have seen showed a true depiction of Faerie."

"So, how much farther is it to Ynis Maw?" Tania asked, pulling her cloak tighter around her.

"We won't get there today," Edric said. "But we should tomorrow."

"So, let us ride!" Cordelia called. "Ride like the north wind!"

Tania patted Tanzen's neck and the three animals dashed along the clifftop toward the looming mountains.

No one could sleep. The night was pitch-black and full of a moaning wind. They huddled together in their cloaks, listening to the blustery air as it hissed and howled among the rocks. But it was not the sound of the wind that disturbed them the most.

Tania had been on watch when she had heard it first: a deep, ponderous noise in the blackness, as if some huge thing was dragging itself through the hills. And then had come the laughter and the crying and the shouting, voices on the wind, far off but eerie and distressing. A strange red glow had tipped the hills. Tania had crept over to a big hunk of rock and had peered over it. She had seen a herd of black horses galloping through the night on spindly insect legs, their manes and tails formed of leaping red flame. Trembling with fear, she had crawled back to where the others were lying.

Soon, they had all been awake, clinging together as the ground groaned under the weight of the slow, monstrous slithering thing. Tania didn't dare to try and imagine what was causing the noise; it was bad enough knowing there was something huge and alive out there without having images of it in her mind.

She was never so glad in her life to see the first faint, gray hint of dawn come creeping over the eastern hills.

XVIII

The morning was strangely calm as they rode along the coast of Fidach Ren. They saw no trace of the things that had disturbed them in the night. The land was barren and raw, as if the soil and crust of the country had been stripped back to reveal its bare bones. There were no trees now, the only living things were wind-torn scrub and bracken, and sharp-edged grasses that thrust up out of the stones like knives.

The sky was a dreary gray sheet above their heads, occasionally tossing down a scattering of cold rain as they rode along. The noise of the waves hammering on the black rocks was so constant that Tania was hardly even aware of it anymore. She rode with her head bowed, weary of this endless journey, exhausted by this terrible land. Their food was almost all gone. They ate a meager midday meal, not even bothering to stop for rest. Tania knew the others felt the same way she did: They all just wanted this to be over and done with.

She was brought sharply out of her lethargy some time in the middle of the slate gray afternoon. She lifted her head, peering at something that she thought at first was a bird flitting low across the sky a little way ahead of them. It was gone in an instant, diving among the rocks before she was able to focus properly, but as she stared into the distance she quickly realized that the thing had been two or three times farther away than she had initially thought; if it had been a bird, it had been a very large and a very strange-shaped one.

A little while later she saw another shape go skittering across her eye-line, low against the horizon, flying from crag to crag, black against the featureless sky. "What was that?" she asked.

"Winged things," Cordelia replied. "Not birds."

They moved warily now, slowing their unicorns to a walk as they found themselves descending into a valley whose steep black walls rose sheer around them. Tania heard a sharp cry from somewhere above. She stared at the black crags that surrounded them. There was a shape up there: something squatting on a broken-toothed peak. A watchful silence filled the valley, as if the hills were holding their breath. They rode on, down and down into the winding valley, the unicorns moving slowly as they picked their way over the uneven ground.

"They are all around us," Cordelia murmured. "I think they mean to attack. Would that we had swords to defend ourselves."

"We might be able to outrun them," Edric said.

"We cannot ask the unicorns to gallop over such terrain," said Cordelia. "They would have broken legs for their pains."

The tension rose as they made their way along the valley. Tania's head ached with the strain. She felt like yelling out to the creatures—anything to break the deadly, volatile silence. Stones rattled and clicked under the hooves. The creatures didn't show themselves. The silence screamed.

There was a sudden rattle of stones behind them. Tania looked over her shoulder. Rocks and boulders were tumbling down the hills at their backs. And suddenly the air was full of flying creatures, shrieking and shouting and hurling stones at them.

A stone struck Tanzen on the neck. He reared, whinnying in fear, his forehooves kicking at nothing. Another stone struck him and he lurched to one side. Tania slipped from his back, trying to clutch at the long mane as she fell. But it was useless. She came crashing to the ground as Tanzen went bounding back up the valley in a flurry of clattering hooves.

She got to her feet. The air seemed full of flying stones. She put her arms up to shield herself. A stone cracked on a rock by her foot. Another grazed her shoulder. She stumbled back as she saw Cordelia's unicorn rise on his hind legs and then slip sideways. Cordelia was thrown to the ground. Zephyr struggled to get back onto his feet, and then, with a whinny of fear, he raced away in pursuit of Tanzen. Drazin went plunging past Tania, almost knocking her off her feet. Edric was not on her back. Then Tania heard his voice.

"This way!"

She spun around. Edric was on higher ground, and close by where he was standing, she saw a cave mouth in the valley wall. She and Cordelia scrambled over the stones, crouching to avoid the missiles that were falling all around them. Tania saw a stone hit Edric's back and bounce off. He fell and she ran to help him get up.

"I'm okay," he said, gasping. "Get into the cave!"

A few moments later the three of them were under the shelter of the low roof of the cave. For a while the stones still peppered the entrance, spinning and skipping, sometimes ricocheting in and almost hitting them.

Tania crawled to the cave mouth. "Stop it!" she shouted. "We haven't done anything!"

The rain of stones came to a halt. Surprised, Tania looked at her companions. "That worked better than I'd expected," she said. "Do you think they understand English?"

"Try it," Edric suggested.

Tania kept herself under the lip of the cave entrance. "Hello?" she called. "We're friendly. We just want to talk to you?"

She waited for a response. None came. She looked at Cordelia and Edric. "I'm going out there."

"No, you can't," Edric said.

"What else is there?" Tania asked. "We can't stay here forever."

"Then I'll go," Edric said.

"No, I will. It's no safer for you than me." Tania stood up and walked out into the open again. She hadn't said so, but she felt a kind of distant kinship with these creatures. They had *wings*—light, gossamer wings that were the same as the ones that had grown from her back only a few weeks ago.

"Please don't hurt us," she called. "We only want to talk to you."

The valley was silent. Perhaps the winged creatures had gone?

Then a solitary shape rose above a nearby boulder. Its wings cupped the air and it jumped lightly onto the boulder's top, crouching low, knees bent, one hand gripping a stone and the other reaching down, fingers touching the rock for balance. Tania stared at it in amazement. It was shaped like a person, but it was utterly alien, quite unlike anything she had ever seen before.

"Hello," she said, her mouth suddenly dry.

The creature was female. She wore a simple tunic of grayish brown material, and her legs and arms were bare. The iridescent wings rose high above her head as she stared at Tania with huge sea green eyes set in a narrow, triangular face. Tania guessed that she would be about five feet tall if she was standing up, her body lithe and slender, her arms and legs fine-boned and her skin a curiously shiny ivory color with a thin tracery of pale blue and green over it, as though the skin was so thin that the veins were showing through. Long unkempt blue-green hair hung over her shoulders.

"What art thou?" The voice was high and keening, and when she opened her mouth Tania saw that the small teeth were needle-sharp and pointed.

"My name is Tania. My friends are Cordelia and Edric." Tania held out her open hands. "We won't hurt you."

The creature's head tilted and she grimaced, her feet shifting uneasily. "Hurt us?" she echoed. "No, truly thou shall not hurt us, Fid Foltaigg."

"I'm sorry," Tania said, stepping slowly toward the creature. "What does that mean—what you just called me?"

"Thou art Fid Foltaigg," said the creature. She rose to stand erect, her hand tapping at her breast-bone. "We are Lios Foltaigg."

"I don't know what that means."

Tania became aware of a dozen or more of the creatures, rising now from cover and surrounding her—both male and female, all dressed similarly to the first one, all with the same slim bodies and oddly beautiful triangular faces, all with shining wings on their backs.

"Thou art the unfinished ones," said the creature. "Where is thy pride?"

"My pride?" She looked around and a sudden understanding hit her. "Oh! You mean my wings. I don't have any. I did have, but they . . . well, I lost them."

She felt a hand on her back. One of the male creatures had crept silently up to her, his face filled with curiosity. "Thou wert winged," he said. "I feel the ghosts of thy wings at thy back. Their loss haunts you."

"Yes, it does," Tania admitted. A few more creatures approached her and gazed at her with questioning eyes. She saw Edric and Cordelia standing at the cave mouth. "I don't think they're going to hurt us," she said to them.

She looked back at the first female. "What's your name?"

"Clorimel Emalion Entarrios," said the creature.

"Wow," said Tania. "That's a lovely name."

"Thou art tamers of the horned beasts," said Clorimel, glancing nervously in the direction the unicorns had fled. "I have not known such a thing before. Thou hast especial sorceries."

"Not really," Tania said. "They were only helping us. They're not really tame."

"Why art thou in our land?" asked the male who had come up behind her. "It was promised to us for all time. The Sun came to earth and gave Fidach Ren to Lios Foltaigg for eternity—for us alone, untroubled by Fid Foltaigg." He waved a hand. "Thou shouldst depart."

"That we cannot do, by your leave," Cordelia said, walking forward to stand beside Tania. "Not until we have fulfilled our quest."

"What is thy quest?" asked Clorimel.

"We've come here to rescue King Oberon from Ynis Maw." Edric joined them. "We were told you might be able to help us."

"None may come to Ynis Maw and none may go," said Clorimel. "That is the ancient law, given to us by the Sun."

"Please listen to us," Tania begged. "Bad things are happening in the south. We've traveled all the way from the other end of Faerie to get here. I don't know how much of this you'll understand, but there's a really bad man down there and unless you help us, he's going to take over the whole of Faerie. There's only one person who can stop this from happening, but he's trapped on Ynis Maw."

"We were told that there are legends concerning your people," Cordelia said. "Legends that say you have a secret knowledge and a secret power. Are you the Karken En Ynis Maw?"

A low murmur came from the creatures. More of them had come out of cover now, and a few of them had surrounded Cordelia and Edric and were staring at them with puzzled eyes and reaching out with thin fingers to touch their clothes.

"We are Karken En Ynis Maw," said Clorimel. "This name was given to us by the Sun in the time before time. We are the guardians of the Black Isle. None may come and none may go. While we hold true to our pledge then the land of Fidach Ren will be ours forever."

"I believe you," Tania said. "But if you don't help us, bad people will come here, and they won't care about any promises that were made to you. They won't care at all. They'll take this land away from you and they'll probably kill you all."

"Tell me," Cordelia asked. "What is the meaning of the words 'Fid Foltaigg'?"

Clorimel pointed to them. "Thou art Fid Foltaigg—unfinished people," she said. "We are Lios Foltaigg—complete people."

"She means the wings," Tania said. "We're incomplete because we don't have wings."

Cordelia looked shocked but said nothing.

Clorimel pointed to Tania. "Thou art Alios Foltaigg. *Half finished*—half Lios." She frowned at her. "Thou art between things. Thou hast one foot on the land and one foot in the sea. The Sun is in thy right eye and the Moon in thy left. That is the engine of thy sadness and thy destiny."

Tania felt a shiver run down her spine at this. Clorimel seemed to have sensed the core of her unrest—that she was half human and half Faerie—and she seemed to pity her for it. "Will you help us?"

"What wouldst thou have us do?" Clorimel replied.

"Do you have black amber?" Tania asked. "We need black amber to break the Isenmort bonds that hold Oberon in his Amber Prison."

Clorimel gazed blankly at her. Tania guessed that she had never even heard of black amber.

"Hopie was wrong, it seems," Cordelia murmured. "These people cannot help us. It has all been in vain."

"We should still go to Ynis Maw if they'll let us," Edric said. "We can't come all this way and then turn back without finding the King."

"Well said, Master Chanticleer," said Cordelia. She turned to Clorimel. "Will you allow us safe passage across the water to Ynis Maw—or will you seek to thwart us?" she asked. "Know you that we will not willingly depart from this place until our quest is fulfilled. Blood may be spilled if you hinder us."

Tania gave Cordelia an anxious look—this wasn't the time to be issuing threats. She held out her hands to Clorimel. "Please help us," she said. "You'll be helping yourselves, too. Trust me: If you do this for us, we'll make sure you're never bothered by Fid Foltaigg again. And you'll be helping us to destroy the bad people in the south. Will you help us?"

Clorimel sprang into the air, her wings vibrating as she flew in a spiral above the rearing walls of the valley. With whooping cries and calls the others leaped into the air and followed her, their wings shimmering like rainbows, their slender bodies light as feathers. Tania felt a terrible ache inside her: a longing to leap from the hard cold ground and soar and swoop with them. But all she could do was to crane her neck and watch them as they hovered in the sky.

They hung in the air for a long time, speaking together, obviously debating whether they should break their ancient law. At length they broke apart and began to circle downward, landing lightly on the rocks all around them. Clorimel came down in front of Tania, hovering a little above the ground so that their faces were level.

"We shall do as you ask, Alios Foltaigg," she said. "For the sake of our homeland and for our long peace. But if thou prove'st false, then shalt thou all be killed."

Tania nodded. "That won't happen," she said.

"Thou shalt travel to Ynis Maw," said Clorimel. "Follow us."

The Lios Foltaigg took to the air again, drifting on the wind like leaves as Tania and the others made their heavy-footed way down the winding valley. They came around a sharp bend and suddenly the world opened up in front of them. The valley tipped steeply to a wide rocky bay where the gray-green sea smashed against the land with a sound like splintering glass. Out across a mile or so of choppy waters, Tania saw a black hump of land rising from the sea.

"Behold the Black Isle," said Clorimel. "Behold Ynis Maw!"

XIX

Tania stood on the seashore, staring over the waves at the sinister black fist of Ynis Maw. Edric and Cordelia were at her side, and many Lios Foltaigg were gathered nearby. Tania's mind was filled with thoughts of Gabriel Drake, of how Oberon had exiled him to that bleak hunk of rock—and of how the Sorcerer King's evil power had set him free once more.

"We could really use Zara right now," said Edric. "She could whistle up a couple of turtles to ferry us over there." He looked at Tania and his voice lowered to a whisper. "Do you think these people would carry us?"

Tania pulled her eyes away from the dismal island. "I suppose we could ask," she said. "But they're really small—I'm not sure they could manage it."

"And how will we return with the King?" Cordelia added. "And how will we bring him safe to our Mother? Even when we set foot upon that cursed isle, I deem our troubles are but beginning." She smiled grimly. "A worthy challenge, indeed!"

Tania had the bad feeling that she was right. All the problems and dangers that had beset them so far were just the preamble to the huge unanswerable question of what to do once they found Oberon. Without black amber, they had no way of freeing him from the iron-bound Amber Prison.

There was a whirring sound in the air behind them. Tania saw one Lios Foltaigg descending toward them in long spirals. He landed lightly, his small feet hardly disturbing the stones.

"Thy steeds are galloping south," he said. "They move at great speed. They will not return."

"Thanks for letting us know," Tania said. She hoped Tanzen and his companions would get safely back to their home. She looked at Clorimel. "We need to get to the island and it's too far to swim."

"There is a boat," Clorimel said. "It is old, very old. It may not bear thee after all this time."

"A boat?" Tania said in surprise. "Where?"

"It lies in a cave not far from here."

"Take us to it, by your mercy," Cordelia said. "And let us test its seaworthiness."

With a delicate unfurling of her wings, Clorimel lifted from the ground and drifted feather-light across the shoreline. Tania and the others followed, as did several Lios Foltaigg, rising and skimming the stones with the soft whirr of their shimmering wings. They came to a place where the dark cliffs reared up into the sky and the waves broke in a welter of foam.

Clorimel led them over sea-wet boulders hung with slippery weed.

A dark crack appeared in the cliff face. The cave had a shingle floor and reached back into the cliff beyond the sunlight. Lying to one side just inside the entrance was a slim black rowboat.

Edric leaned over it, his hands on the gunwale. "It seems to be intact," he said. He looked at Clorimel, who was standing by the cave mouth. "When was it last used? What was it for?"

"It is not of our making, nor was it ever used by Lios Foltaigg," she answered. "The minions of the Sun did once on a time use the vessel, but I know not its purpose, save that it is said that the blood of the stones is food for the Sun."

"What does that mean?" Tania asked.

Clorimel cocked her head. "It means what it means," she said. "No more, no less. Is the boat serviceable?"

"I think so," Edric said. He looked at Tania and Cordelia. "Help me get it down to the shore?"

Between the three of them, they managed to haul the boat out of the cave and down through the stones. Tania saw that a pair of oars lay in the keel. Clearly at some time someone had used this boat to get to and from Ynis Maw. Oberon had no need of a boat to send exiles to the Black Isle—he did that with the power of his Mystic Arts. So who had used the boat and why?

They pushed the boat into the sea. Edric waded in waist deep, fighting the waves as they tried to drag the vessel away from him.

"I see no water seeping through the boards," Cordelia said. "I think the hull is sound."

Edric held the boat as steady as he could while Tania and Cordelia climbed on board. It rocked and bucked on the waves, but they were able to help Edric in without mishap. Cordelia took an oar and fended the boat off the rocks. Edric joined her in the stern and together they managed to push off. Tania sat in the narrow prow and Cordelia at the stern while Edric took the middle seat and began to row with long, firm strokes. Tania could see on his face the effort it was taking for him to get the bobbing boat under control. He gritted his teeth, fighting the waves, plying the oars expertly as the boat moved away from the shore.

"It's working," Tania encouraged him. "You're doing it."

He nodded, the sweat standing out on his forehead as he lunged forward, lifting the oars in a wide arc out of the sea, then heaved back, twisting the blades as he plunged them into the waves and dragged them through the water. It was several minutes before he managed to row the boat away from the shore and beyond the breaking, foam-capped waves. As he rowed them out into the gray-green sea, Tania saw that a few Lios Foltaigg had lifted off from the shore and were following, hanging as buoyant as thistledown above them.

It wasn't an easy crossing. The sea fretted at the small boat, spitting foam at them, jolting them this way and that as if a spiteful intelligence was at work, determined to force them off course. Tania clung to the side and looked over her shoulder, watching the black shore of Ynis Maw come closer.

They made landfall in a flurry of sucking foam. Drenched to the waists, they fought against a sea that seemed to be trying to pull the boat away from them and leave them stranded. But at last they managed to drag it clear of the hungry waves onto a sloping shore of black shingle. Tania stared up at the slick black rocks that jutted from the top of the beach. They shone under the gray sky, their dull sheen ghostly and sickly.

Cordelia gazed up to where Lios Foltaigg hung in the air a little way off the coast. "Do they come to spy upon us or to give us aid?" she asked suspiciously.

"I don't know." Tania looked up, cheered a little by the sight of the delicate people floating like curiously shaped kites, gazing down with their almond-shaped sea green eyes while their dragonfly wings held them aloft and away from all harm.

She envied them at that moment more than she could have said.

Clorimel circled lower. "We shall help thee in thy search," she called down. "Tell us what it is that thou seek'st."

"That's really kind of you," Tania said. "We're looking for a large amber ball. There's a man inside it."

"Thank you for your aid," said Cordelia. "Courtesy unlooked for is a great boon."

Clorimel nodded and rose to rejoin the others. Tania watched as Lios Foltaigg darted off one by one over the island, vanishing inland above the cliffs. She heard a crunching of shingle and turned to see that Edric and Cordelia were making their way up the slope of the beach. She followed them toward the greasy-looking rocks.

It was hard work to get up that first frowning wall of cliffs, and Tania's arms and legs were trembling from the strain of the climb by the time they finally stood on the top and saw Ynis Maw stretching out in front of them.

"A desolate place, indeed," said Cordelia. "A fit kingdom for a traitor."

There were some signs of life among the knife-edged cliffs and jagged valleys: a few bleak wind-scoured bushes and spiked grasses that jutted from the black rubble. The island lifted in uneven terraces toward a cracked dome of fanged rock. The hills looked as if they had been battered and broken by gigantic hammers, the land ripped open and wounded by monstrous axes.

Edric's hand slipped into Tania's. His voice was low and full of horror. "I know what Drake did to you, and what he tried to do to us all, but I wouldn't wish this on him . . . not *this*."

Tania didn't want to talk about Gabriel Drake—this place was dreadful enough without that. Besides, they had come here for a reason. "Where should we look first?" she asked. She had always imagined that once they had reached Ynis Maw, she would be able to sense her Faerie father's presence—like a kind of warmth or a feeling of well-being in the air. But there was nothing.

"The Amber Prison might be out in the open somewhere, but it could just as easily be hidden away in a valley or a cave," Edric replied. "We'll have to look everywhere."

"Then let us begin," said Cordelia. "Do we stay together or search alone?"

"We should keep together," Tania said, uneasy at the thought of being alone in this ghastly place. "I know it'll take longer, but I don't think it's a good idea to split up."

"So be it." Cordelia began to pick her way through the rocks.

They searched for a long time, climbing down into steep-walled valleys, making their way over wolf-fanged ridges, scrambling among the ruination of pulverized rock. Now and then Tania saw one or two Lios Foltaigg moving across the sky, but any hopes that the flying folk would quickly find the King had ebbed away. The world darkened as battalions of storm clouds streamed in from the north.

Cordelia eyed the clouds. "If we do not find the King while the daylight lasts, what then?" she asked, voicing a concern that Tania had been feeling for some time. "Do we sleep on this cursed island, or must we return to the mainland?" She lowered her voice. "I have seen things," she said. "They keep away from us and try to stay hidden, but I have seen them, flitting among the rocks—watching us, following us."

Tania looked at her in alarm. "What kind of things? Animals?"

"Nay, not unless there are beasts on this isle that walk upon two legs and clad themselves in ragged garments."

Tania's eyes widened. "You mean *people*?"

"The wretched remains of things that once were people," Cordelia said. She looked at Tania, and there was a strange light in her eyes. "Thought you that only the Traitor Drake had ever been banished to this place?" she asked. "Nay, sister—there are others."

A cold chill ran down Tania's spine. She glanced around, half expecting to see crazy-eyed faces peering out at her from among the rocks.

"There are still a few hours of daylight left," Edric said. "We don't have to decide yet."

A high-pitched call, like the cry of a seagull but with words in it, came drifting down to them. Tania stared up into the gray sky. Three Lios Foltaigg were hovering near the coastline, two males and one female.

"Maybe they've found something," Tania said, renewed hope kindling in her.

"Or maybe they're giving up," Edric said grimly.

They scrambled over the rocks, coming to a high cliff that overhung the sea. The three winged folk came closer. The female was Clorimel.

"The Sun sleeps in a cave upon the north side of

the island," she called down. "Ithacar and Uriban have seen him. He lies in an orb of yellow light and slumbers with both eyes open."

"*Oberon!*" said Tania. "They've found him." She called out, "Can you show us the way?"

"That we can," Clorimel called. "Come, it is not far."

The Lios Foltaigg led them around the west coast of the island until they came to a cave-pocked valley in a ring of broken hills.

"Merciful spirits!" Cordelia said. "Do you see the light?"

An amber glow brightened the mouth of one of the caves. They scrambled down the hillside, Tania's eyes fixed on that amber light, praying that they would find the King alive inside the cave. It was little more than a scoop hollowed out of the cliffs, the roof low and rugged, and the floor of gray shale. But the amber radiance lit up the walls, so that as they stepped over the threshold it looked as if the cave was made of dark gold.

The Amber Prison hung in the air, a few inches off the ground. It was wrapped around with a network of gray metal bands through which the trapped light welled. A figure lay within. Cordelia let out a low sob, her hands coming to her face. Tania stepped forward, trembling as she remembered how she had found Edric trapped in such a globe.

Oberon lay on one side. He was clad in a robe of dark fur trimmed with white. His eyes were open in his handsome bearded face, but his gaze was fixed on nothing and there was no life or animation in the sky blue irises. One arm was lifted, the hand stretching out, the open palm upward, as though he had been frozen in amber at the moment of trying to defend himself.

Tania drew closer. A single tear ran down her cheek as she stared through the brutal metal straps at the face of her Faerie father. There was no fear in his expression, but the emptiness in his eyes drained all the hope from her. She bit her lip, hearing Cordelia's sobs behind her.

Edric came up beside her. He said nothing.

For a few moments they just stood there, staring at the amber globe. Then Tania stretched out a hand to touch it. A blue spark leaped from the iron bonds, burning her fingers like a flame, shooting barbs of agony up her arm. She snatched her hand away with a cry of pain.

"I can't even touch it," she said, her voice shaking with emotion. "We've come all this way and I can't even touch him." She fell to her knees, anger and frustration and fear overwhelming her at last. "What was the point?" she shouted. "It's all hopeless. It's all completely hopeless!"

XX

Night came down over Ynis Maw like a black lid. There were no stars, no hint or gleam of light, save for the sad amber glow that beamed like trapped yellow moonlight from between the iron bands that enwrapped Oberon's prison.

None of them could bear the thought of leaving the King alone there for another grim night of sleepless, petrified banishment. There was little comfort in the cave, but they made the best of it, Edric and Cordelia curling up to sleep on the shale floor while Tania took first watch. She huddled in her cloak at the cave mouth, her back to the cold stone, her eyes aching as she peered into the nothingness that lay beyond the amber glow. Bleak thoughts filled her mind. They had no black amber to melt the Isenmort bonds—no metal to destroy the Amber Prison. How were they to set Oberon free when they couldn't even touch the shining sphere?

A faint pattering sound brought her out of her brooding thoughts.

Patter, patter, patter. Like distant running feet.

She thought of the half-mad creatures that Cordelia had seen—the banished people. Were they out there in the night? Were they closing in on them?

The pattering grew louder, and a heavy drop of rain splashed on Tania's hand. Dark dots began to stain the gray stone beyond the cave mouth. Darts of rain lit up like jewels as they cut down through the amber light. Tania drew herself a little deeper into the cave as the rain began to fall more persistently. Soon, the rock was slick with running water, the rain pelting down with a hiss that was like snakes and lizards.

Thunder growled and forks of lightning cracked the night open, making brief hectic silhouettes of the surrounding hills. The storm clouds were emptying themselves over Ynis Maw. They were in for a restless night.

Tania awoke to a sky full of grim, ruddy-colored clouds. It was as if the sky had rusted over from the rain; the grisly light made the black rocks look like bloody bones thrusting up out of pools of gore. She was still huddled in the cave mouth, stiff and aching. She got to her feet, wrapping herself in her cloak and stepping out of the cave. The rocks around her shone wetly red and dark red water splashed underfoot. She looked around, remembering the banished folk and wondering what their lives must be like on this terrible barren hunk of rock.

"And they won't ever die," she murmured.

"They'll be here forever." The immortality of the Faerie folk could be a curse as well as a miracle.

Her mouth was dry. She reached for the water bag that hung at her waist. It was limp and empty. She needed something to drink, but she couldn't bring herself to fill her bottle from the bloodred rain pools that had formed overnight.

She walked a little way off, searching for a less tainted water source. A small pool had formed under the lip of an overhanging rock. The water was dark and still, but not bloodred. She knelt, taking the stopper from her bottle to scoop up some water. As she bent over the pool she saw her own reflection gazing darkly up at her.

"Is that really me?" she whispered. The hair was draggled and unkempt, the face pale, the hollow eyes full of sadness. It was the face of someone who had witnessed horrors—the face of someone who had come to a place of utter despair.

And then it was as if the universe stumbled for a moment—as if time had stuttered.

"Tania?"

She stared into the pool. The face had changed. It was her face but not her face. The lips moved again and a voice spoke in her head.

"Tania, it's me."

"Titania?" Tania said breathlessly, leaning closer to the water.

"I've been trying to reach you for days," Titania said from the surface of the pool. "Where are you?"

"We're on Ynis Maw," Tania replied. "Are you all right?"

"Yes, we are all safe and well. Eden's spell is keeping us hidden."

Misery filled Tania's voice. "Everything's gone wrong," she said, the words thick in her throat. "We've come all the way here, but now . . ."

"I know, I know," said the soothing voice. "Do not worry, Tania. I have spoken with Hopie. She told me everything that happened."

Tania rubbed tears from her eyes. "A lot more has happened since we left her."

"You can tell me about it when you get back," Titania said. "But now you have to listen to me, Tania. I'm going to tell you a great secret. Probably the greatest secret in Faerie. I did not dare to tell it to you before now, in case something went wrong and you fell into the hands of the enemy." There was a brief pause, then: "The black amber mine is on Ynis Maw."

Tania stared down into the rippling face of her mother. *"Wha-at?"*

"In the center of the island there is a deep crater; the mine is inside the crater. The black amber will break the Isenmort bonds from Oberon's prison, and once they are broken, I believe he will have power enough to destroy the Amber Prison from within and free himself."

Tania's head was spinning. "You're kidding me? The mine is *here*?"

"Yes, it is," Titania said. "I wanted to tell you days

ago when you were all here talking about the black amber, but I did not dare." Tania remembered the Queen's reflective silence at the table back in Rafe Hawthorne's cottage; so that's what she had been thinking about. And Clorimel's strange comment suddenly made sense now: *The blood of the stones is food for the Sun.* Oberon was the Sun, and the black amber was the blood of the stones. The rowboat must have been used to ferry black amber from the mine thousands upon thousands of years ago.

"There is a problem," the Queen continued, breaking into Tania's thoughts. "The mine has a guardian."

"What kind of guardian?" Tania asked in a daze.

"I do not know," Titania said. "The King put it there a very long time ago. You have to assume it will be dangerous."

"It can't be any more dangerous than some of the things we've already dealt with," Tania said. "Listen, I'm going to go back now and tell Edric and Cordelia about this. And then we'll find the mine and rescue the King." She reached her hand toward the water. "Thank you," she said softly. "Thank you so much."

Her Faerie mother's hand reached up toward her. "I wish I could have told you sooner."

"No, I understand." Their fingertips met for a moment on the surface of the water and the reflection broke into expanding rings of ripples. The Queen was gone.

Tania sprang up and ran back to the cave, the red rainwater spraying high in her wake.

Edric and Tania lay on the rim of the cracked crater that formed the heart of the island. It had been a laborious climb up through the splinters of the black rocks, but at last they were looking down into the pit of Tasha Dhul.

They had left Cordelia with Oberon. It had been against her wishes to allow them to face danger without her, but they had convinced her that she should stay with the King. Edric's words had the greatest effect.

"The King can see us," he had told her. "I know— I've been in an Amber Prison. Stay here with him. He'll be comforted by it."

The sides of the crater tumbled down to an oval depression studded with holes and black-mouthed caves. There were the remains of an old trackway to the left of where they were lying. It wound down the steep slope and made its way across the floor of the gorge, ending at a great backward-leaning cavern mouth.

"I wonder what the guardian is," Edric mused. "A person or some kind of animal?"

"I don't think Titania knows. It was put here thousands of years ago. Perhaps it's dead."

"Do you think the King would have used a guardian that was going to die?"

"I guess not." Tania frowned. "Can you see anything moving down there?"

"No, I can't. But that doesn't mean it's not there."

They got to their feet and stepped over the crater's rim to begin the descent into the gorge. Loose scree slipped away under their feet and they held hands to help each other as they slipped and slithered downward, but soon they were safely on level ground. They walked cautiously along a beaten path across the valley floor. Above them heavy clouds rolled in, blotting out the sun. An unnatural darkness came over them, like twilight at noon.

"I wish we had swords," Tania whispered.

"I wish we had a rocket launcher," Edric responded. She looked at him and they clasped hands even more tightly.

As they came in under the high mouth of the cavern, rain was beginning to fall. The mine-workings stretched back into a darkness that was like a gaping throat. Pools of dark water gathered in pits and ruts in the ground. Walking deeper into the cavern, Tania began to notice that the overarching walls were streaked with black threads that glinted in the weak light. Behind her she could hear rain falling steadily.

Edric let go of her hand and walked off to one side, picking his way over the spreading pools of water. She followed, finding him crouched in shadows, holding a few small shards of black amber in his open palm.

He looked up at her. "This is all we'll need," he said. "Doesn't this seem a bit too easy to you?"

"I like easy." She crouched at his side. "I'm thirsty—do you think the water in here is fit to drink?"

"I don't see why not. It's only rainwater."

Tania cupped her hand and scooped up some of the icy cold water. It tasted slightly odd—as if there were minerals or something in it—but it was refreshing and not unpleasant. She drank a couple more handfuls and then filled her water bottle.

Edric had stood up. He was staring intently down the great black throat of the cavern.

"What's wrong?" she asked.

"I thought I heard something."

She stood up, tying the water bottle to her belt. "We should get out of here."

Now she, too, heard the sound of movement in the darkness. They shrank together, staring into impenetrable nothingness.

A shape began to form at the far end of the cavern. Malevolent red eyes glinted.

"Run!" Tania shouted. She had seen those eyes before—in a nightmare.

But before they could move, the thing pounced forward into the light. It stood on four clawed feet and must have been six feet high at the shoulder. The monster had the rough-haired body and mane of a lion, but its hindquarters were bare of fur and covered in black scales. Its tail reared up, thick and segmented, lifting above its back like the tail of a scorpion, the barbed tip dripping thick yellow poison.

But the most horrible part of the monster was its face: It was the distorted and twisted face of a human being, all the more appalling because it *was* almost human. The terrible bulging eyes burned red, the wide mouth was open, the lips drawn back to reveal jagged yellow fangs.

"A mantichore!" Edric whispered. "The guardian is a mantichore!"

Tania bent down and picked up a stone. With a fierce sweep of her arm she launched the missile at the creature. It was a good shot: The rock struck the monster on the forehead. But it didn't even seem to be aware that it had been attacked. It let out another deafening roar and gathered itself to leap.

They ran.

"Don't look back," Edric said, gasping as they sprinted over the uneven ground.

"The black amber?" Tania said.

"I've got it in my tunic."

They raced out of the cavern and into the hammering rain. The storm clouds seethed, as if the sky was convulsing above their heads. Tania heard the scrape and clatter of claws on stone behind them. She heard the monster's heaving breath, the thud of its feet on the ground. It sounded as if it was getting steadily closer, but she didn't dare look back for fear of tripping.

"This way!" Edric shouted, darting to one side. He was slightly ahead of her as they hit the sloping wall of the gorge. The stone was like broken black glass in the rain.

She scrambled up the rise, using hands and feet. Lightning forked across the sky. She heard the monster bellowing. They were almost at the top now; she had no thoughts beyond reaching that sharp ridge.

"Come on!" Edric urged.

Her foot slipped on stones as sharp as knives. She fell onto one knee, crying out with the pain.

"Get up!" Edric shouted down. "It's closing in on us! I'll have to let go of you! I need both hands to get up this next bit." His wet hand slid out of hers and he scrambled to the ridge. She got to her feet, deadly cold and soaked to the skin.

A deep snort sounded behind her. The mantichore was almost upon them.

"Tania!"

She looked up into the needling rain. Edric was crouched on the crater's edge, reaching down toward her.

This was the moment in her nightmare when Edric turned into Gabriel Drake.

Tania hesitated, not daring to take his hand. Living the nightmare.

"Tania!" He stretched down farther, his fingers spread. And then, before Tania could pull herself together, he overbalanced and fell, tumbling past her down the side of the crater.

He managed to bring himself to a halt but the mantichore was only a couple of meters below him, ploughing its way through the rain, its eyes furnace red, its bellows louder than the thunder.

Tania didn't stop to think. She had put Edric in danger; that was all that she knew. She stood up on the steep slope, turning, catching her balance for a moment, and then jumping down. She crashed feet-first into the mantichore's head just as its jaws were about to lock on Edric's arm. Her weight knocked the monster back, but one of its claws raked across the back of her hand, drawing blood. Its great talons scrabbled on the loose stones as it slid down the hill-side, still roaring, its scorpion tail thrashing. Tania hit the ground with stunning force, only just managing to grab hold of a jutting edge of rock to stop herself from plunging down in the mantichore's wake.

Edric was sprawled on the slope, his tunic torn open. He staggered to his feet, pulling her up. Together they scrambled up the last few feet to the top of the crater. Once they had reached the rim, Tania looked back into the teeming rain. The mantichore was bounding up after them again, roaring and gnashing its teeth, the fearsome tail poised to strike. Edric grabbed Tania's hand and pulled her headlong down the outside of the crater.

Tania lost her footing on the scree and crashed to her knees with a gasp. Edric stopped to help her up. They were at the foot of the crater now, the cone rearing above them. While Tania struggled to get her feet under her Edric snatched up a rock and stood over her, ready to hurl it at the monster.

But the mantichore had not followed them. It stood on the lip of the crater, black against the seething sky, pacing back and forth with its tail quivering and its jaws gaping. As Tania stared up it bellowed and clawed at the ground. Stones rattled down. She got to her feet. "It isn't following us," she said, gasping. "Why?"

"It guards the mine," Edric said. "We're not in the mine anymore."

Tania let out a breathless gust of laughter. "Then we did it! We've got the black amber."

Edric's voice was suddenly full of anguish. "No," he said. "We haven't."

She looked at him in confusion. He made a helpless gesture with his hands, and she looked down. His tunic had been ripped open when he fell trying to reach down to her; the precious nuggets of black amber were gone, lost inside the crater.

"No!" She stared at him in horror. "We have to go back."

"We can't," Edric said. "We only just survived the first time. The mantichore will be waiting for us now."

"But we were so close," Tania cried. "I don't believe this is happening."

Edric reached for her, taking hold of her wrist and looking at the scratches left by the mantichore's talons. "You've been hurt."

"It's only a cut. It's nothing."

"It isn't *nothing*. It might be poisoned. Let's get away from here and wash it out."

Tania was too miserable to protest. As they stumbled away through the falling rain she could hear the mantichore bellowing into the stormy sky.

* * *

"We have lost a battle, not the war," Cordelia said. "The creature may be fearsome, but we will find a way to defeat it."

Tania looked bleakly at her. "What makes you think that?"

Cordelia frowned. "Because we *must* prevail," she said.

Tania wished that she had Cordelia's confidence. How were they going to get anywhere near Tasha Dhul with that monster on the prowl? And how would they defeat it? By throwing rocks? She already knew how effective that would be.

"Keep still," Edric said gently as she flinched away from where he was dabbing her wounded hand with a corner of his tunic.

"It stings," she said. "Leave it alone, Edric. It'll be fine."

"No, it won't," he insisted. "At least let me wash it."

She handed him her water pouch. She winced as he let the cold water run over her wound. The cut wasn't particularly deep, but it ran the length of the back of her hand and it was quite sore.

"I have a plan," Cordelia said. "All three of us will go to Tasha Dhul next time. I shall show myself, drawing the monster off, while you two enter the mine and steal away with the black amber."

"And what if the thing kills you while we're doing it?" Tania asked.

Cordelia's eyes flashed. "Be assured that I will do all in my power to prevent that from happening."

Tania shook her head. "It's too risky. We need to think of a better way."

Cordelia walked over to the cave mouth without saying anything and sat down with her arms wrapped around her legs and her chin on her knees, staring out into the distance with a grim look on her face.

"Shall I bandage it for you?" Edric offered, examining the cleaned cut.

"No, it's fine."

"Best to be on the safe side."

"Stop fussing, Edric." Tania pulled her hand away. She stood up, resting her fingers in his hair for a moment. "Honestly, I'm all right," she said.

"Really?"

"It's just . . . you know . . ." She turned and walked deeper into the cave. She stood in front of the Amber Prison, gazing into the King's frozen face. Titania had said he should have the power to get free once those iron bands were gone. Tania wanted so much to release him from that terrible prison—she wanted it so much that it was like a pain in the middle of her chest.

Tears burned behind her eyes. No, she wouldn't cry. She refused to waste her anger like that. She wanted to hold on to it, to use it to find the strength to do what they had come here to do. She reached out her hand toward the Isenmort bands. She didn't care how much it hurt. She deserved to be hurt for not doing better. Gritting her teeth, she pressed her hand against the iron.

A whiplash of pain ran up her arm and into her

shoulder, but it was nothing like as intense as it had been the last time she had dared to touch the Amber Sphere. She stared at her hand; wisps of gray smoke were rising from where her skin was pressing against the metal. The Isenmort was fizzing and melting where her hand touched it. Her *wet* hand! Her hand that was wet from the water she had brought from the mine.

Tania pulled her hand away, snatching the water pouch from her belt and emptying it over the Amber Sphere. The metal crackled and spat, melting away like ice on hot stone. "Edric! Cordie!" she called, stepping back as a cloud of gray smoke dimmed the amber globe.

"What did you do?" Edric asked.

"It was the water from the mine," Tania told them. "Whatever makes black amber work against metal must be in the water, too."

"Did I not tell you we would find a way?" Cordelia said, resting her hand on Tania's shoulder.

"You did," Tania admitted.

The cloud of gray steam faded and the light of the Amber Sphere filled the cave again.

"Father!" Cordelia called. "Awaken!"

But the King lay unmoving in the globe, his glazed eyes staring at nothing.

"He should wake up now," Tania said. "Titania said he would wake up and break out." She reached for the globe, spreading the fingers of both hands over the warm surface, bringing her head close to the shining amber shell. "Oberon, wake up!" she called.

"Please, Father, wake up!"

For a long time nothing happened. Then very slowly Tania became aware that the surface of the globe was growing warmer under her hands, and the amber light was becoming brighter. So bright that she had to close her eyes against it.

She heard Cordelia's voice. "He awakes!"

The surface of the globe was now too hot for her to touch. She stepped back, her arm up to cover her eyes, her whole body beaten back by wave after wave of fierce heat.

An explosion of dazzling light knocked Tania off her feet. She sat up, blinking, seeing only a white blaze in front of her eyes, as though lightning was playing in her brain. Gradually her vision cleared. The globe was gone, shattered to a million pieces. Oberon lay limp on the ground.

Cordelia was already at the King's side, brushing his hair off his forehead. "Father? Wake up now. You are free."

Edric and Tania came closer. The King didn't move. Tania saw that his eyes were closed and his face was deathly pale.

Cordelia looked up at them, tears running down her face. "He is dying!" she wept. "All is in vain! Our great father is *dying*!"

Part Three

The Power

of Seven

XXI

A somber group gathered at the shoreline of Fidach Ren. It had been a heartbreaking and arduous task to carry the unconscious King across the island to the waiting boat and to lay him gently in the bottom while Edric rowed them back to the mainland. There were only two consolations: He was breathing and his pale skin was warm to the touch. Tania gazed down at his face, at the golden curls of his hair and the close-cut golden beard. At the high slanted cheekbones and at the closed eyes that she knew were a vivid, piercing blue, as bright as a clear summer sky.

For the first time in many days, Tania's thoughts drifted back to her other father and mother in the Mortal World. She had lost track of the days, but she knew that they would soon be returning from their holiday in Cornwall—returning home to find the house trashed in the battle with the Gray Knights, to find Tania gone again without explanation, and to discover that Edric was also missing. She imagined their horrified reaction, visits from the police, Edric getting the blame again. . . . Tania shook her head, trying to dislodge the disturbing images.

Lios Foltaigg swarmed around the sleeping king, crying out in their high, shrill voices.

"The Sun is dead," said Clorimel, weeping. "Our land shall fall in fire and ice, Lios Foltaigg will wither and burn, and the long ages shall devour even the memory of us."

"He isn't dead," Tania said. "He's just exhausted. We have to get him away from here."

"We must take him to his Queen," Cordelia said. "And pray that she has the power to wake him and to make him whole again."

"Will he not ride upon the horse of air?" Clorimel asked, kneeling at the King's head. "Will he not call up the four winds to bear him hence?"

"He has not the strength for that," Cordelia said. "Have you no carriages or wagons to carry him?"

"We are Lios Foltaigg," Clorimel replied. "We need no carriages—the air is our chariot, the breeze our gallant steed."

"That doesn't help us!" Tania burst out. "For goodness' sake, if we can't take him back to where the Queen is waiting for him, he *will* die, and the Sorcerer King will win, and *everything* will be destroyed."

Clorimel darted away from her in alarm, her long slender neck arching as she stared at Tania. "Thy anger is as the sea, thy need as the earth parched for rain," she said. "Thou alone art Alios Foltaigg—we shall aid thee." She sprang into the air, calling out strange words. Moments later the air was full of winged people, rising and swarming away inland.

"What can they do to help?" Edric asked as they watched the Lios Foltaigg leave. "The Queen is two hundred leagues away. How can we get the King to her?"

"We shall bear him upon our backs if needs must," said Cordelia.

The three of them sat beside the King, waiting in silence while the waves beat endlessly at the forlorn shore and the clouds scraped slowly across the sky.

The first Tania knew of the return of the Lios Foltaigg was the soft whirr of wings. She looked up; a group of the flying folk were descending toward them from the sky, some of them carrying something large and oblong in shape. As they swooped closer Tania realized it was a kind of hammock made of woven grasses. Loops of twisted grass had been woven into the fabric along both sides to form handles.

"We cannot pass beyond the borders of our own land," Clorimel told them. "But we shall bear the Sun as far as we may. Then thou must speak with the Fid Foltaigg of the southlands and seek their aid on thy journey."

"Thank you," Tania said. "Thank you so much."

It took ten Lios Foltaigg to lift the King once Tania and Edric and Cordelia had laid him on the hammock of woven grass. They slung the grass loops over their shoulders and rose into the air, carrying him along close to the ground so that Tania and the others could walk beside him as they made their way up the long valley that led from the coastline. Clorimel gave food to the travelers: dried fish and hard flat bread and the rubbery leaves of a dark, salty vegetable. It didn't taste of much and it all smelled of the sea, but they were grateful of it as the day wore on and they plodded along the deep valleys of Fidach Ren. Many of the flying folk traveled with them, the stretcher-bearers changing as the hours passed.

They rested at midday. Tania and Edric sat together on a rock. Tania nibbled at the edges of a piece of the hard bread, trying not to think about how slow their progress had been through the morning, nor of how many mountainous miles still lay ahead of them. Cordelia stood on a high tooth of rock, staring into the south.

She jumped down after a while and came to sit next to Tania and Edric. "'Tis most curious," she said. "The wind has shifted to the south. It is faint and far, but I can sense something." She smiled, putting her hand inside her tunic and taking out the pipes that Bryn had given her. "Something is coming, I believe."

"What kind of something?" Tania asked.

Cordelia put the pipes to her mouth and blew. A single high, floating note hung in the air. "You will see," she said. "Good fortune may favor us yet."

It seemed to Tania that the landscape hardly changed as they plodded on through the afternoon. Even when they came to a high hill, all that she could see ahead were more mountains stretching away forever into a blue-gray mist. Edric and Cordelia were walking on either side of the King's stretcher. Tania was a little behind, Clorimel flying at her shoulder. Other Lios Foltaigg filled the air, talking softly together in their high, clear voices.

"Do you come this far inland very often?" Tania asked Clorimel.

"Not often do we leave the seashore," Clorimel replied. "We are the Karken En Ynis Maw. We have our duty to perform in the Great Song."

"It's so bleak here." Tania sighed.

"This is our land," Clorimel said. "Our home. In the spring, when the air comes in fresh and sweet from Ynis Boreal, life is good indeed."

"And in the winter? Isn't it very cold?"

"Cold? Aye, it is cold, but the Fimbulstorm brings us deep blankets of snow to keep the chill winds away, and we shelter in our caves in the cliffs and tell the old tales by firelight." Her eyes grew dark. "Once all were winged," she said. "Once on a time all were Lios Foltaigg."

"What happened?" Tania asked, fascinated. "How did that change?"

Before she could reply, a cry from high in the air made Clorimel look upward. One Lios Foltaigg was hovering above them, pointing into the south.

"Something comes," Clorimel said. She rose swiftly into the air; all around her more of the winged folk were also spiraling upward.

Cordelia turned to Tania, and her face was wreathed in smiles. "He comes!" she said. "I knew it was so, but I knew not how swift he might reach us."

"Who's coming?" Tania asked.

"The unicorn-friend," Cordelia said, her eyes shining. "Bryn is coming!"

It was a while before Tania heard the first faint murmur of thundering hooves, and yet more time passed before she saw the unicorns galloping toward them through the hills. There were twenty or more of the noble stone gray animals in the herd, and Bryn was riding on the leading one. Cordelia ran forward to meet them as they came nearer. Edric and Tania followed her, but the Lios Foltaigg held back, laying down the King and rising uneasily into the air.

The unicorns came to a turbulent halt and Bryn jumped down. "Well met!" he called, and Tania saw that his eyes turned first to Cordelia. "We were still a league away when I heard in my mind the call of the pipes, my lady. Then I knew you were close by and we came at the gallop."

"I felt that you were near, Master Lightfoot," Cordelia said. "The pipes have mystical powers, I think."

"They are of wych-willow," Bryn said. "'Tis said that the wood is bound about with charms." He looked up dubiously at the flying people. "Are all safe?"

"We are," Cordelia replied. "And as you see, we have met friends in the north, despite your fears. They are the Lios Foltaigg and they are neither savage nor murderous."

Bryn bowed low. "Then I hope they will forgive me for my foolish words," he said. "I spoke out of ignorance and would gladly learn better."

The Lios Foltaigg began to descend warily to the ground, but only Clorimel dared to come close to the unicorns. "Friends of Alios Foltaigg are welcome in Fidach Ren," she said. "But do not fear to tell tales of our savagery—such stories are a bulwark between us and the inconstant world."

"Then the secret of your courtesy will be safe with me," Bryn promised, bowing again.

"But what are you doing here?" Edric asked him. "What made you follow us?"

"On the night that you departed, I was visited by ominous dreams and visions of peril," Bryn replied. "With the dawn I gathered my friends and tracked you as swiftly as I might." He suddenly seemed to become aware of Oberon lying on the Lios Foltaigg's stretcher. "Spirits of mercy!" he cried. "I pray that the King is not dead!"

"He lives yet," said Cordelia. "But we must take him to the Queen. Can you help us?"

Bryn frowned. "Unicorns cannot bear him down all the long leagues of Faerie," he said. "But the fief-dom of Shard lies not five leagues southeast of this place. The crofters there are solitary folk and wary of strangers, but they are good and trustworthy, and loyal to the House of Aurealis. We will be able to beg a wagon from them to take us to Caer Circinn. And from there the south roads are wide and straight through the Earldoms of Llyr and Anvis."

"That sounds like a long journey," Tania said. "Perhaps someone should ride on ahead to let everyone know what's happening." She turned to Bryn. "Would a unicorn take me that far?"

Before Bryn was able to answer, one of the unicorns detached itself from the herd and trotted up to Tania, bowing its sculpted head and fixing her with an intelligent, knowing eye.

"Tanzen!" she cried as the animal nudged his long head against her shoulder. "It is you, isn't it?" She patted his neck. "I'm so glad to see you again."

"I met with Drazin and Zephyr and Tanzen in the southern wilds," Bryn said. "They said you had been attacked by flying things."

"That was a misunderstanding," Edric said. "The Lios Foltaigg helped us to get to Ynis Maw."

"But we cannot travel beyond the southern borders of Fidach Ren," Clorimel said. "From there others must take on the burden of the sleeping Sun."

"I will do that willingly," said Bryn.

Cordelia stepped forward, whistling between her teeth. Zephyr trotted up to her. She stroked his neck, looking over her shoulder at Tania. "Two may travel more safely than one alone," she said, and then she turned to Edric. "Will you journey to Shard with Bryn and see to the King's comfort and safety?"

"Of course, my lady," he said.

"Then Tania and I shall go on ahead to bring the news to the Queen," Cordelia said. "And you shall bring the King south as quickly as you may."

"It might not be safe to go into Esgarth Forest," Edric said. "The Gray Knights will probably still be there."

"That is wise counsel, Master Chanticleer," said Cordelia. "We shall make for Caer Ravensare instead. It is the traditional meeting place of the lords and ladies of Faerie in times of trouble. The Earl Marshal Cornelius should be in attendance, and it is to be hoped that many knights and warriors will have gathered there also." She looked at Bryn. "I have no parting gift for you, Master Lightfoot," she said. "Save the hope that we shall meet again in better times."

"I could wish for nothing more," said Bryn. Cordelia looked into his eyes for a moment and Tania saw a faint blush color her sister's cheeks.

Then Cordelia turned away. "Come, sister," she said. "Mount up and ride with me."

"Just a moment," Tania said. She ran to where the King lay. She knelt by his side and gently kissed his forehead. "I'll see you again very soon," she whispered. She stood up, looking at Edric. "Keep him safe," she said.

"I will."

She touched his chest with her fingertips. "And keep yourself safe, too."

He smiled. "I will if you will." They slipped quickly into each other's arms and held each other for a few moments.

Tania broke away from him and she and Cordelia mounted their unicorns. Tania took one final look at Edric before touching her heels to Tanzen's flanks. The powerful beast turned and sprang away along the valley, galloping hard with the south wind in its flying mane.

XXII

Tania and Cordelia halted their unicorns on the brow of a low, round hill. A white road lay beneath the unicorns' hooves; above them the sky was clear and bright. A warm wind ruffled their hair and lifted the long fine manes of their steeds. They were six days out from Fidach Ren.

"Behold Caer Ravensare and Passion Meadows," Cordelia declared. "Did I not tell you it was something to marvel at?"

The meadows seemed to stretch out forever, flooded by an ocean of tall waving poppies that danced and rippled in the breeze. The colors left Tania speechless. At one moment the huge blossoms flowed in streams of magenta and fuchsia and orange, then all would change with a breath of air to an undulating carpet of lilac and purple and mauve. Another gust of wind, and the flowers shimmered into hues of green and turquoise and aquamarine that flooded in turbulent eddies before clashing against currents of saffron and topaz and ocher.

The white road led down the hill and through the ever-changing blossoms to a tall castle of shining crystal, as blue as moonstone. Even from a distance, Tania could see that the castle had been built for beauty rather than warfare. The ornately decorated walls and battlements were festooned with swaths of greenery and overgrown with leafy vines, speckled and clouded with cataracts of many-colored flowers. In the meadows around the castle, clusters of tents had been set up sporting fluttering pennants of white and yellow and sky blue. Tania saw horsemen and knights moving purposefully among them, as well as laden wagons and many carts and carriages.

"The armies of Faerie are mustering," Cordelia said. "That is good!" She made a clicking noise with her tongue. Zephyr reared up beneath her and went galloping down the hill.

For a few moments Tania was too bewitched by the shifting rainbow patterns of the flowers and too thrilled by the sight of the floral castle to react, but then she gave Tanzen a gentle nudge with her heels and followed Cordelia down the white roadway to Caer Ravensare.

Sentries must have given word that they were approaching, because as Tania and Cordelia passed under the gateway of the castle and came into a courtyard that was like a blooming garden, they found many people had gathered to greet them.

A tall, broad-shouldered man with ruddy hair and a red beard stood on the steps of a great keep. He was flanked on either side by tall young men with raven hair and handsome dark-eyed faces. With them Tania saw Hopie and Lord Brython, as well as Zara and an old gray-haired man leaning on a stick: Eden's husband, Earl Valentyne, Tania assumed. She stood gazing at the elderly man in surprise; she had known that Eden's husband was much older than her, but the stooped earl looked *ancient*. But there were others who took her attention, many highborn lords and ladies of Faerie who had come here with their knights to help defend the Realm against the Sorcerer King.

Tania and Cordelia dismounted. Grooms stood nearby, eyeing the unicorns nervously and unwilling to come too close to the fearsome horns.

"They will do you no harm," Cordelia told them. "Lead them to the finest stalls in Ravensare and give them food and water." She patted Zephyr's neck. "Take your rest, great-heart; you have earned it, you and your brother. I will come as soon as I may to speak with you and to make sure you are being well-treated." She linked arms with Tania and walked with her to where the others were waiting.

"Cordelia and Tania, you are most welcome," boomed the red-haired man, striding down the steps toward them. He took Tania's hand and bowed to kiss it. "We have not met since you returned to us after your long wanderings in the Mortal World," he said. "I am your father's brother, your uncle Cornelius."

"Hello," Tania said. "I'm really happy to meet you." She looked into his fierce blue eyes, realizing now that she was closer just how much he resembled the King. He turned after a moment, gesturing toward the dark-haired young men. "These are my stepsons, Titus and Corin, and this is my wife, the Marchioness Lucina."

The marchioness was a graceful woman with flowing ash blonde hair and eyes that reflected the blue of the crystal walls of the castle. "Many greetings," she said. "Our halls are made merrier by your presence."

"Thank you," Tania said, but before any more introductions could be made, a whirlwind of blue satin came flying down the steps and Zara caught hold of Tania and Cordelia and danced in a jubilant circle with them. "I am so glad to see you both!" she cried, her eyes glittering with happy tears. "I feared for your lives, truly I did!"

"Hush, Zara," Hopie said, coming up behind. "Remember that you are a princess."

"I am a sister first!" Zara exclaimed. "And a daughter." She looked into Tania and Cordelia's faces. "How fares our father? Does he yet live?"

"Indeed he does, although he is weak and will not wake," Cordelia said. "The last news we had of him was two days ago. Bryn Lightfoot sent a goshawk to us to say that they had reached Caer Circinn and that Earl Ryence of Minnith Bannwg was to provide them with wagons and an escort south."

Hopie frowned. "Then they are still many days

away," she said. "I had hoped for better news. We dare not move against the Sorcerer without Oberon, and yet we have heard only this morning that an advance guard of Serpent ships has arrived at Fortrenn Quay and that two thousand Gray Knights have disembarked to swell the army of Lyonesse."

"Is the Queen still safe?" Tania asked in alarm.

"We have spoken with her through a water-mirror," said the Marchioness. "She and the refugees are secure in the Hunting Lodge under Eden's glamour. But the Gray Knights still swarm the forest, and they dare not leave their sanctuary."

"And now more Gray Knights come to join the chase," Cordelia said. "I like this not. How are we to unite our father with the Queen if all the spears and swords of Lyonesse lie between them?"

"This is but one of the many issues we must debate before we can act against the Sorcerer," said Cornelius. He looked at Cordelia and Tania. "You must be weary and hungry from your long journey. I would have you rested and refreshed before we speak more." He turned to the others. "We shall meet in the Rose Garden when the sun is at its zenith," he declared. "And may good fortune look down upon our deliberations, for the fate of Faerie lies in our hands."

The Rose Garden lay under the tall many-windowed walls of the castle keep. Slender paths wound through beds of red and white roses, leading to a grassy central area where carved wooden chairs formed an oval around a raised pond of still, clear water. More roses climbed trellises, and yet more hung from the sills of the windows, so that the whole of the garden was bright with their heavy blossom and the air was sweet with their scent.

Tania looked around as people began to gather. Hopie and Brython were there, as were the Earl Marshal Cornelius and his wife and sons. Cordelia sat nearby with Zara. Earl Valentyne sat alone, both hands leaning on his cane, his eyes hooded and brooding. She also saw sad, grieving Lord Gaidheal seated with several other lords and ladies, representatives of almost every earldom in Faerie except for Weir and the far north.

The Earl Marshal began the meeting. "Scouts have returned from the south," he announced. "They have brought grave news. The armada of Lyonesse has been sighted off the coast of Udwold: a thousand Serpent ships, their red sails like a tide of blood upon the ocean. It cannot now be many days before a great army sets foot on our land."

"A thousand ships?" said Brython. "Their army will outnumber us twenty-fold. Our only hope is to meet the Sorcerer King in battle and to destroy him before the armada makes landfall."

"But how may we do that?" asked Corin. "He will not move against us until all his forces are arrayed, and once that is done he will come upon us with such strength that we may not be able to withstand him."

"Oberon will have the power to challenge the

Sorcerer King once he is healed," said Hopie. "But he is many days' journey from here, and he cannot be made well until he is reunited with the Queen."

"How do we get them together?" Tania asked. "Titania is trapped in the forest. Isn't there some way of getting her out of there so she can go and meet up with him?"

"Not unless we can conceive of a way to draw the Gray Knights from Esgarth," said the marchioness. "That is our only hope."

"Why should he withdraw from Esgarth Forest and engage in battle?" asked Earl Valentyne, his voice dry and cracked. "He will sit at his ease in the palace until all is in readiness and victory is assured." He looked sharply at Tania and Cordelia. "How long will it be, do you think, before Oberon arrives in the south?"

"Two days," Cordelia said. "Maybe three. But without the Queen I do not believe he will be able to help us against the Sorcerer. We should not wait for him. We should gather all our forces and march around the west flank of Esgarth Forest. We must set up our banners on Salisoc Heath and challenge the Sorcerer to meet with us in the field."

"I believe the Princess speaks truth," said Cornelius. "We must head south and make the challenge. But the children of my brother and the blessed Titania should not travel with us. They will remain here in Ravensare until the battle is done, for good or ill."

Cordelia's eyes flashed. "That I will never do!"

"I neither!" declared Zara. "I can fight with a

sword as well as any knight here." She looked at Hopie. "Would you lurk in Ravensare while others go to war?"

"I would not," Hopie replied.

Tania sat in uneasy silence as the debate moved back and forth among the lords and ladies. Apart from the princesses themselves, everyone seemed to think that she and Zara and Cordelia and Hopie should keep out of harm's way, but at the same time no one seemed to be able to come up with a method of getting the Sorcerer King to pull his knights out of Esgarth Forest. And so long as the forest was full of the Gray Knights, how would Oberon and Titania be reunited?

Tania didn't want to have to fight. She had seen enough of battles in Kymry Bay, but hiding away while everyone else went to war seemed so cowardly, and so utterly useless. Gradually, an idea began to form in her head—a way of getting the Sorcerer King to fight them. An idea that she didn't like at all. She sat silently for a while, hoping that someone else would come up with a better plan.

No one did.

"I know what we should do," she said.

All the faces turned to her. She swallowed hard. "The Sorcerer King will only fight us if we offer him something he can't refuse," she said. "A really good bait." She paused for a moment. "I think the only bait he'd be interested in would be *us*." She gestured toward Hopie and Zara and Cordelia. "*We* should lead the Faerie army down to the palace. I think he'll jump at the chance of killing four of Oberon and Titania's daughters."

An uneasy murmur ran around the gathering; the only people who didn't look shocked or dismayed were her three sisters.

"I will not put you in such danger," Cornelius said at last. "It is a brave offer, Tania—but an impossible one."

But then a quiet, strong female voice seemed to speak out of the air. "I do not agree, Cornelius."

"Titania?" Cornelius said, staring around.

"She speaks from the water," said Hopie, getting up and moving toward the raised pond. "Mother?"

Now everyone came surging up from their seats and gathered around the pond.

"What are your thoughts, Your Grace?" asked Brython.

"If the princesses head our army, it will convince the Sorcerer that Oberon is not a threat to him," said Titania. "He would see it as madness for us to go into battle without the King if we had any hope that Oberon could be restored to us. He will think that we've grown desperate—that we are assaulting the palace in the hope of rescuing the King from the dungeons. The Sorcerer will think we believe the King still to be there. He does not know that we have released the King from his prison on Ynis Maw and that he is on his way to us."

"I would not put your daughters in jeopardy," said Cornelius.

"I do not ask you to," said Titania. "I ask that you give command of the Faerie army to Princess Tania. This is her moment, Cornelius. I believe that the battle with Lyonesse can only be won by her."

Horrified, Tania stared down at her mother's image. "No," she said. "That's not what I meant. I can't lead an *army*."

A sharp sound caught everyone's attention. Earl Valentyne had tapped his cane on the stone lip of the pond. "The Queen is right," he rasped. "Many ages ago, I read ancient texts concerning the Sorcerer King, books that even the Great Library of the palace does not possess. I had long forgotten them, but the Queen's words have brought them back to mind." He looked slowly around the ring of people. "Do you know why the Sorcerer of Lyonesse was not killed in battle by King Oberon when the serpent banners fell a thousand years ago?"

"It is because he is enwrapped with powerful spells," the marchioness replied. "None can end his life."

"Not true," said Valentyne. "The ancient texts do not say that he *cannot* be killed; they say that he cannot be killed by one of Faerie born nor by the hand of a mortal." He nodded toward Tania. "The princess was not born in Faerie, and yet she is not wholly mortal. She alone of all of us stands with one foot in the Immortal Realm and one in the Mortal World. It is my belief that only she can defeat the Sorcerer King."

Tania listened to him in silent astonishment, remembering that Clorimel had said something very similar, speaking of her as Alios Foltaigg. What was it she'd said? *Thou art between things. Thou hast one foot on the land and one foot in the sea. The Sun is in thy right eye and the Moon in thy left. That is the engine of thy sadness and thy destiny.*

"Do the ancient texts speak of a sure victory?" Hopie asked.

"Nay," said Valentyne. "They do not." He looked at Tania. "I do not say that this is a safe path, my lady," he warned. "And I do not say that a bright future lies beyond it, but this destiny is yours, Princess Tania—if you would take it."

"You would not take it alone, sweet sister," said Cordelia. "Choose this path and I shall stand at your side."

"And I," said Zara.

"I believe that all things have a purpose," Hopie said, looking solemnly at Tania. "Maybe it is that your strange journey of life was predestined so that you alone of all of us would have the potential to destroy once and for all the threat of the Sorcerer of Lyonesse."

Tania gazed at her sisters, and then at the other waiting faces. Oddly, she felt less shocked than she would have imagined. It really did feel as if everything that had come before—her disappearance from Faerie all those centuries ago, the mysterious procession of her past mortal lives, and her return to Faerie at this particular point—had all happened to bring her to this place at this time.

"Okay," she said. "I'll do it." She took a deep breath. "I'm ready to fight."

It was later that same day. The late-afternoon sun was pouring in long golden rays through the windows of a vast white chamber. The earl marshal's son Titus had brought the four princesses here, to the Great Armory of Ravensare, to fit them for armor and weapons. At dawn tomorrow the Faerie army would be on the move.

Tania still couldn't quite believe the speed with which things had changed. At one moment she had been assuming that the earl marshal would have all the responsibility on his shoulders—and then, in a dizzying whirl, everything was upended and it was her thoughts and plans that everyone was listening to. She wished she had Edric to talk to, or her dad—not Oberon, but the father she had grown up with in London. He always knew how to make her feel better when events threatened to overwhelm her. But he was far beyond reach. Whom could she confide in now? She sat quietly to one side, watching her sisters. Hopie and Titus were examining a large wall map and talking quietly. Zara was practicing swinging a long crystal sword, the blade glowing brightly in the raking beams of honeyed sunlight. Cordelia was hunting among the hanging racks of armor for something suitable for the battle.

The Faerie armor was very similar to that which Tania had seen at Caer Kymry: breastplates and shields of a hard shelly substance, ivory white on the outside and with a mother-of-pearl sheen within. And there was a whole array of shell helmets, and racks that were hung with mail made of tiny linked shells, hard and impenetrable as chain mail. Swords and spears and axes and maces were displayed on the walls and in standing frames. Tapestries hung between the long windows, showing scenes of battle—pictures of the fall of the Sorcerer King over a thousand years ago, when the Faerie armies had finally overcome him and he had been taken prisoner.

And now he was free again, and Rathina was at his side, and Tania was trying to come to terms with the idea of leading an army into battle against him.

Cordelia strode toward her, a breastplate under her arm. "Come, Tania, see if this will fit you."

Tania stood up and allowed Cordelia to strap her into the shell armor.

"Is it comfortable?"

"Not exactly," Tania said.

"But it will protect you." Cordelia rapped on the plate with her knuckles. "And it will allow you to swing a sword." She smiled darkly. "I have spoken with Zephyr and Tanzen," she said. "They wish to bear us into the battle, Tania. Imagine that! Riding against Lyonesse upon wild unicorns of Caer Liel. What a thing to do!"

"I hope they don't get hurt," Tania said. She swallowed hard. "I hope no one gets hurt."

"There is faint hope of that," Zara said, coming up

to them with the sword in her hand. "But we will give better than we receive, I trow, and by tomorrow's eve, we will be wading knee deep in the gray dust of the Sorcerer's vanquished army." She spun on her heel. "Titus, come away from my dour sister now and help me to choose armor that is both sturdy and becoming."

Titus turned from the map and smiled. "I shall, my lady," he said. "But the choice will be hard to make."

"Why so?" asked Zara, linking her arm with his and walking with him to the armor racks.

"Because I would have you protected head to foot by armor that is a hand's span thick," he replied. "And yet I would not choose any covering that might prevent me from seeing the beauty and glory of your face."

"A sore challenge indeed, my lord Titus," Zara said, grinning at Tania and Cordelia over her shoulder. "But all must suffer in warfare."

"Is there a budding romance going on there?" Tania asked Cordelia.

"Mayhap," said Cordelia. "It would be good if Zara were finally able to choose between the earl marshal's two stepsons and put an end to her endless prattle about their virtues and qualities."

Laughing, Tania stepped up onto the platform where Hopie was perusing the map of Faerie. Her sister looked gravely at her. "You have taken on a great burden, Tania," she said. "All of Faerie hangs in the balance now, and it is for you to tip the scales in our favor."

"But no pressure, huh?"

Hopie frowned.

"Never mind. It was a bad joke." Tania looked at the wall map. It was incredibly detailed, with the saw-toothed mountains painted brown, the forests shaded in green and the rivers and lakes washed with blue.

"At dawn the army will skirt the western eaves of Esgarth Forest," Hopie said, describing a smooth arc with her arm. "We will bivouac upon Salisoc Heath." She smiled at Tania. "It is a place of great memory and portent, for it was there that the Sorcerer's armies were routed long ago."

"Then what happens?" Tania asked, lowering her voice. "I know I'm supposed to be in charge, but I don't have any idea how to organize a battle."

"You have lords and generals enough at your back to array our forces," Hopie told her. "But I suspect that we will prepare to make the challenge to the Sorcerer King at sunup the following day. That will give his scouts ample time to run back and inform him of our coming—and of the fact that it is you and I and Cordelia and Zara who are leading the army and not the King."

"And then?"

Hopie put her arm around Tania's shoulders. "Then you will learn how deep within you run the veins of Royal courage, sweet sister," she said. "And we will do battle for the Immortal Realm."

XXIII

Servants woke Tania before dawn and she ate breakfast with the earl marshal's family and her sisters before being led back to her chamber to put on her armor. Over a light tunic of threaded shells she wore a breastplate and back-plate of flattened white shell, tied over her shoulders and at her waist. Long curved shells protected her legs and arms, and a high-pointed, curling conch shell was put on her head, the lip coming down low on her neck and curving around to protect her cheeks. Finally, she was given a crystal sword for her belt.

She stood for some time, looking at herself in a mirror, wondering how an ordinary sixteen-year-old girl from London had turned in a matter of weeks into a princess warrior of Faerie. She smiled wryly at her martial reflection. *Life can be really weird, sometimes.*

"They are ready for you, my lady." She turned at the voice and walked out of her room. The shell armor was surprisingly light and had been carved and shaped to allow ease of movement. She followed the serving girl down through the building. Tanzen was waiting in a courtyard. Tania mounted and rode toward the gatehouse. All around her, from every window, people were cheering and throwing petals and flowers down on her.

She didn't know what to expect as she came out under the gatehouse. She halted, her breath taken away by the sight that greeted her.

The slanting rays of the rising sun glinted on the helmets and spear-points of a thousand Faerie knights as they stood or sat astride their horses in wide battalions that straddled the white road leading to the main gate of Caer Ravensare. Seated on horses in front of the ranks of knights were the Earl Marshal Cornelius and Marchioness Lucina with their two sons mounted beside them, ready to lead the knights of Ravensare into battle. To their left the knights of Talebolion and Mynwy Clun were fronted by Lord Brython and Hopie and Earl Valentyne, and on the right flank Tania saw Lord Gaidheal and Cordelia and Zara, with other lords and ladies of Llyr and Dinsel and Udwold, leading a force of knights who had gathered here from many parts of Faerie. All were clad in full armor, and all were looking straight at Tania.

At their backs the fields of poppies were a sea of turquoise and aquamarine and heliotrope, sparkling with a network of white and pearl blossoms like stars on an earthbound sky.

After a few moments Cordelia urged Zephyr forward and trotted up to Tania. "A fine morning, sister! How do you like your army?"

Tania tore her eyes from the gathered ranks of knights and gazed at her sister. "What happens now?"

Cordelia smiled. "We ride south," she said. "Come, your sisters and your captains await. Ride with me."

Tania touched her heels to Tanzen's sides and followed Cordelia's mount along the white road toward the waiting army. "Don't leave me alone," she whispered to Cordelia as they rode side by side. "I don't know what I'm doing."

Cordelia glanced at her. "That is good, Tania. I would fear for our lives if you thought otherwise."

They came to the end of the parade of knights, and their two unicorns began to wade into the great meadow of poppies. Tania heard a noise like thunder at her back. She turned her head and saw that the knights of Faerie were following. Moments later, as the sun climbed into the eastern sky, all the poppies suddenly burst into wave after wave of daylight colors, sending an eddying flux of scarlet and yellow and orange and lilac and sapphire blue in ever-expanding ripples to the far horizon.

"Thus does Faerie go to war," Cordelia murmured. "May the spirits of the Immortal Realm bless us in our endeavors."

It took most of the day to circle the western flank of Esgarth Forest and to bring the army at last to bivouac on the high swell of Salisoc Heath. Below them they could see the palace, some ten miles south of their encampment, following the winding line of the river. The waters of the Tamesis were a dull gray, as though the river suffered the same sickness as the land. Despite their distance from the palace the ground underfoot was dead, the grass withered, the lifeless heather straggling on the earth, the trees at the forest's eaves shrouded in brown tatters.

"The Sorcerer's influence is spreading," the earl marshal said, standing at Tania's side as they looked down at the palace. "We come not a moment too soon."

Tents and pavilions and corrals were set up through the long afternoon. Swift birds were sent out to north and south and east and west on Cordelia's instructions, returning to give news of what was happening. Meanwhile, Gray Knights could be seen galloping hard in the south and away to the east, coming and going from the Sorcerer King.

The best news for Tania came late in the afternoon, when the shadows were long and the sun an orange ball in a sky banded with yellow and red cloud. A peregrine falcon came in from the northeast, skimming down the sky like an arrow. The Gray Knights had withdrawn from Esgarth, he told Cordelia; Eden and Sancha and many of the people who had been hiding in the Hunting Lodge were already heading through the forest toward Salisoc. Queen Titania was not with them; she and Rafe Hawthorne and a few trusty men had gone north, making for Ravensare and intending to follow the road north through Anvis to meet up with the wagons and riders that were bringing King Oberon south.

Tania sat on padded silk cushions on the floor of a large circular pavilion. A white wooden pole held up the heavy cloth of the roof, lifting the panels to a point fifteen feet above her head. Colored rugs filled much of the floor space, leaving only a small stretch of withered brown grass by the closed cloth panels of the entrance. Cushions formed a circle on the rugs, and inside the circle platters of food and jugs of Faerie cordial had been laid out. It was evening, and globes of soft blue light hung from the tent pole, giving off a gentle glow, while spiced incense sticks sweetened the air.

Tania's sisters sat around her, eating and talking quietly. Zara had finished her food and she was sitting to one side with her head bowed, playing a small handheld harp that filled the pavilion with rippling streams of music.

Cordelia and Hopie were there, too, but Tania looked with particular fondness at Sancha and Eden, glad to be reunited with them after all those long days of peril and adventure. They had arrived in the early evening, and the reunion of six of the seven daughters of Oberon and Titania had been full of joy and hope.

"What of the morrow?" Eden asked, looking at Tania. "Are all plans now set?"

"The earl marshal's advice was that we should

send heralds to the palace at dawn," Tania told her. "They'll challenge the Sorcerer King to bring his army out and fight with us. He thinks we should announce ourselves as the Army of the Six Princesses."

"That is good tactics," said Hopie. "Hopefully it will convince the Sorcerer that neither Oberon nor Titania ride with us. How many Gray Knights face us?"

"The latest news I have heard is that they number close to three thousand," said Cordelia. She smiled grimly. "And we are a thousand. How can we not take the day?"

"You say the Army of the *Six* Princesses?" Eden mused. "I wonder. . . ."

Sancha looked up sharply. "We *are* only six," she said. "I will not acknowledge that traitor woman as kin."

"A fallen sister is a sister still," said Hopie. "She is of our blood, Sancha, and nought can change that." She looked at Eden. "But why do you ask?"

"Before we parted the Queen told me to remember the Power of Seven," Eden said. "I asked her what it meant, but she said she did not know. All she knew was that there was an ancient text that spoke of the Power of Seven."

"I heard Gabriel's father use the same expression in Caer Liel," said Tania. "When Gabriel told him that Rathina had turned traitor, he said the Power of Seven could never be invoked."

"So the Power of Seven is linked to Rathina," said Zara. "Most curious."

"Or linked to all of us," said Eden. "*We* are seven— or would be if Rathina were with us."

"That she will never be," Cordelia said.

"I have read of this Power," Sancha said. "Our mother is right. It is spoken of in an ancient text indeed. I had almost forgotten it."

"What does it mean, Sancha?" Eden asked.

Sancha thought deeply for a few moments. "It is of no consequence," she said at last. "I remember clearly now. Lord Aldritch was right: The Power cannot be invoked."

"Tell us all the same," said Tania.

"It speaks of a healing power, a power of life over death that can be harnessed when the seven children of a seventh daughter come together in love and harmony," Sancha said. "Our mother is the seventh daughter of the House of Fenodree, and were we not cursed with a traitor for a sibling, we also would be seven." She looked around the ring of her sisters. "I know not what that power may have been, but it is lost to us."

"As are many things." Eden sighed.

Zara's gentle melodies had been forming a soothing backdrop to their talk, but suddenly the music stopped and they heard Zara gasp. "What miracle is this now?"

She was sitting near the closed entrance to the pavilion, staring down at the ground where a crescent of short bright green blades of grass was pushing up through the brown tangle of dead grasses. Tania watched in amazement as daisies and buttercups strained upward and opened their white and yellow flower heads as though nature was creating in a few moments the work of hours or days.

"Sorcery!" cried Cordelia, leaping up and snatching at her sword. "This is the mark of Lyonesse! They come upon us in the night!"

"Nay, sister," said Eden, also getting up. "This is not death—this is life. This is new life."

"It must be Oberon," Tania said. She scrambled to her feet and ran to the entrance. She pulled back the flap and stared expectantly into the night.

A cloaked and hooded figure stood a little way off.

"Father?" Tania called, but she wasn't so sure now—the figure was too slight, too slender to be the King. Her voice wavered. "Who is that?"

The figure stepped forward. The hood was thrown back.

"Well met by moonlight, dearest sister," said a well-known voice as the figure came within the light of a hanging lantern and Tania saw the familiar features of Princess Rathina.

XXIV

Tania stared at her sister, too surprised even to draw breath.

Rathina's once beautiful face was smeared with grime and shadowed with bruises; her flawless skin was an unhealthy skull white, her radiant black hair tangled and lank. But it was in her eyes that Tania saw the most harrowing damage. Rathina had the eyes of someone who had stared into an abyss of horror and whose mind had been seared by what she had seen there.

"A warm welcoming would be too much to ask," Rathina said, her voice low and weary. "But I would speak with you."

Tania came to her senses. "I don't have anything to say to you," she said, her voice trembling. "Go. Go now, before—"

Tania heard a movement behind her. "No, Rathina," Eden said, her voice soft but compelling. "Do not go. Enter, I bid you. There is much we would discuss with you."

She reached out, her open hand beckoning. Rathina grimaced and struggled briefly as she was pulled forward by Eden's power, her arms pinned to her sides, her legs stiff, feet dangling. Tania stepped aside as Rathina was drawn into the pavilion. The other princesses were on their feet now, staring at their sister as Eden compelled her to move to the middle of the tent and lifted her so that she hung like a puppet in the air.

"How did you get past the sentinels?" Cordelia demanded. "What sorcerous wiles did you use?"

"I used no sorcery," Rathina said, her voice strained. "You taught me how to move unseen, Cordelia. Do you not remember our pilgrimages into the forest to watch the deer and the wild boar? I would be a poor scholar not to have remembered the wood-skills you passed on."

Zara had her hands over her mouth, her eyes haunted as she looked up at her sister. "How *could* you?" she murmured. "How could you have done those terrible things?"

Sancha made a move forward, her face dark with hatred. Hopie stopped her with a hand on her shoulder.

"You have done much harm, sister," Hopie said to Rathina. "Do you come here to atone or to triumph over us?" Her dark eyes narrowed. "Or are you come as an emissary from the Sorcerer, sent to beguile us with treacherous offers?"

"None of those things," Rathina said. "I come to beg your mercy."

Sancha gave a snarl. "Mercy?" she spat. "You have unleashed desolation on our land; you have schemed to break us utterly. How many are dead at your hands? With how much innocent blood is your soul stained? You will get no mercy here. Were it in my power, you would be blasted to dust and scattered to the four winds for your wickedness."

"Peace, Sancha," said Eden.

Sancha turned on her, eyes blazing. "Peace? It is because of her that my Library was burned. It is because of her that our Soul Books are turned to ash." Her voice rose. *"Our Soul Books are destroyed!"*

Hopie put her arms around Sancha and drew her away, stifling the aching sobs that were heaving up from Sancha's chest.

Tania stared at Rathina. Pain showed in her sister's eyes. But was it real pain, or was it pretense?

Eden made a small movement of her fingers and Rathina came down to the ground. "You already have my mercy, sister," Eden said gently. "You would know were it otherwise."

Rathina fell to her knees. "I never was an ally of the Sorcerer King," she cried. "I beg you to believe that if you believe nothing else."

"I saw you in the Great Hall!" Tania said, her voice shaking. "I saw you sitting next to him when Lady Gaidheal was murdered. You didn't care about any of those people he was hurting."

"How did you see?" she asked. She glanced at Eden. "A glamour!" she said. "You used a glamour to

pass unseen." Her eyes turned pleadingly to Tania. "Then you saw how the Sorcerer abused and tormented me. He only allowed me to live for his own amusement, to see how his actions wounded me. Had I fought against him, he would have killed me."

"And were you not better off dead than at his side upon our mother's throne?" Cordelia said. "I would have died a thousand times before I would have given aid to that creature."

"Yes," Rathina murmured. "I know that you would." She looked around at her sisters. "Do you think I do not know how you hate me? Yet with all that, none of you can hate me as much as I hate myself. You do not know what it is to be torn asunder, to be split in twain by desire and longing and desperation. To be tortured by a love that burns like a fire in your heart. You cannot know!"

Tania felt pity welling inside her. She had experienced firsthand the awesome powers of Gabriel Drake; she knew what it was like to stand stripped of all willpower and all control under the force of those deadly silver eyes. And although Drake had not put an enchantment on Rathina, her overwhelming love for the wicked Faerie lord was as powerful as any spell.

Tania walked toward Rathina and knelt in front of her. Rathina lowered her head, her shoulders shaking. "Look at me," Tania said. Reluctantly, Rathina raised her eyes. "Do you still love Gabriel?"

"No." Rathina's voice was only just above a whisper.

"Tell the truth."

Rathina sobbed. "Yes." She reached out for Tania. "Yes, I do still love him. For pity's sake, protect me from myself!" she cried. "Keep me from him till this madness passes!"

Tania put her arms around Rathina and let her bury her head in her shoulder. For a while she knelt there, stroking her sister's tangled hair while the misery and agony and horror came pouring out of Rathina's quivering body. Tania was torn by her sister's return; she didn't know what to think about it. Even before Rathina had brought down all this evil upon them, Tania had been given good reason to hate and distrust Rathina. But she couldn't forget either that this wretched woman had once been her closest friend in all of Faerie.

She looked around at her sisters. Sancha's face was stony with hatred. Cordelia looked angry and confused. Zara was weeping. Hopie's expression was uncertain, as though she was caught between compassion and despair. Only Eden's face showed a glimmer of understanding. Tania thought she knew why: Eden had known pain and anguish down the years; she knew what it was to suffer for your deeds.

"What would you have us do, Rathina?" Eden asked.

Rathina lifted her tear-streaked face. "Put an end to my misery," she said, choking. "Free me from Lord Drake, that is all I ask."

"Only you have the power to do that," Hopie said. "Speak again."

"I cannot live with the horror of what I have done," Rathina said. "I would fight any foe if I were assured that death would be my reward. Oblivion is all I seek."

"Granted gladly!" said Sancha. "And that by mine own hand had I a bright blade to do the deed."

"No," Zara murmured. "Look at her, Sancha—she is broken. What would killing her avail?"

"What are our choices?" Cordelia asked, looking at her sisters. "To imprison her until the battle is lost or won? To send her under escort to Ravensare? Eden? Do you have the power to banish her to some faraway place where she can do no more harm?"

"I do not," Eden said. "And I would not use it if I had." She turned to her kneeling sister. "Rathina? Would you be as one with us on the morrow? Would you fight at our side?"

"No!" Sancha shouted. "You would forgive and forget? Never!"

"Sancha is right," Cordelia said. "She cannot be trusted. We have no proof that she has not come here on some dark errand from the Sorcerer. This could all be a sham."

"It is not," Rathina said. "You have my heart's word on that."

"How did you get away from the Sorcerer?" Tania asked.

"He is preoccupied with tomorrow's battle plans," Rathina replied. "He was busy with his captains—with Gabriel Drake and with other fell leaders. I made a pretense of going to my bed. I slipped by the guards as soon as I could." She lifted her head and held Tania's gaze. "I am not lying to you," she said.

Hopie turned to Eden. "Why should we trust her to ride with us against Lyonesse on the morn? Is that not madness?"

"Short of utter madness, I would hope," Eden said. "See, all around us the Power of Seven awakes and thrives. Would you not have that power with you when you ride against the Sorcerer King tomorrow?"

Tania looked to where Eden was gesturing. The carpet of fresh young grass and of blossoming daisies and buttercups had spread all around the tent now, and the flowers and slender blades of grass were even pushing up through the weave of the rugs so that everywhere the ground was patched with spreading pools of green and yellow and white.

"Is this the Power of Seven?" Cordelia asked. "The power of life in the midst of death? It is glorious and gladdening to the heart, but will it aid us in battle?"

"I do not know," Eden said. "But when our mother spoke to me of it, I believe she had hopes that Rathina would come to us. Would you turn her away or fetter her—or would you have her ride with us into battle and thus win the day?"

"Eden is right," said a subdued voice. It was Sancha. Everyone turned to look at her. "The victory of new life over the crawling death of the Sorcerer King is a great and a glad thing. It will put heart into our army and will cause dismay to our enemy. We must use it if we can." She stood up and walked to where Rathina was kneeling. "Get up," she said.

Rathina climbed to her feet, her head bowed so she did not have to look at Sancha.

"Lift your head!" Sancha commanded. Rathina raised her chin and looked into Sancha's face. "Hear me well, sister," said Sancha. "You do not know what harm you have done."

"I do know," Rathina murmured. "And I repent it."

"No!" Sancha spat. "Believe me, you do *not* know how deep the wounds will be ere all is done." She took a breath and continued. "I do not trust you, Rathina, but without you the Power of Seven cannot be. You will ride with us against the evil of Lyonesse when the sun rises tomorrow. But if you seek to betray us or to thwart us or to do us harm, know this." Her voice became deadly cold. "I will strike you down, sister. Even though it be the doom of my own soul, I will end you!"

A chill ran up Tania's spine. She had no doubts that Sancha would prove true to her threat.

"So be it," Eden said. "It is late and we should be abed."

"Where will Rathina sleep?" Hopie asked. "And who will stand guard over her?"

"She will sleep in my tent," said Zara. "And none shall watch her. If she is gone in the morning, then we will know her heart is untrue."

"Thank you," Rathina murmured. "I will not fail you."

"See that you do not," said Hopie.

Rathina looked at Tania and the misery in her eyes was almost too much to bear. Tania held her gaze for a few moments, then Rathina looked away.

Tania didn't want to think of the nightmares that must be churning inside her sister's head. She just hoped that with her sisters around her Rathina would find the strength to resist her blind devotion to Gabriel Drake. If not . . .

If not, then Rathina might prove to be the deadliest danger of all.

Tania awoke from a fretful half-sleep. Thoughts of Rathina were tumbling through her mind, preventing her from resting properly. Could Rathina be trusted or would she betray them again? *And even if she's genuinely sorry and she really wants to put things right, could I ever really trust her again?* It was an impossible question, and deep in her heart, all that Tania really wanted was for the seven of them to be together as if all this evil had never happened. And she knew that could never be.

The candles in her tent had burned low, but by the silence that surrounded her, Tania could tell that it was still nighttime. She lay for a while staring up at the stooping roof of the tent. She was less scared of the coming battle than she had expected. It was almost as if the very idea of putting on her armor and charging into an army of Gray Knights was so outlandish that her brain refused to accept the reality of it. Her mind was behaving as if this was all a dream—as if she'd wake up in the morning in her own bed in North London and find that these weeks as Princess Tania of Faerie were just an elaborate fantasy.

At least that was preferable to the alternative: that her sisters would find her in the morning whimpering with fright and totally incapable of doing anything.

She got up and poured herself a cup of water. Faerie water. Thirst quenching and delicious. She noticed a pricking under her bare feet. Blades of bright green grass had thrust up through the carpeting and the ground was studded all over with flowers. And more growing things had climbed the walls of the tent: long thin tendrils of leafy greenery from which hung star-shaped flowers with pink and white petals. It seemed that the Power of Seven was still gaining in strength. At the very least that must mean that Rathina was still with them—for good or for bad.

Tania pushed through the tent flap and stepped out into the night. The camp was quiet and still under the floating half-moon. A little way off she could hear the movements and sounds of the horses in their paddock, and through the ranks of tents she saw guards standing watch. She could not have said why, but something led her over the lush flower-strewn grass toward Sancha's tent. She found her sister sitting on a grassy hillock outside the billowing canvas, her shoulders hunched, her eyes staring sleeplessly down the long slope of the heath to where the flickering red lights of the palace pierced the blackness.

Tania sat at her side. "Can't sleep?"

"No."

"Me neither." She sighed. "My brain won't stop."

There was a pause, then Sancha's head turned, her eyes hidden in black shadow under her brow. "I would not speak of my thoughts," she murmured. "I cannot speak of them."

"Why not?" Tania urged. She saw shining tears pouring down Sancha's cheeks. "Sancha, what's wrong?"

"I cannot say," she said, weeping. "It is too awful."

Tania put her arm around Sancha's shoulders. "Talk to me about it," she said gently. "Please."

Sancha wiped her eyes with her sleeve. "Do you remember when we were in the Library together? When the Soul Books burned?"

"Yes." Tania remembered it vividly—how could she ever forget those unearthly screaming voices as the flames consumed the books? "I know you're very upset about the books . . . but . . . but they're only *things*, Sancha. Things can always be replaced."

"You do not understand," said Sancha. "The books hold in their pages the whole of a person's life—not only those things which have happened, but also that which is yet to come. The books speak to me, Tania. Although each book can be read only by the one whose life lies within the covers, I can read them all— that is my gift . . . and it has become my curse."

"Why a curse?"

"I have never sought knowledge of the future

from the books," Sancha said. "I always closed my eyes and stopped my ears from learning what is to come—that is a burden I would not wish to bear. But when the books burned, I heard one voice that would not be silenced." She swallowed and Tania felt her fingers gripping fiercely into her arm. "I heard death crying out from the burning pages. . . ."

Tania gasped. "Whose death?"

"I must not tell you," Sancha said, crying. "But tomorrow on the battlefield, death will take a great soul. A beloved soul." She pulled away from Tania. "Leave me, please, leave me! I have told you too much. I will not speak of it anymore. It is not meant for you to know such things!" She scrambled to her feet and pushed her way into her tent.

Tania got up, meaning to follow her sister—to ask more questions. But she had taken only two paces when she came to an abrupt halt. Why wouldn't Sancha say who was going to die? If she would only tell her, then maybe she'd be able to protect them or even stop them from getting into the battle in the first place. But then a terrible thought struck her and she stared after Sancha, her throat suddenly dry. What if the victim was someone who *had* to be at the front of the battle, someone whom it would be impossible for Tania to allow to stay out of harm's way?

"It's me," she whispered. The starry sky whirled around her head, the half-moon flashing across her eyes like a strobe light. "I'm the one who's going to die."

She stumbled back to her own tent and fell onto her bed. She lay like that for an eternity of misery, too wretched even to cry. Then she turned onto her back, staring up at nothing. Silent tears flowed now, pouring down the sides of her face into her hair.

"I wish Edric was here," she murmured. "I'd like to have seen him again. Just once more before the end."

She turned onto her side, her face lost in the pillow as she gave way to the depths of grief and despair.

XXV

"It is a fine dawn, indeed," Eden said. "Alas that it is the harbinger of such a deadly day." She turned her head, looking into Tania's face. "You are very quiet, sister—do thoughts of the approaching battle darken your spirit?"

"No," Tania replied. "I'm fine." She touched her hand against Tanzen's neck and he began to walk down the long eastern slope of Salisoc Heath.

She had not slept, except for maybe a few snatched moments in that strange in-between time when night and day stood in the balance and all the world held its breath. A servant had come into her tent shortly before dawn to help her into her armor. She had stood silently in the candlelit tent, allowing her to strap on the breastplate and back-plate and attach the greaves and cuisses to her legs and the vambraces to her arms. And all the while it had been as if this was happening to someone else. Even when the sword belt had been buckled around her waist and she had felt the hilt of a crystal sword under her hand, it still hadn't seemed real.

She had felt drained of all emotions, as if she was hollow, just a shell of skin over a great gaping void. It was as if her mind was floating in a white cloud while her earthbound body went through the motions of being alive. Even when the sun lifted its shining arc over the eastern downs and the early light leaped like flying sparks from shield rim and spear-point of the arrayed Faerie army, they meant nothing to her. Even the fact that the heath was now alive with grasses and heathers and bright flowers gave her no cheer. She had mounted up and ridden to the front of the army, past the captains in their armor, past her sisters, all else on horseback save for Cordelia, who sat solemnly astride Zephyr.

Tania brought Tanzen to a halt on the edge of the heath and gazed out at the Sorcerer King's forces. Eden was at her side. There was no order or organization in the army of Gray Knights that swarmed on Puck's Heath. They looked to Tania like some kind of disease—like a sickness held briefly in check, but ready at any moment to pour out over the land. The Morrigan hounds wove between the emaciated legs of the hideous gray horses like black maggots, baying and howling. The ground under the army of Lyonesse was brown and dead; the tide of greenery ended in the valley between the two high heaths.

Tania and Eden rode down into the valley, flanked by heralds who carried the Royal standards of

Faerie—a yellow sun on an azure background and a white moon on a field of darkest blue. As they brought their steeds to a halt in the lap of the vale, where green grass gave way to brown decay, five horsemen broke from the melee on Puck's Heath and came cantering down toward them. Four of the Gray Knights bore banners: a black serpent on a red background. The fifth wore a black cloak that spread out like wings as he rode down the hill.

The Gray Knights wore the perpetual grin of Lyonesse on their pale, haggard faces, and in their eyes was the red glow of battle madness. But it was the smile that played on the lips of the fifth rider that would normally have chilled Tania to the core. The knights brought their horses to a halt only a few yards from where Tania and Eden were waiting.

"Brave heart!" Eden whispered to Tania as Gabriel Drake spurred his horse to walk forward. He came to a halt only a yard from Tanzen. The unicorn snorted and stamped a forehoof, but stood his ground.

"Well met, my bride," Drake said, his voice sliding through the air like a silken snake. "Our last meeting left me with a pain I will never forget." He put a hand to his shoulder, where Titania had stabbed him with the black sword back in the Palmers' house in North London. "Your half-mother, the Queen, kept you from me then, but I do not see her today. Perhaps you have hidden her away in the hope of protecting her." He laughed softly. "A forlorn hope, my lady. So, have you come to swap final marriage vows with me, Tania?

Are we to be fully united at last?"

Tania lifted her chin and looked Gabriel Drake in the face. There was nothing she needed to say to him. She lifted her arm to signal the herald to speak.

"The seven princesses of the Royal House of Aurealis, rightful rulers of the Immortal Realm of Faerie, demand of the Sorcerer of Lyonesse that he and his armies quit this land now and forever," called the herald in a high, clear voice. "Safe passage will be allowed for all those that lay down their arms. If the Sorcerer of Lyonesse refuses, then he and his armies shall be swept from Faerie and all those not destroyed utterly shall be imprisoned in amber for eternity."

A heavy silence followed. Gabriel Drake stared into Tania's eyes as if he was trying to reach into her heart with his will and freeze it in her chest. She looked steadily back at him and for the first time she felt no fear as she gazed into those shining silver eyes. She was going to die today—either at the hands of one of the Gray Knights or on Gabriel's sword. Sancha had seen it. There was nothing to be done, except to die as bravely as she could.

His smile faltered and a look of unease flickered over his face. "You have changed, my lady," he said. "Something cloaks your mind from me. It is not an enchantment, I would know it if that were so. It is something else. Something within you." He sat up, smiling again. "I care not," he said. "It is of no matter how you shield yourself from me, be it for a moment or a day: Your fate is inevitable. I will have you for my own, my lady, body and mind, spirit and soul."

He seemed to be waiting for her to respond, and her continued silence clearly confused him. He looked up the hill to where the Faerie army was gathered. "I see you have a new recruit to your little band of sisters," he said with a twisted grin. "Do not put too much trust in Rathina, my lady—she does not have full possession of her mind." He raised his hand and curled his fingers. "I hold her heart in thrall. When the moment is ripe, I will speak but a single word and she will turn on you."

Still Tania said nothing, simply holding his gaze until it was he who had to look away.

Then Eden spoke, and her voice was steady and fearless. "Will your new master not come forth and see how green grows the grass on Salisoc Heath?" she asked. "With Rathina at our side death shall never have victory in this land."

Gabriel smiled at her. "You would make us tremble with talk of new grass, my lady? I know of the Power of Seven. It is a soft power, a feeble power—it has no cutting edge. Nay, my lady, were each grassy blade a blade of crystal and were each pretty flower a Faerie knight, still would the scythe of Lyonesse cut you down. The King will come forth, my lady, have no doubt of that—but before that time comes, the flowers of Faerie will all be weeded away." He lifted his arm and gestured to one of the Gray Knights.

The creature began to speak, its voice thin and shrill. "The High King of Lyonesse, in reparation for his unlawful imprisonment at the hands of O[...] Aurealis, takes now this land of Faerie unto his for all time. The former Queen and all of her daugnters will surrender themselves to his mercy and the armies that have gathered to oppose him will disarm and disperse. One hour only does the King give for compliance with this demand, and refusal to obey will be dealt with most harshly."

"Those are our most reasonable terms," Gabriel said. "None other shall be given." He looked from Tania to Eden and back again. "And do not mistake me, your royal highnesses: If you seek battle, your army will be destroyed and none shall survive to remember you." He bared his teeth. "And when the slaughter of this day is done, the knights of Lyonesse will go forth throughout the land and not a man nor a woman nor a child will be spared the wrath of their passing. We will make Faerie a desert." His eyes shone with an evil light. "One alone will be allowed the gift of life," he declared. "I would not have my bride killed. No, Tania—you will live on forever at my side." The smile widened. "You will never be free of me, Tania! Did you not know? We are bonded for all time!"

"No, Gabriel," Tania said quietly. "We aren't." And now it was her turn to smile. "Don't you get it?" she said. "Today is the day I'm going to break the bond between us once and for all."

Gabriel narrowed his eyes, his face transformed by anger and uncertainty. He drew back his lips and opened his mouth as if to speak, but she didn't give him the chance; she touched her heel against Tanzen's flank and he carried her rapidly back up the long slope of Salisoc Heath, Eden and the heralds cantering after her.

She heard Gabriel's voice calling: "The only way you will ever be free of me is with your death, Tania!" he shouted. "If that is your choice, then so be it. Today you will die!"

Tania gave a breath of laughter. "Tell me something I don't know, Gabriel," she muttered.

Eden caught up with her. "I know what you fear, sister," she said. "But death is not the only path."

"Yes, it is," Tania replied calmly. "But don't worry, I'm not afraid. I'm not afraid at all." She urged Tanzen into a gallop, pulling out her sword and brandishing it in the air as she rode toward her waiting army. Her only regret at that moment was that her parents would never know what had happened to her.

"The talking is done!" she shouted, galloping wildly along the face of the Faerie army. "In the name of King Oberon and Queen Titania and the Seven Princesses of Faerie, follow me!"

Tanzen turned, rearing up on the brow of the hill and letting out a piercing neigh. And then he went galloping back down the hill, and behind her Tania heard the gallant shouts and the clashing of swords and spears on shields as the Army of the Seven Princesses poured like a shining wave down the long hill at her back.

XXVI

Tania fought mechanically, her body moving with a fluid, passionless skill as she urged Tanzen into the throng. Her shield rang with blows, swords and spear-points glanced off her seashell armor and her curled conch shell helmet, and all the while arrows sang in her ears and her head was filled with shouting, with the neighing of horses, and the maniacal baying of the Morrigan hounds. She thrust and parried with her sword, blocking a sweeping sword-strike, bringing her own weapon in under the defenses of her enemy and striking swift to the heart. And then she was moving on, not waiting for the Gray Knight's body to explode into dust before she was engaging another with the shining play of her crystal blade.

Tanzen acted as one with her, the wild unicorn of Caer Liel rising and falling among the hordes of Lyonesse, hooves pummeling and teeth biting and the spiraling horn slashing and stabbing at the mobbing hounds and the Gray Knights on their bony undead horses.

Tania fought without fury and without emotion. Even when Tanzen carried her to where the Gray Knights were massed most thickly, plunging through the crowded creatures as though breasting a rising tide, she felt nothing. She swung her sword, fending off a hound that leaped at her throat, hearing it whine as her crystal blade bit deep. She ducked to avoid a swinging mace, slashing upward, her sword severing the arm at the elbow. The arm cartwheeled through the air and came thumping back onto the stump, the mace still gripped in the skeletal fingers. Tanzen wheeled to one side, his head coming down, his spiral horn thrusting into the neck of the rider's gray steed while Tania leaned into the plunge and her sword pierced the Gray Knight's chest. Tanzen turned again, tossing a Morrigan hound high into the air. Tania's sword sliced its head from its body as it fell.

She had only one thought in her mind—to find Gabriel Drake in all this mayhem and madness and to do her utmost to kill him before he killed her.

The surge of the battle moved away from her and she found herself in a strangely empty eddy of the battlefield. Tanzen turned in a slow circle, snorting and stamping as if eager to get back into the melee. All around her, the knights of Faerie were hammering at the gray legions of Lyonesse, but Tania could see that the tide of battle was slowly turning in the Gray Knights' favor. The Faerie banners were waving valiantly, but they had been pushed back up the long gradient of Salisoc Heath, and there were many—far too many—Faerie knights lying in the long grass, staining the green to a dark, livid red.

Tania shook her head to get the sweat out of her eyes. Where was Drake? She had not seen him since the two armies had first clashed—and she had no idea of how long ago that might have been. Time didn't mean anything in all this deadly chaos. She could see the grim banners of Lyonesse on the rise. And in the air around one of the serpent banners, she saw falcons and eagles circling, diving constantly, harrying the standard-bearer.

"Cordelia!" she exclaimed.

Her sister was there, high upon the back of her leaping unicorn, her sword a white blur as she fought her way toward the banner. Gray Knights galloped toward her, their inhuman shrieks carried on the wind. A single hack of Cordelia's sword sent the serpent banner tumbling. Tania caught her breath as, moments later, she saw the Gray Knights surround her sister. For a few moments Cordelia and Zephyr fought savagely, but then an unlucky spear-thrust caught the unicorn in the side. He reared up, his neck arching back as he cried out to the sky in a high, sweet, piercing voice. And then he fell and Cordelia was lost among the Gray Knights. The birds flocked to her aid. Swords bit the air, arrows flew, spears stabbed upward. Many of the birds fell, but still they came.

For the first time that day Tania allowed herself to

feel something real. And what she felt was *fear*. A terrible fear—not for herself, but for her sister. She heard Sancha's voice in her head. *Tomorrow on the battlefield, death will take a great soul.*

Not me! Cordelia! She was talking about Cordelia!

She had been so caught up with the image of herself as the *special* one—the most important of the seven—that it had never occurred to her that someone else might be the target of Sancha's prophecy.

"Tanzen! To Cordelia!" she called. The wild unicorn roared up the hillside like the north wind. Tania clung grimly to his back as he fell upon the Gray Knights. They went slashing and hacking through them, buffeted by sword and spear as they fought their way toward Cordelia.

She glimpsed her sister through the crowding knights. Cordelia was on her feet, standing over her fallen unicorn with a sword in either hand, the crystal blades whirling while her enemies swarmed around her, their monstrous steeds screeching as Cordelia cut their legs from under them and sent their riders tumbling. Birds attacked the milling knights, flying into their faces, talons raking at their eyes, curved beaks pecking. But the undead creatures of Lyonesse could only be destroyed by a strike to the heart, and too many hemmed Cordelia in now, blocking the whirl of her swords with their own blades, closing in on her for the kill.

Cordelia lost her footing and fell. Screaming their triumph, the Gray Knights closed over her. Tania urged Tanzen forward, leaning over the unicorn's head to stab and thrust at the knights that surrounded her sister. She was aware of someone at her side; someone on a bay horse—a rider in Faerie armor, a spinning sword, a shouting voice, a familiar face twisted in rage.

"With me!" Rathina howled, hacking her way through the Gray Knights.

Together, Tania and Rathina cut a path through to their fallen sister. Cordelia staggered to her feet and swung herself onto Tanzen's back behind Tania. Horse and unicorn reared and turned, heaving through the enemy, bursting out of the throng and cantering into clear ground.

"Are you okay?" Tania said, panting, twisting her head to look at her sister.

"I am unhurt," Cordelia said. "But it was an opportune rescue. I fear they would have butchered me else. Alas for Zephyr, I could do naught to save him. Come, find me another steed. I have a great debt to repay to the filth of Lyonesse."

"I wouldn't have been able to reach you without Rathina," Tania said, looking across to where her dark-haired sister sat astride her horse, catching her breath.

"Aye," Cordelia said, nodding to Rathina. "That was bravely done."

"A drop in the ocean of my debt to you all," Rathina said grimly. She tugged on her horse's reins. "Much is still to be done." She kicked her heels and the animal went galloping back toward the enemy. "I shall see you anon!" she called back. "On the field of victory, or not at all!"

"Have you seen the others?" Tania asked Cordelia.

"That will be Eden," Cordelia said, pointing down the hillside to an embattled huddle of knights. In the middle of the throng the air was livid with blue-white flashes, like spears of landlocked lightning. "I have not seen Zara and Sancha since the battle began," Cordelia continued. "But Hopie is upon the hill, ministering to the wounded. Lord Brython stands guard over her like an oak tree, wielding a double-handed axe and allowing none to come near."

The two armies had broken into many smaller groups spread over the heaths and the vale between. There was some savage fighting going on almost under the eaves of the forest where the Earl Marshal Cornelius and his sons were attacking a serpent banner. The valley itself was like a deadly, boiling cauldron: knights of both armies pressing at one another while the hounds circled and pounced, pulling down horses where they could, while the shrieks and calls and cries of the conflict rose horribly into the air.

The Moon banner and the Sun banner of Faerie had become separated: The Moon banner was to the rear of the battlefield, protected by Earl Valentyne and his knights, but the banner with the yellow sun on its sky blue background was partway up the slope of Puck's Heath, the knights protecting it pressing forward toward the crest. Tania saw a small valiant figure galloping up the side of Puck's Heath toward the Sun banner, sword raised and shining in the light. Zara!

But a group of Gray Knights was racing across the sloping ground, closing in on her from behind, like storm clouds chasing down the summer sun—and their leader was wearing a black cloak that spread out behind him like bat wings.

"They're going to catch her!" Tania shouted.

Cordelia leaped from Tanzen's back. "Go to her aid!" she called, slapping the unicorn's hindquarters. "I will find a steed and be with you as soon as I may."

Tanzen surged forward, his mane streaming out as he galloped full tilt down the hillside and across the valley to the rise of Puck's Heath. Tania screwed her eyes against the shrilling air, her sword gripped tight in her fist as she leaned into the rushing wind. Running quicker than any horse, Tanzen soon closed the gap between them and Drake's Gray Knights. Tania knew that these were the deadliest enemies on the battlefield, armed with swords of Isenmort, protected by black amber, led by the evil renegade Lord of Weir. But she didn't care—she had been afraid of Drake for far too long. He had invaded her dreams and made her life a bitter torment. But one way or another his hold over her would be broken today.

Tanzen didn't flinch as he went crashing into the side of Gabriel's horse, his long horn piercing the beast to the heart. But the force of the impact threw Tania from his back. Earth and sky wheeled around her, but she kept her wits and hit the ground in a curled roll, her armor absorbing the shock so that she was on her feet in seconds, a little dizzy from the fall, but crouched sure-footed with her sword ready.

The collapse of Gabriel's horse had thrown his knights into confusion, some of the hideous animals falling headlong, others bucking and swerving to avoid the chaos. Gabriel had been catapulted over his horse's head and was lying motionless on the ground with his cloak over him like a shroud.

With a cry Tania ran toward him, her helmet falling off so that her long red hair was released into the whipping wind. She stood over him, feet spread, her sword raised in the high ward. This was the moment to set herself free. A simple lunge and Gabriel's dominion over her would be finished forever.

But she hesitated. She believed herself capable of killing him in a fair fight, but to thrust a sword into his body while he lay helpless at her feet? Every instinct in her shouted out against it. She lowered her sword, stepping back. She was aware of a group of Faerie knights thundering up the hillside, Sancha and Rathina at their head. They broke against Drake's disordered Gray Knights, fighting desperately against the Isenmort swords. Gabriel stirred, heaving himself up on his arms, shaking his head, struggling to get his feet under him.

"Get up!" Tania shouted.

Gabriel pulled himself to his feet. He swayed, his cloak swirling around him, his face dazed. Then he looked at Tania and the silver glint in his eyes was like knives in her heart.

"Pick up your sword," she said.

"Gladly," he said, stooping and sweeping up his sword of shining steel. "You were ever a fool, Tania. Now meet a fool's end!" He ran at her, his sword aimed at her throat.

She parried his blow and sidestepped, her smooth side sweep almost managing to slash him as he stumbled by her. He was quick, his blade coming up, ringing on hers as he fended off her attack. Now they faced each other again, their eyes locked—his a deadly silver that clashed and sparred against the gold-flecked green of hers. He leaped forward, sword extended. She turned his thrust aside, spinning and striking fast, her sword cutting through the billows of his cloak, striking solid flesh. He let out a shout of pain, stumbling to his knees. Tania saw that there was blood on the edge of her sword.

He was up again in an instant, slicing the air with his sword, holding her at bay. She could see that she had hurt him—he stood bent over to one side with a grimace of pain on his face. But through the pain he still smiled that vile, knowing smile. Seeing the smile and looking into those silver eyes again, she beat and beat and beat down on his faltering blade, howling with an anger she had never known herself capable of as she forced him onto his knees.

At last he let his sword fall away and knelt there, his arms limp, blood spreading over the gray mail on his side, staring up at her with eyes that were like twin full moons in an empty sky. She lifted her sword, trembling with rage.

"Our bond does not end with my death, Tania," he said. "Remember, we are bonded for all time. Murdering me will not set you free. I will haunt you down all the long ages."

She stared at him, shaken by his words in spite of her rage.

Then his eyes moved away from her face, seeming to focus on something behind her. A smile curved his mouth. He spoke a single word, like a breath on the air. "Rathina!"

Something hit Tania from behind, something that knocked her sideways, jarring her sword out of her hand and throwing her to the ground. She was vaguely aware of the stamping of hooves and of movement above her as a rider brought a horse to a sudden halt and swung from the saddle.

Tania lay winded on the ground as she saw Rathina step in front of Drake, her face grim and set, her sword held in both hands. "I cannot let you do this," Rathina said. "Leave him, Tania—I do not wish to fight with you, but I shall if you seek to do him any more harm."

"No!" Tania groaned, staring into her sister's face. "Rathina, no!"

"I cannot help it," Rathina said, her voice cracking with something close to madness. "I am *his*!" She glanced over her shoulder at him. "No more blood need be shed, Gabriel, my love," she cried. "It is not too late. Let us quit the battlefield—let us leave this Realm entirely and be forever as one."

Drake rose to his feet, his eyes shining, his face twisted with a malevolent smile of triumph. "Did I not warn you, Tania?" he said. "Did I not tell you she would turn on you?" He pushed indifferently past Rathina, making her stumble to one side, his sword ready in his fist as he strode toward where Tania lay.

Tania reached blindly for her sword. But she was too late—his booted foot came down on her wrist, trapping her arm. And then, even as his sword cut down toward her, a shape came darting in from the side: a small, slender shape that pushed in under his blow, standing between Tania and her impending death.

Tania saw Faerie armor. Flowing golden hair. A sword raised to fend off the falling blade. There was a clash as iron sword struck crystal. The crystal blade shattered, the iron sword plunged downward, piercing the breastplate, thrusting through to the hilt, the bloodied blade jutting from the arched back.

Tania scrambled to her knees as the weight of the collapsing body crashed against her, falling into her arms. The helmet tumbled from the golden hair, the neck strained back, the face ash white, the glazed blue eyes staring up into the sky. Tania let out a cry as she stared down at the beautiful, lifeless face of her fallen sister.

XXVII

"Zara! *Zara, no!*"

Tania was half aware of figures looming and floating around her like living shadows. The sounds of the battle came into her head, booming and thundering, terribly loud but somehow distant. She stared down into the glazed sapphire eyes, remembering the first time she had met her sister, standing at her chamber door, dressed in a yellow gown and smiling like all summer. She saw Zara seated at the spinetta, her mouth open in song. Dancing with a handsome lord in the Great Hall of the palace. Playing her flute and calling up a wind to fill the sails of the *Cloud Scudder*. Standing on the shoreline of Kymry Bay, the echo of her voice suddenly clear in Tania's ears. *We shall defeat this evil, Tania—I know we shall. And you and I will dance again in the Great Hall of the palace and play duets upon the spinetta and the lute once more.*

A cold rage filled Tania's mind, freezing out fear and grief as she gently put Zara's body aside and stood up. All around her, and down the long slope into the valley and up the rise of Salisoc Heath, the fresh green grass began to brown and wither and the flowers to die. The Power of Seven was lost forever.

Drake stood poised, blood dripping from his blade, watching with hooded, taunting eyes as Tania stooped to pick up her sword, so sure that he would defeat her that he let her arm herself again before he attacked. But Tania was not alone. Sancha stood beside her, tears pouring down her face, but her sword ready. Drake lunged forward with a shout, the edge of his blade flicking Sancha's sword aside. He hammered his shoulder into the princess and threw her to the ground. Tania stepped back, fending off his flashing sword. But she stumbled, falling backward over Zara's body.

He stood over her, victory in his eyes. But before he could strike, a huge dark shape came plunging in from the side, knocking him off balance.

It was Rathina, on horseback again, her sword slicing the air. She screamed out a single word. "Murderer!"

Drake was adder quick. Even caught unawares and thrown half off his feet, he turned and brought his sword whistling upward. The two blades rang as they clashed, but Drake's blow was the more powerful. Rathina's sword spun out of her hand. Following his attack through, Drake stabbed at her horse. The stricken animal came crashing down, legs kicking, hurling Rathina from the saddle. She sprawled on the ground, gasping and weeping.

Drake gave her one contemptuous glance then turned again to Tania. Behind him Tania saw Rathina lift herself to her knees, groping for a sword. Her fingers tightened around a hilt. She picked it up, gripping it in both hands. She clambered awkwardly to her feet, coming up behind Drake and shouting aloud as she raised the shining weapon: "For Zara!" She thrust the sword into his back right up to the hilt.

For a moment Drake hung in the air, pinned to the shining blade, his face petrified at the moment of triumph. Then he slumped forward, sliding off the sword and dropping soundlessly to the ground.

Rathina stared down at him, her face as white as bone. "For Zara!" she said again. "And to be free of you! My love could have saved us! It could have redeemed us both!"

Sancha stumbled to her feet. "Rathina!" she called. "The sword—it is Isenmort! Let it go! You will be killed!"

Tania had seen the blade gleam as her sister had lifted the sword, but she had not realized that Rathina had picked up one of the Sorcerer King's Isenmort swords, dropped by a slain Gray Knight. Rathina stared at her hands in alarm and fear—she had obviously been unaware of the deadly nature of the weapon when she had picked it up.

"It does not burn," she murmured. She looked at Sancha, lifting the bloodied sword. "It does not burn me at all!"

Sancha stared at her. "Your Gift is revealed at last!"

she said. "You have the power to touch Isenmort without harm."

"I wish for no Gift! I deserve no *Gift*!" Rathina tossed the sword aside and stumbled forward, falling onto her knees by Zara's body. "I am sorry!" she said, weeping. "I am so sorry!" Sobbing aloud, she gathered her dead sister in her arms, burying her face into Zara's neck.

Tania got to her feet. She had expected to feel glad at Drake's death, but her relief was mixed with horror and dismay and regret and a deep, bewildering sense of loss, as if some fragment of her own spirit had died with him. And Zara had fallen—Sancha's terrible prophecy had come true. But there was no time to grieve now—many of Drake's Gray Knights were still alive upon the hillside, and the princesses were far from safe.

In fact, so much had happened so quickly that Tania was surprised to see that the fight was still raging all around them. The reality of their peril was brought home to her as an unhorsed Gray Knight came lurching toward her brandishing a spear. Acting almost on instinct, she knocked the spear aside with her sword and aimed a darting thrust at the creature's chest. The undead knight's eyes still glowed with red madness as her sword pierced his heart and his body erupted into ash.

More of the Gray Knights came and for a short time Tania was forced to focus on the simple act of staying alive and of keeping her screeching enemies away from where Rathina crouched, huddled over

Zara's body. But Tania was not alone. Sancha fought at her side and more Faerie knights came galloping to their aid, led by Cordelia and Eden.

The battle against Drake's knights was hard and vicious, but suddenly Tania found herself standing among the empty gray mail of the last of the dreadful creatures while the dust of her final kill drifted on the air. The battle still raged furiously over the two withered heaths, but in this one place the gathered princesses were given the bitter gift of a few moments to mourn for their fallen sister. Hopie was the last to arrive, galloping up with Lord Brython at her side. She jumped from the saddle and stood with her sisters over Zara's body while silent tears flowed down her cheeks.

Rathina was still curled on the ground over Zara. Brython took her by the shoulders, gently lifting her away from the dead princess, scooping Zara up in his arms and getting to his feet as if she weighed no more than an infant. No one spoke a word as Brython cradled Zara against his chest and walked toward his horse.

A Faerie Knight took Zara from Brython and held her as he climbed into the saddle. Then the delicate body was lifted again into Brython's arms.

"I will bear her into the forest," he said, his voice cracking. "She will be safe there till all is done." He set off at a steady canter toward the dying eaves of Esgarth Forest.

Rathina got to her feet. "I would have given my own life to save her," she said, crying. "I would render up my very soul to have her alive again. I have brought this upon us!" She stared down at Gabriel Drake's body. "I am more monstrous far than he! I cannot bear it!"

Tania stepped forward and put her arms around Rathina's shoulders, holding her close. "You're not a monster," she said. "You're my sister."

"This battle is far from won," said Eden. "The very air is full of dread and the ground trembles in trepidation." A look of terror came over her face and she pointed down toward the palace. "Oh, sweet spirits of earth and water, look! *Look!* He comes! The Sorcerer comes!"

Tania turned, and as she did she felt a tremor in the ground and a moment later she was struck by the fierce hot breath of a furnace wind that came roaring up from the south. The Sorcerer King of Lyonesse galloped toward them on a huge bloodred creature that was like an evil mingling of horse and reptile, hairless and scaled, its body lined by rows of hooked ridges and crests, its eyes blacker than the darkest night. And where the beast's hooves fell, the ground smoked and was left blackened so that a burned path seemed to follow in its wake.

"His captain is slain!" Cordelia shouted, lifting her sword in defiance. "He comes to avenge the death. Come, sisters—stand firm."

Tania released Rathina and the six sisters formed a line across the hillside. Tania gripped her sword, her mouth dry as she watched the King rushing toward them. The Sorcerer was clad from head to foot in dark red armor, and his bloodred cloak cracked, streaming out behind him as he rode. From beneath a high helmet crested with a rearing snake, his terrible white face stared out, the fuming eyes filled with boiling fire. As he came closer he lifted a long red sword and the air shrieked as if wounded by the blade's edge.

Tania's knuckles whitened. She felt like a child standing on a bleak seashore as a great breaking wave curls above her.

And then the King was upon them, his red blade scything the air as the hideous beast crashed into the line of princesses. Tania was knocked back, her sword ringing on the Sorcerer King's armored leg, the jarring impact numbing her arms. She saw Cordelia strike at the misshapen beast as it thundered past, her sword stabbing at its throat. But the blade snapped halfway to the hilt as it struck against the armored scales and Cordelia was flung aside as the creature turned and reared, its huge hooves beating the air.

One hoof struck Sancha, sending her spinning to the ground. Eden came in under the beast, shouting in a high voice with her hands raised, palms upward. Blue lightning sparked from her fingers, cracking in the air and wrapping around the head of the monster so that its bellowing changed to a scream of agony and rage. The Sorcerer King's sword slashed downward, slicing through Eden's lightning, gathering it and rising again, drawing the power with it so that the whole blade was alive with writhing blue light. Then he pointed the blade at Eden and the crackling energy struck her forehead and drove her to the ground.

Only Tania, Rathina, and Hopie were still on their feet. The King lunged toward Tania, his sword ripping the air wide open. She lifted her blade and found Rathina suddenly at her side, her sword also raised against the crashing blow. Together they managed to deflect the great red sword, fending it off as the beast thundered past. The King gave a shout of rage. Tania saw that Hopie was in the creature's path, her face bold and brave as she swung her sword and flung it at the King's head. It glanced off his helmet and Hopie was only just quick enough to hurl herself aside as the creature's pounding hooves bore down on her.

Rathina leaped recklessly after the beast, shouting defiance. The king pulled on the reins and the monster turned, its mouth wide as it bellowed its anger. Tania saw Rathina standing in its path, her sword above her head, gripped in both hands, the level blade pointing forward. And even as Tania shrank from the sight of her sister being trampled Rathina thrust the sword into the gaping mouth of the beast, forcing the blade down the open throat and leaping to one side as the dying monster stumbled and fell.

But the King didn't share in its crashing fall. As the beast died under him he lifted out of the saddle and hung in the air, the billows of his bloodred cloak opening and spreading wide behind him. And it was only in that moment that Tania realized with a shock of intense horror that the cloak was a pair of red, leathery wings: thin-veined membranes stretched between curved skeletal fingers of bone.

He hurtled down, his eyes blazing, his huge sword aimed at her heart. Again, Rathina came to her aid, bounding in as the King swooped, beating his sword aside. His arm swung and his armored fist struck her on the back, driving her onto her hands and knees. He came pounding down to the ground in front of Tania, the hideous wings lifted high over his back. She stepped back, her eyes on his face, her sword held out to parry his next blow.

"Your sisters lie vanquished at my feet," the King intoned. "Your mother has no power and your father is my captive." He smiled, and it was the same smile that Tania had seen so often on Gabriel Drake's face: evil and cruel and bitter cold. "Would you face me alone, half-thing? Would you die alone?"

"Not alone!" shouted a voice.

Tania turned to see Edric galloping up the hill on Drazin's back. Behind him Bryn and a whole herd of wild unicorns were racing toward them.

The Sorcerer King hissed like a snake, his wings curling as they lifted him into the air again. His sword sliced down, cracking against Edric's raised blade and almost tipping him from Drazin's back. Howling with rage, the King lunged at Tania, raining blows down on her sword so that she was beaten to her knees. Her foot slithered under her and she fell sideways, but the king's death-blow was warded off by Edric; he had thrown himself from Drazin's back and had forced his sword between them.

As she scrambled to her feet, Tania was aware that a strange, expectant hush had come over the battle-field. Even in the turmoil of her battle with the Sorcerer King, she saw that many faces were looking northward. She turned her head. At the edge of the forest a golden light was growing, bright as the dawning sun. As she watched, the light became stronger, shining out brilliantly. She stared into the light, her heart lifting as she saw Oberon and Titania step out from among the trees.

At last the King had come. At *last*! But even from that distance, Tania could see how heavily Oberon leaned on the Queen. Was he strong enough to fight the Sorcerer King?

Tania heard a gasp of pain; she turned and saw that the Sorcerer King had beaten Edric to the ground. One heavy armored foot was upon Edric's back and his sword was poised for the kill.

"No!" Tania leaped forward. Her sword was deflected by a side sweep of the Sorcerer King's arm. It fell out of her hands as his armored fingers caught her around her throat, almost choking her as he brought her attack to a sudden wrenching halt. He lifted her into the air, her feet kicking. She clutched at his arm with both hands, unable to breathe. Red and black lights exploded in her eyes.

But even as the darkness grew in her mind and the light of Faerie began to fade from her eyes, Tania felt something strike her from the north, something that poured over her like the warmth of the summer sun. Something that seemed to fill her with golden light, running through her veins, filling her limbs with new energy and tingling over her skin.

She felt the Sorcerer King's fingers snatch back from her throat, but instead of falling, she found herself floating in the air, surrounded by a golden corona that threw out rays of bright amber. And where the beams of light struck the ground, green blades of grass leaped up, sprinkled with yellow flowers. She turned her head and saw an undulating river of thick gold light spinning out from Oberon and Titania, joining them to her and feeding their power to her. Tania opened her mouth, letting the force of Sun and Moon together explode out of her in a long shout. Tendrils of golden light flickered at her fingertips as she held up her hands, creating intricate webs that went shooting in all directions.

As the threads of gold spun from her fingers they seemed to seek through the air for the Gray Knights and the Morrigan hounds of Lyonesse. And where they struck home, the knights exploded in ash and the hounds shriveled to lumps of black rock, the battlefield ringing to the sound of empty falling armor and the crash of downfallen steeds.

A cradle of golden light gathered around the Sorcerer King, enmeshing him in a network of shining tendrils that thickened and spread until he was lost in a globe of burning gold. Tania could hear his howls of anger and see his shadow thrashing about wildly. She felt a final rush of power, of golden potency that poured out of her eyes and crashed against the golden sphere, detonating it into a million sparkling fragments that mushroomed into the air and fell like glittering rain.

And where the Sorcerer King had been standing there remained only a smoky ball of shriveling darkness that waned and wasted and was gone.

Tania gazed around her in amazement. All the brown and withered land was coming alive, the tide of green life spreading in a great expanding circle around her, washing up to the forest and turning winter to summer in a shining moment, sweeping down to the palace and filling the ruined gardens once more with color and beauty. But the flood of new life did not end at the palace walls—it burst over them in a gushing, tumbling wave, and everywhere that it touched it washed away the stains of the burnings and scoured the red and black disfigurations from the walls and erased all traces of the Sorcerer King's brutal dominion. Shattered windows became whole again, broken roofs rose, and tumbled walls remade themselves.

But the healing went deeper than that, and it seemed to Tania that although the palace walls were solid, she could see right through them as if they were made of glass and she saw furniture being remade and slashed pictures mended and all the beautiful ornamentation of the palace recreated as new, even to the burned Library, where the ruination of the fire ran backward in time and ash turned to paper and cinders to leather and embers to soaring shelves that teemed with a multitude of restored books—including all the Soul Books that had been destroyed.

And all the time this was happening, Tania could hear music ringing in her head. Music the like of which she had never heard before, music she had never even dreamed of. The loudest music of all came from the sun, its great, glad, glorious voice ringing out over the world, leading a multitude of other voices: the bass of distant mountains, the sweet descant of rivers, the harmonious cadences of tree and leaf and grass and blossom, the song of air and earth and sky and water, all burgeoning together in her ears into a thrilling symphony. The power and the song and the light grew inside her until she felt that she could not bear it anymore, until she felt as if her body and mind would explode from the intensity of it.

At the last possible moment the funnel of golden power that linked her to the King and Queen wavered and dimmed, and Tania floated down to earth, the impossible light growing pale, the music of the world drifting away beyond hearing, the mystical strength that had threatened to tear her apart at last fading away.

She saw Edric standing in front of her.

"Wow!" she said. "That was really—" But before she could finish the thought, she toppled forward into his arms and fell unconscious into a warm golden void.

XXVIII

"Grieve not overmuch, my children," King Oberon said gently. "Death is a bitter wound to endure for those who must remain to mourn, but it is not the end of things, indeed it is not."

Tania stood with Edric and the rest of the survivors of the battle on a long sloping lawn that ran down through blossoming cherry trees to the bank of the River Tamesis. The long and dreadful day had turned into a beautiful evening, the western sky banded with rosy clouds through which the rays of the setting sun extended like the spokes of a gigantic wheel. All along the riverbank the dead of Faerie lay at rest under sheets of white satin. Three hundred and seventeen knights had been slain on the battlefield, and many more were injured, gathered in a white pavilion that had been erected by the river, their wounds tended by healers working under Hopie's guidance.

The valiant fallen steeds of Faerie had not been forgotten. Cordelia had organized a group of knights to bring the bodies of the dead animals to the river to lie in state under white satin, all save for Zephyr, who was shrouded in the Sun Banner of Faerie and whose head was pillowed by the black serpent banner of Lyonesse that he had helped to bring down.

All that remained of the Morrigan hounds were fists of hard black stone scattered on the heaths. Of the undead knights of Lyonesse, not one had survived; they and their fleshless steeds had blown away on the warm south wind. And good news had come to the survivors on that same south wind: The armada of Lyonesse had turned back, the hag Queen Lamia losing heart and hope when she learned that her evil husband was no more.

The body of Gabriel Drake had been brought down from the heath. He lay under a gray shroud far from the dead of Faerie, and no one went near him or spoke of him.

Of the highborn of Faerie, all had survived except for Lord Gaidheal, who had ridden his horse into the thickest of the enemy, reckless of his own life in his desire to avenge his murdered wife. The earl marshal had been wounded, as had his son Titus, but both were able to be with the King and Queen and their daughters and Lord Brython and Earl Valentyne and Corin and the marchioness as they stood around the bier of Princess Zara in the golden evening light. Silent tears flowed down Titus's cheeks, and Tania saw that he could not bring himself to look at Zara's face.

Tania was still feeling light-headed from the aftereffects of the Mystic Power that Oberon and Titania had gifted her with. After the death of the Sorcerer King and fainting into Edric's arms, she had only the memory of floating on cushions of white cloud till she had awoken several hours later on Salisoc Heath to find Edric sitting over her, holding her hand. She was holding his hand again now, gripping it tightly as she gazed down at Zara's pale, peaceful face.

Oberon and Titania stood at Zara's side, their heads bowed. The princesses and their husbands and the other members of the Royal Family gathered around the simple table of white wood. The King still leaned on Titania and Tania guessed that what power the Queen had been able to give him had been spent in the gush of golden light that had given her the strength to destroy the Sorcerer King. She just wished that the power had come to her a few minutes earlier and that she had been able to use it to save Zara.

She looked at Eden, who was standing at her side. "Can't we bring her back?" she whispered. "What about the Power of Seven? Sancha said it was the power of life over death."

"Zara is lost to us, Tania," Eden replied. "We are but six now; the Power of Seven cannot be called upon ever again."

"But you could use your own powers, surely?"

Eden turned her sad eyes toward Tania. "To call back a Faerie spirit from the Blessed Land of Avalon were a wicked deed," she murmured. "Would you have our sister walk among us as if she were a Gray

Knight of Lyonesse? For that is how she would return."

Tania swallowed. "No, I wouldn't want that." She looked down at Zara. "Is that place you mentioned like . . . well, like *heaven*, then?"

"Avalon?" said Eden. "Oh, yes, very heaven indeed."

Tears welled in Tania's eyes. "Will she be happy there? Will she be able to sing?"

"Let us hope so," Eden said. "Hush now, darling. It begins."

A silence came over all the people gathered on the riverbank. The copper disk of the sun kissed the distant hills and the land was suddenly steeped in rich, deeply colored shadows. At that moment Tania became aware of a tingling in the air and of the soft hymning of voices that seemed to come drifting up out of the grass all along the river. The ethereal singing grew until the air shimmered with it. And then a single dulcet voice soared above the chant, rising and rising in a bittersweet carol of such loveliness that Tania found tears pouring down her cheeks.

It was Zara's voice, leading the song as it swelled to fill all of the land and all of the endless Faerie sky.

As the song reached its zenith fluttering streams of white mist were drawn up from the bodies of all the fallen, Faerie knight and animal alike, coiling and spiraling upward, twining together and filling the sky. And as the light ascended so the bodies of the dead faded away and the coverings of white satin settled gently over the emptiness where they had once lain.

But the illumination that came from Zara as her body turned to pure light shone brighter than all the rest, and it was radiant with all the colors of the rainbow. Instead of flowing upward it coiled around King Oberon, enclosing him in a cloak of multicolored light that swirled faster and faster about him like a whirlwind until, in a rainbow blur, it entered his body and vanished.

The King gasped, his back arching, his hand coming away from Titania's shoulder as the rainbow light filled him. His head tilted back and he gave a shout of joy as arrows of red and blue and green and indigo and yellow and orange and violet light sped upward from his eyes, coloring the hanging curtains of white light like a scattering of jewels. And in the patterns of sapphire and emerald and ruby and topaz, Tania thought for a moment that she saw a Faerie host riding on jeweled steeds, and at their head, Zara seated astride a unicorn. She seemed to turn and look down at them and smile for a moment before the winds of heaven blew the vision away and the white river and the colored stars poured away into the west and were lost in the heart of the setting sun.

The evening had darkened to a warm and star-filled night filled with the honeyed fragrance of evening primrose and the spicy-sweet aroma of night scented stock. Torches had been set up all along the river and the Faerie folk sat in groups in the grass, eating a simple supper and talking quietly together in the lee of the tall palace walls.

Tania sat in the grass with her Faerie family and with Edric at her side. Eden was with Earl Valentyne and Hopie with Lord Brython. Tania was intrigued by the difference between the two couples. While Hopie and Brython were loving and intimate, Eden and her ancient husband behaved like strangers, exchanging an occasional polite word, but clearly not at ease with each other. Tania guessed that theirs had probably never been a love-match, more likely a union founded on the earl's great wisdom and Eden's thirst for knowledge.

Bryn Lightfoot was also there; he had eagerly accepted Cordelia's invitation to eat with the Royal family, and the two of them were sitting close together.

Tania remembered the King's words. *Death is a bitter wound to endure . . . but it is not the end of things.* Tania felt the truth of that keenly. Zara would never sing with her again, they would never play duets together, but her sister was not entirely lost—she existed still, and not only in Tania's heart and memory; hopefully her voice and her music could still be heard in the Land of Avalon that lay beyond the setting sun. It was a comforting thought, and although it didn't stop Tania from mourning, it took the bitterness out of her grief.

It was wonderful to Tania to see the King looking so glad and healthy again as he sat with his Queen. They held hands and gazed often into each other's eyes as though some private, silent conversation was taking place between them, a reuniting of their spirits after five hundred years of separation.

Rathina sat between Hopie and Sancha, her face unbearably sad. Tania knew that it would take a long, long time before the dark clouds cleared from Rathina's heart, but she intended to be here to help Rathina recover.

"What are you thinking?" Edric asked her. "You look miles away."

Tania turned and smiled at him. "I was more than miles away," she said. "I was back in the Mortal World."

He looked thoughtfully at her. "Is that where you want to be?"

"Yes and no," Tania said. "How long have we been here? How long since we left London?"

"I've lost count," Edric said. "But it must be fourteen or fifteen days, at least."

Tania nodded. "That's pretty much what I made it. My mum and dad will have got back from Cornwall by now. Can you imagine what it must have been like for them to find us gone again and the house half wrecked? It's got to have hit them so much harder than last time. They'll be going out of their minds."

"You must go back there and let them know you're all right," Titania said.

Tania gave a start, not realizing that anyone else had been listening to their conversation. "What on earth can I tell them this time? They'll have got home to find your car crashed in the garden, the back door smashed in, dead birds all over the kitchen floor, and who knows what else chaos in the house. There's no way for me to explain all that away."

"Then do not explain it away," said Oberon. "Tell them the truth of who you are."

"I'd love to," Tania said. "But I don't think they'll believe me. They'll think I've gone crazy."

"Then they should be given proof that you are not crazy," Titania said. She smiled. "Do you think they'd believe *me* if I told them who you really are?"

Tania stared at them. "You'd come back with me and talk to them?"

"Nay!" Oberon exclaimed. "I will not allow the Queen to enter the Mortal World again. That is a peril she shall never endure, so long as the Sun and the Moon rule the heavens."

"No, of course not," Tania said, her spirits sinking a little. "I understand."

"But there is another way," Titania said, resting her hand on the King's arm. "A way that won't leave your mortal parents in any doubt about the truth."

Tania looked at her in confusion.

"Can you not guess the answer to this riddle?" said Eden. "You must enter the Mortal World and bring your other mother and father into Faerie."

Tania looked at the King. "Can I really bring them here?"

"Of course you must," said Oberon. "Your mortal parents are as much a part of you as are the Queen and I. And therein lies your strength, Tania, in the blending of Faerie and mortal blood that flows in your veins. That is what has shaped your destiny, my daughter."

"The ancient texts spoke truly," Sancha added. "Not by Faerie nor by mortal could the Sorcerer King be slain."

Titania put her hand on Tania's. "It was your dual nature that gave us victory over Lyonesse. Nobody but you could have done it, Tania. Nobody."

Tania smiled. "Can I go and get my parents right now, please?" she asked.

"Go upon this instant with my blessings upon you," Oberon said.

Tania scrambled to her feet. She looked down at Edric. "Coming?"

He smiled up at her. "You bet I am."

XXIX

Titania made a soft clicking sound with her tongue, drawing back on the reins so that the horse-drawn carriage came to a jangling halt among the aspen trees that grew around the Brown Tower. She turned, smiling at Tania and Edric, who were sitting together in the back.

"I'll wait here for you," the Queen said. "Good luck."

"Thanks," said Tania as she and Edric got down from the carriage.

Above their heads the velvet sky was so heavy with starlight that Tania felt as if she could have reached up and snatched down a handful of silver. Warm forest scents wafted over them and from somewhere nearby came the piping call of a nightjar.

Edric walked toward the door of the tower and pushed it open. Tania hesitated a moment, looking up at her Faerie mother. "This is going to be so weird," she said. "My two mums and my two dads meeting one another."

Titania laughed. "It'll be interesting, that is certain." Her face became solemn for a moment. "Are you absolutely sure that you want to live in Faerie?" she asked. "It is a huge decision to make. You can still change your mind; no one here will think the worst of you if you do."

"Are you kidding?" Tania said. "This is where I belong. I feel as if my whole life up to now has just been a kind of . . . I don't know . . . a kind of *prelude*, a preparation. I feel as if my real life starts right here and right now. Does that make any sense at all?"

"It does," Titania said.

"Besides, I've got a lot of remembering to do, and a whole lot of exploring. I want to rediscover every inch of Faerie. But first of all, I want to visit Leiderdale—Zara told me it was her favorite place in all Faerie. I think she'd like me to go there." She looked cautiously at the Queen. "And I'd like to go back to Fidach Ren and speak with Clorimel again."

A strange light glowed in the Queen's smoky green eyes. "Oh, yes?" she said. "What do you want to speak to her about?"

"Well . . . she started telling me how a long, long time ago, all the people of Faerie had wings for the whole of their lives. I want to find out more about that. I want to know what happened, what changed."

"Ahh." Titania nodded. "That will be quite a quest, Tania."

"Do *you* know what happened?"

Titania shook her head. "No, but the legends say

that the answer lies in the Western Ocean." Her voice took on a lilting quality, as if she was reciting poetry. "Beyond the flaxen coasts and heathered glens of Alba, beyond the emerald hills of Erin of the enchanted waters, beyond even dragon-haunted Hy Brassail, far, far away in the land of Tirnanog, the answer lies, where the Divine Harper spins his songs at the absolute end of the world." Titania smiled down at her. "That's what the legends say."

Tania gazed up at her, spellbound for a few moments. "Then maybe that's where I'll have to look," she murmured. "If Edric will go with me."

"Right now, going into the Mortal World and confronting your parents is going to be enough of an adventure for me," Edric called from the doorway of the tower.

"Yes, of course. Sorry." Tania gave Titania one last, affectionate look as she entered Bonwyn Tyr. "I won't be long," she called.

"I will be here," her mother called back.

Hand-in-hand, Tania and Edric mounted the winding stair to the upper floor of the watchtower. They stood in the middle of the wooden floor, bathed in starlight, listening to the whisper of the aspen leaves.

Tania looked at him. "Ready?"

Edric nodded. Tania took that impossibly simple side step and moments later the two of them were standing in darkness in Tania's bedroom in London. Breaking her grip on his hand, Tania walked to the door and switched on the light. At a first glance everything looked disarmingly ordinary. There was her new computer and her bulletin board and posters—all her familiar possessions in all their familiar places. The bed was rumpled, but the mattress on which her three sisters had slept on their first night in the Mortal World had been removed and the bedclothes tidied away.

"They're definitely back, then," Tania said.

"Looks like it."

Tania reached for the door handle. She saw that the lock was broken. She swung the door open, revealing deep scores and grooves on the outer panels, damage done when the swords of the Gray Knights had cut and hacked into the wood. She swallowed hard as she stepped onto the unlit landing. She switched on the light, moving to the banister rail and staring down into the hall. The lower parts of the house were silent and dark.

Edric was standing in the doorway. She turned to look at him. "I don't think anyone's here," she said. "Maybe the place was such a mess that they went to stay with relatives or something."

"Maybe," Edric said. "So? What do we do now?"

"Find them, I guess."

A small sound made Tania turn and peer along the landing: a soft, subdued sound, as of bare feet on a thick carpet. A moment later the door of her parents' bedroom opened and she saw her father standing there, wrapped in a dressing gown, blinking in the light, his face crumpled from the pillow.

"Dad—it's me."

"Anita?" His voice quavered as he stared at her in disbelief. *"Anita?"*

She ran toward him and caught him in her arms. "Yes. I'm back," she said. "Please, please don't ask any questions right now. Where's Mum?"

"Is that Anita?" called a voice from the darkness of the room.

"Yes, it's me," Tania called, letting go of her father and running into the bedroom. She grabbed her mother's hand. "You have to get up now," Tania said. "You have to get dressed—both of you."

Her mother gasped. "What happened to you? The house! We thought burglars—but then we found out you didn't go with the Andersons to Florida. We thought you'd been kidnapped or murdered or—"

"I'm fine, Mum," Tania interrupted her. "Please— get up now and I promise I'll explain everything."

"Everything?" her father said from the doorway. "For heaven's sake, Anita, have you got any idea of the state the house was in when we got back?"

"She *can* explain, sir," Edric said.

Tania's father turned, his face darkening. "You!" he spat. "I might have known you'd be involved in this."

"Stop it, please!" Tania demanded. "I'm going to explain everything to you, I promise. But you have to trust me just for a little while longer—and you have to get dressed." She took a breath, looking from her mother to her father. "I'm going to take you somewhere, and when you get there, you'll understand everything. Now put some clothes on, *please!*"

For a moment she thought her father wasn't going to do as she asked, but then, with a last angry glare at Edric, he walked back into the bedroom and began to pick up his clothes.

"I'll wait outside," Tania said. She switched on their ceiling light and walked out onto the landing, closing the door behind her. She looked at Edric, shaking her head.

He smiled encouragingly. "So far, so good," he said.

"You think?" Only sheer willpower was stopping her from running to the bathroom and throwing up.

Two or three minutes passed before the bedroom door opened and her mother and father came out fully dressed. Her mother looked confused and upset, and her father's face was dark with barely suppressed anger.

"Well?" he said. "Let's get this over with."

Tania walked toward her room, Edric stepping back through the doorway.

"In here, please," Tania said.

Her father frowned. "What is this nonsense, Anita?"

"Trust me, please."

"No more lies, Anita," her mother said. "I couldn't stand any more lies."

"No, no more lies," Tania promised.

Her mother came to the door, her father following reluctantly.

Tania led them into the room. "I'm sorry for everything I've done to you recently," she said. "But there is an explanation, and I'm going to show it to you right now." She moved between them, taking them both by the hand.

Her mother gave a gasp of surprise as Edric took her other hand.

"Okay," Tania said, her heart pounding so loudly that she could hardly hear herself speaking. "I'm going to take a step, and when I do, I want you to move with me."

"Anita!" growled her father.

She looked at her mortal mother and her mortal father. "Trust me!"

Holding her parents' hands tightly in hers, she took that enchanted side step and led her mortal parents and Edric into the Immortal Realm of Faerie.

"Good grief!" she heard her father gasp as the curved stones walls of Bonwyn Tyr appeared in front of them. "Good *lord*!"

Her mother's hand tightened in hers, her eyes widening in amazement.

Tania laughed out loud with pure joy. "And believe me when I tell you, Mum, Dad, this is only the beginning!"